Ghostly Echoes

The Jackaby Series by William Ritter

Jackaby
Beastly Bones
Ghostly Echoes
The Dire King

Ghostly Echoes

A Jackaby Novel

William Ritter

ALGONQUIN 2017

Published by
Algonquin Young Readers
an imprint of Algonquin Books of Chapel Hill
Post Office Box 2225
Chapel Hill, North Carolina 27515-2225

a division of
Workman Publishing
225 Varick Street
New York, New York 10014

First paperback edition, Algonquin Young Readers, August 2017. Originally published in hardcover by Algonquin Young Readers in August 2016.
Printed in the United States of America.
Published simultaneously in Canada by Thomas Allen & Son Limited.
Design by jdrift design.

LIBRARY OF CONGRESS CATALOGING-IN-PUBLICATION DATA
Names: Ritter, William, [date] author. | Ritter, William, [date] Jackaby series.
Title: Ghostly echoes / William Ritter.
Description: First edition. | Chapel Hill, North Carolina : Algonquin Young Readers, 2016. | Series: A Jackaby novel | Summary: "Jenny Cavanaugh, the ghostly lady of 926 Augur Lane, has enlisted the services of her detective-agency tenants to solve a decade-old murder–her own. Fantasy and folklore mix with mad science as Abigail Rook and her eccentric employer, R. F. Jackaby, race to unravel the mystery"–Provided by publisher. | Audience: 7 to 8. | "Published simultaneously in Canada by Thomas Allen & Son Limited"–Title page verso.
Identifiers: LCCN 2016009022 | ISBN 9781616205799 (HC)
Subjects: LCSH: Private investigators–Juvenile fiction. | Murder–Investigation–Juvenile fiction. | Cold cases (Criminal investigation)–Juvenile fiction. | New England–History–19th century–Juvenile fiction. | CYAC: Private investigators–Fiction. | Murder–Investigation–Fiction. | Cold cases (Criminal investigation)–Fiction. | New England–History–19th century–Fiction. | LCGFT: Detective and mystery fiction. | Paranormal fiction.
Classification: LCC PZ7.1.R576 Gh 2016 | DDC [Fic]–dc23
LC record available at https://lccn.loc.gov/2016009022

ISBN 978-1-61620-744-1 (PB)

10 9 8 7 6 5 4 3 2 1
First Paperback Edition

For Justin,
whose past was sometimes dark,
but who makes his future bright.

Ghostly Echoes

Chapter One

Mr. Jackaby's cluttered office spun around me. Leaning heavily on the desk, I caught my breath in shuddering gulps. My head was throbbing, as though a shard of ice had pierced through one temple and out the other, but the sensation was gradually subsiding. I opened my eyes. The stack of case files I had spent all morning sorting lay strewn across the carpet, and the house's resident duck was cowering behind the legs of my employer's dusty chalkboard, shuffling anxiously from one webbed foot to the other.

One lonely file remained on the desk at my fingertips—a mess of fading newsprint and gritty photographs. My pulse hammered against the inside of my skull, and I concentrated, trying to slow my heartbeat as I propped myself up on the desk. Before me lay the police report, which described the grisly murder of an innocent woman and the mysterious disappearance of her fiancé. Beneath it was tucked the lithograph of a house, a three-story building in a quiet New England port town—the same house in which I now stood, only ten years younger—it looked simpler and sadder back in 1882. Then there were my employer's collected notes, and beside them the photograph of a pale man, his lips curled in a wicked smirk. Strange men stood behind him wearing long leather aprons and dark goggles. My eyes halted, as they always did, on one final photograph. A woman.

I felt sick. My vision blurred again for a moment and I forced myself to focus. Deep breath. The woman in the picture wore an elegant, sleeveless dress as she lay on a bare floor, one arm outstretched and the other resting at the torn collar of her gown. A necklace with a little pewter pendant hung around her neck, and a dark stain shaded her chest and collected around her body in an ink-black pool. Jenny Cavanaugh. My friend. Dead ten years, and a ghost the whole time I had known her.

The air in the room shimmered like a mirage, and I pulled my gaze away from the macabre picture. Keeping one hand on the desk to steady myself, I raised my chin and straightened my blouse as a spectral figure coalesced before me. My pulse was still pounding in my ears. I wondered if Jenny could hear it, too.

"It's fine. I'm fine," I lied. *I am not fine*, every fiber within me shouted. "I'm ready this time." *I am anything but ready.* I took a deep breath. The phantom did not look convinced. "Please," I said. "Try it again." *This is a bad idea. This is a terrible idea. This is–*

And then the office vanished in a blinding haze of mist and ice and pain.

Jenny Cavanaugh was dead, and she wasn't happy about it. Another week would mark the passing of ten years since death had come prowling into her home. It would mark ten years since it had dropped her on her back in the middle of her bedroom, her blood spilling across the polished floor. Her fiancé, Howard Carson, had vanished the same night, and with him any clues as to the purpose or perpetrator of the gruesome crime.

Perhaps it was due to the approach of such a morbid anniversary, but in all the months I had known her, Jenny had never been so consumed by her memories as she had become in the past week. Her carefree attitude and easy laugh had given way to tense silence. She made an effort to maintain her usual mask of confidence, smiling and assuring me that all was well. Her eyes betrayed the turmoil inside her, though–and there were times when the mask fell away completely. What lay beneath was not a pleasant sight.

R. F. Jackaby, my employer and a specialist in all things strange and supernatural, called those moments *echoes.* I cannot begin to fathom the depths of Jenny's trauma, but I glimpsed into that icy darkness every time I witnessed an echo. Everything Jenny was fell away in an instant–the woman she had once been and the spirit she had become–until all that was left was a broken reflection of her last living seconds. Fury and fear overwhelmed her as she relived the scene, and all around her spun a storm of ice and wind. The unfathomable forces that held a soul intact had come untethered in Jenny, and what remained was something less than living and something more than human. The first time I watched her fall into that cold place had been bad enough, but it was far from the last. The further we pursued her case, the more frequently and violently the echoes overcame her.

Jenny regarded these moments with frustrated embarrassment after she regained her composure, as might a sleepwalker upon waking to find herself on the roof. She became increasingly determined to hone her spiritual control so that she might find answers to the questions that had haunted her since her death, and I became increasingly determined to help.

"Tread lightly, Miss Rook," warned Mr. Jackaby one evening, although he was usually the last person to exercise caution. "It would not do to push Miss Cavanaugh too far or too fast."

"I'm sure she's capable of much more than we know, sir," I told him. "If I may . . ."

"You may not, Miss Rook," he said. "I've done my research: Mendel's treatise on the demi-deceased; Haversham's *Gaelic Ghasts.* Lord Alexander Reisfar wrote volumes on the frailty of the undead psyche, and his findings are not for the faint of heart. We are churning up water we ought not stir too roughly, Miss Rook. For her sake and for ours."

"With all due respect, sir, Jenny isn't one of stuffy Lord Reisfar's findings. She's your friend."

"You're right. She isn't one of Lord Reisfar's findings, because Lord Reisfar's findings involved pushing spectral subjects to their limits just to see what would happen to them—and that is not something I intend to do."

I hesitated. "What would happen to his subjects?"

"*What would happen,*" answered Jackaby, "is the reason Lord Reisfar is not around to tell you in person."

"They killed him?"

"A bit. Not exactly. It's complicated. His nerves gave out, so he abandoned necropsychology in favor of a less enervating discipline, and was shortly thereafter eaten by a colleague's manticore. He might or might not still haunt a small rhubarb patch in Brussels. Cryptozoology is an unpredictable discipline. But my point stands!"

"Sir—"

"The matter is settled. Jenny Cavanaugh is in an unstable condition at the best of times, and finding painful answers before she is ready might send her over an internal threshold from which there can be no return."

I don't think my employer realized that Jenny had crossed an internal threshold already. Until recently, she had always been reticent about investigating her own death, shying away from solid answers as one who has been burned shies away from the flame. When Jackaby had first moved his practice into her former property, into the home in which she had lived and died, Jenny had not been ready. The truth had been too much for her soul to seek. She had made a decision, however, when she finally enlisted our services to solve her case–and, once made, that decision had become her driving force. She had waited long enough.

Now it was Jackaby who seemed to be dragging his heels to help, but his unavailing attitude only made Jenny more determined to help herself. To her dismay, determination alone could not give her a body, and without one she could do frustratingly little to expedite the case. Which was why she had come to me.

Our first spiritual exercises had been fairly benign, but Jenny still felt more comfortable practicing when Mr. Jackaby was away. We had known each other only six short months, but she had quickly become like a sister to me. She was self-conscious about losing control, and Jackaby only made matters worse by growing increasingly overprotective. We began by attempting to move simple objects one afternoon while he was out.

Jenny remained unable to make physical contact with anything that had not belonged to her in life, but on rare occasions she had managed to break that rule. The key, we found, was not concentration or sheer force of will, but rather perspective.

"I can't," she said after we had been at it for an hour. "I can't move it."

"Can't move what?" I asked.

"Your handkerchief." She waved her hand through the flimsy, crumpled thing on the table. It did not so much as ripple in the breeze.

"No," I answered. "Not *my* anything. You can't move *your* handkerchief. I gave it to you."

"*My* handkerchief, then," she said. "A lot of good *my* handkerchief is going to do me when I can't even stuff it in a pocket!" She gave it a frustrated swat with the back of her hand, and it flopped open on the table.

We both stared at the cloth. Slowly her eyes rose to meet mine, and we were both grinning. It had been the flimsiest of motions, but it was the spark that lit the fire. We scarcely missed a chance to practice after that.

Not every session was as productive as the first, but we made progress over time. Several fragile dishes met their demise in the following weeks, and the frustration of her failures pushed her into spiritual echoes more than once. With each small setback, however, came greater success.

We expanded our tests to leaving the premises, which Jenny had not done since the day she died. This proved an even more daunting task. On our best round, she managed to plant but a single foot on the sidewalk–and it took her most of the afternoon to rematerialize afterward.

When moving outward failed to yield the results we had hoped for, I began to explore moving inward. I knew that this could be even more dangerous territory to tread, but the following day I asked Jenny to think back and tell me what she remembered about that night.

"Oh, Abigail, I'd really rather not . . ." she began.

"Only as much as you feel comfortable," I said. "The smallest, most inconsequential details. Don't even think about the big stuff."

Jenny breathed deeply. Well, she never really breathed; it was more a gesture of comfort, I think. "I was getting dressed," she said. "Howard was going to take me to the theater."

"That sounds nice," I said.

"There was a sound downstairs. The door."

"Yes?"

"You shouldn't be here," said Jenny.

The shiver rippled up my spine even before I felt the temperature drop. I had come to recognize those words. They came from that dark place inside Jenny.

"I know who you are." Her gown was elegant and pristine, but at the same time it was suddenly torn at the neck and growing darker. She was already fracturing. Jenny's echoes were like a horrid version of the party favors my mother used to buy–little cards with a bird on one side and an empty cage on the other with a stick running down the middle. When you twirled the stick, the bird was caught. A trick of the eye. As Jenny fluttered in front of me, graceful and grotesque, the two versions of her became one, but some part of my brain knew they did not belong together. Her brow strained and her eyes grew wild with anger and confusion.

"Jenny," I said, "it's me. It's Abigail. You're safe. There's no one–"

"You work with my fiancé."

"Jenny, come back to me. It's all right now. You're safe."

"No!"

"You're safe."

"NO!"

By the time she reappeared, I had tidied up all the broken glass and righted all the furniture. She always returned, but it took Jenny time to recover from an echo. I kept myself from fretting by keeping busy with my chores. I sorted through old receipts and dusty case files compiled by my predecessor, Douglas. Douglas was an odd duck. He had had excellent handwriting when he had been Jackaby's assistant. Of course, that was when he had still had hands–not that he seemed to miss them now that they were wings.

When I say Douglas was an odd duck, I mean it quite literally. His transformation into water fowl had taken place during his last official case. Working for R. F. Jackaby came with unique occupational hazards.

Douglas perched on the bookshelf now to watch me while I worked, issuing an occasional disapproving quack or ruffling his feathers when I filed something incorrectly. He seemed to enjoy life as a bird, but it made him no less insufferably fastidious than he had been as a human. Jenny materialized slowly; she was just a hint of shimmering light in the corner when I first realized she was there. I gave her time.

"Abigail," she said at last. She was still translucent, only just visible in the soft light. "Are you all right?"

"Of course I am." I set down the stack of case files on the corner of the desk. Jenny's own file lay open beside them. "Are you?"

She nodded faintly, but heavy thoughts hung over her brow like rain clouds.

"I'm sorry," I said. "I shouldn't have . . . I'll stop pushing you."

"No." She solidified a little. "No, I want to keep practicing." She bit her lip. "I've been thinking."

"Yes?"

"I'm not as strong as you are, Abigail."

"Oh, nonsense–"

"It's true. You're strong, and I'm grateful for your strength. You've already given me more of it than I have any right to ask, only . . ."

"Only what?"

"Only, I wonder if I could ask for a little more."

Possession. She wanted to attempt possession, and in my foolish eagerness I agreed. I managed to convince myself that I was braced to handle Jenny Cavanaugh's spirit entering my mind and sharing my body–but nothing could have been further from the truth; there could be no bracing against the sensations to come. She was tentative and gentle, but the experience proved to be like inviting a swirling maelstrom of pain and cold directly into my skull. My vision went white and I felt as though my eyes had been replaced with lumps of ice. If I cried out, I could not hear my own voice. I could not hear anything at all. There was only pain.

Our first attempt was over as soon as it had begun. I was reeling, my head throbbing and my vision blurry. The files I had sorted were strewn across the floor–all of them but Jenny's. Her photograph, the photograph from her police record, lay atop the pile on Jackaby's desk. Jenny was in front of me before I could gather my wits about me. She looked mortified and concerned.

"It's fine. I'm fine," I lied, doing my best to make it true as I leaned on the desk and tried not to pitch forward and retch on the carpet. "I'm ready this time. Please. Try it again."

I was not ready. Neither was she.

Jenny hesitated for a moment and then drifted closer, smooth and graceful as always. Her hair trailed behind her like smoke in the wind. She reached a delicate hand toward my face, and–if only for an instant–I could have sworn I felt her fingers brush my cheek. It was a sweet caress, like my mother's when she used to tuck me into bed at night. And then the biting cold returned. My nerves screamed. *This is a bad idea. This is a terrible idea. This is–*

The office faded into a blinding haze of whiteness, and together we tumbled into a world of mist and ice and pain . . .

. . . and out the other side.

Chapter Two

It seemed like only yesterday I had been back home in England, packing for my first term at university. Had someone told me then that I would throw it all away and run off to America to commune with ghosts and answer to ducks and help mad detectives solve impossible murders, I would have said they were either lying or insane. I would have sorted them on the same shelf in my mental library as those who believe in Ouija boards or sea serpents or honest politicians. That sort of foolishness was not for me. I adhered to facts and science; the impossible was for other people.

A lot can change in a few short months.

The pain had ebbed to numbness and the blinding light had faded away. I did not remember moving into the foyer, but it was suddenly all around me. I blinked. How long had I been out? I stood in the front room of Jackaby's offices at 926 Augur Lane–of that there was no doubt–but the room was barely recognizable. In place of the battered wooden bench sat a soft divan. The paintings of mythical figures had been replaced by tasteful landscapes, and the cluttered shelves full of bizarre masks and occult artifacts stood completely barren–even Ogden's terrarium was missing. When I had been gassed out of the house by the flatulent little frog on my first day, I would not have expected to be so bothered by his absence, but now I found it most disquieting. The desk stood in its usual place, but it was uncharacteristically clean and empty. Behind it stood a pile of boxes and paper bundles bound in twine. Had Jackaby packed? Were we moving?

The front door swung suddenly open and there stood R. F. Jackaby in his typical motley attire. His coat bulged from its myriad pockets, and his ludicrously long scarf dragged across the threshold as he stepped inside. Atop his head sat his favorite knit mess, a floppy hat of conflicting colors and uneven stitches. I had been secretly pleased to see that particular piece of his wardrobe completely incinerated by an ungodly blaze during our previous caper. I shook my head. It had been destroyed, hadn't it?

"Mr. Jackaby?"

"Yes. This will serve my purposes nicely," said Jackaby, walking toward me.

I opened my mouth, but before I could speak, my employer stepped right through me as though I weren't there. I looked down to find, most distressingly, that I wasn't.

"I'll need to make a few modifications, of course."

I spun and saw that he was talking to Jenny. She hovered by the window, regarding Jackaby with cautious interest. Her translucent hair drifted weightlessly behind her. Her dress was moon-white, its hem rippling gently along the ground beneath her. Her skin was nearly as pale, pearlescent and as immaterial as a sunbeam. "Nothing too drastic, I hope? I understand, of course. You must make the place your own. I had the kitchen remodeled the year I moved in–but it's so darling as it is."

"I'm sure you'll barely notice the changes." He opened the door to the crooked little hallway and paused. "I *will* be making this place my own, Miss Cavanaugh," he said, turning back. "But don't think that makes it any less yours. You will still have your space. You have my word."

Jenny smiled, looking bemused and grateful. "You are a singular man, Mr. Jackaby. What have I done to deserve you?"

"I've been considering that. There is something you could do."

She raised an eyebrow. The room was beginning to fill with mist, but neither of them seemed to notice. "What?" she asked.

"Promise me," said Jackaby, his voice growing faint, "that you will never . . ."

And then, in a rush, the mist was gone and I was in the office again. I was lying on my back and Douglas was standing on my chest craning his head this way and that to regard me with his glossy black eyes. I shooed him off and sat up. My whole body felt tired and numb, with a prickling heat creeping into my extremities. I was back in the present, but I felt like I had spent all day in the snow and then climbed into a warm bath.

Jenny appeared above me. "That was sensational! It worked! Oh, Abigail, are you all right?"

I wiggled my fingers and toes experimentally and felt my face. Aside from the fading numbness, everything seemed to be in working order. "I'm fine. What just happened?"

"Legs! I haven't had honest to goodness legs to stand on in years! And you're so warm, Abigail–I had forgotten how blood feels. It's like being wrapped up in a cozy blanket from the inside." She spun and sighed happily, drifting up toward the ceiling. I had not seen her so content in weeks.

"It worked?" I pushed myself up, leaning on the desk to steady my swimming head. "You mean I was possessed? You were walking me around and everything?"

"Well, not walking, exactly. I kept us from falling down for the better part of a minute, though. You couldn't see it?"

"I saw . . . something else," I said. "I saw you and Jackaby. It must have been the day he moved in. He promised you that you would always have your space in the house."

"He did say that," Jenny said, sinking back to my level.

She regarded me thoughtfully. "You saw my memories? What else did you see?"

"Nothing much. He asked you to promise him something in return—only then I slipped back here. What was it he never wanted you to do?"

"A promise?" Jenny thought for a moment. "I don't remember." She crinkled her brow. "Do you think you could see further if we tried again?"

"I suppose so." Jenny looked completely in control, invigorated, even—but I could not forget Jackaby's cautions about pushing her too far or too fast. "It isn't upsetting to know that I was inside your memories?"

"What's upsetting is knowing that I might have secrets hidden inside me and I can't get them out." Jenny looked at me pleadingly. "Abigail, this could be the answer."

It really could, I had to admit. With practice, possession could grant her the means to leave the house and pursue secrets that had been hidden from her for so long—and at the same time, it could grant me the means to uncover the secrets hiding within.

"All right," I said. Douglas was bobbing back and forth, looking more disapproving than a duck has any business to look. I ignored him. "Let's try again."

This time I was ready for the pain. I leaned into it, and it passed over me more quickly. The blinding whiteness returned, and when the mist cleared, I found myself not in the foyer of 926 Augur Lane but in a drawing room I did not recognize. The sky outside was black, and the room was dim. I had entered a different memory.

"No. That's no good. The output will be half what they asked for," said a man's voice.

"It'll be twice what it should be. There's no way to stabilize at these levels."

Two figures stood directly ahead of me, their attention fixed on a stack of schematics spread over a wide desk. Something about them was familiar. The first was an energetic, handsome man. I felt uncomfortably drawn to him, although I could not say why. And then he smiled and I knew. This was Howard Carson. This was Jenny's fiancé–the man who had loved her–the man who had left.

Across from him stood a man with white-blond hair. He wore a scowl and a three-piece suit, tailored impeccably to his slim figure. "They're not going to be happy about this," said the slender man.

"They'll be a lot less happy if the whole thing blows up in their faces," countered Howard Carson. The thin man grimaced as Carson rattled on about conductivity and tensile strength.

In a chair behind them sat a third man, heavyset with a chubby face and a mustache waxed into thick curls. He said nothing as he fidgeted an unlit cigar from one hand to the other, watching the men work. Beside him stood a prim woman with ink-black hair holding a clipboard and a pen. "Are you getting all of this down?" the big man asked quietly.

"Yes, Mr. Poplin, every word." She remained expressionless, her pen scratching away.

"Good girl."

"Don't forget, boys," came a soft voice from behind me. Before I could turn to see her face, a woman with brunette locks stepped through me toward the desk. I shuddered, or I would have if I had a body to shudder; I would never get used to the sensation of not physically existing. "The copper fittings in the prototype lost conductivity as they tarnished. Silver will cost more, but it will also increase the output over time."

The thin man grimaced. "What do you know about it?" he said.

"She knows quite a lot, actually," interjected Carson. "I told you already that my fiancée has been assisting me with my work. She's as sharp as they come."

Jenny Cavanaugh stepped behind the desk and turned to face the room. Had I been in possession of my own jaw at the time, it would have dropped. The Jenny I knew was a beautiful ghost—but the woman before me, with real weight to her steps and a flush in her cheeks, looked like another person entirely, so vibrant and alive. Her hair framed her face rather than hovering in weightless silver waves. She wore a honey yellow dress, practical and pretty, and around her neck hung a little pewter locket.

"She's quite keen, you know," Carson was saying. "And she's right about the fittings."

"Thank you, Howard." Jenny Cavanaugh and Howard Carson looked at each other for only a moment, but their affection was obvious.

"We discussed this already," said the blond man flatly. "We will move forward with copper." I did not like him. It was more than his sanctimonious sneer. Something within Jenny disliked the man, so I disliked the man.

"If you insist," Howard said, taking a deep breath. "Copper will do."

Jenny was not satisfied. "It would save us all a great deal of time and effort if we knew the exact purpose of our efforts."

The man glared at Jenny. "Our benefactors have provided us with very clear objectives."

"Objectives are not an ultimate purpose. What exactly are your benefactors building?"

"Jenny–" Howard said.

"The future!" declared a new voice, and all eyes turned to the door. "We're building the future, young lady. One shiny cog at a time." The man who stood in the doorway was stout and unshaven. He had coal-black hair and wore a shabby black coat over a black waistcoat. His skin was deathly pale, save for a bluish shadow across his chin and under his eyes.

I knew that face. That was the face we had fruitlessly

hunted across the countryside and back into the shadows of New Fiddleham. That was the last face our client poor Mrs. Beaumont had ever seen before she died. I watched as that face spread its pallid lips into a crooked grin. "Doesn't that sound exciting?"

Chapter Three

You knew him?" I gasped as the dark drawing room faded away and Jackaby's office reappeared, the midday sun streaming in through the windows. I stood up abruptly from the leather armchair and immediately regretted my decision. My vision reeled and I sat back down.

Jenny–my Jenny–hung pale and translucent in the air ahead of me. She had been beaming, but the smile was rapidly melting away. "Knew whom?"

I breathed, holding on to the armrests to keep from falling out of the chair. Slowly the world stopped spinning and the feeling returned to my skin. "How did I get–Jenny, did you possess me all the way into the armchair?"

She nodded, but the pride had left her face. "I knew *whom*, Abigail?"

"That man. The one in the photograph."

Rising more gradually this time, I stepped over to Jenny's open file. My temples were throbbing and the room felt as though it were slowly spinning to a stop. Jenny stood beside me as I tried to pull my mind together. When the world was finally stable again, I looked up to find that she had already fixated on a picture. Her translucent hand brushed the image of her body, sprawled across her bedroom floor.

"Jenny . . ."

"Howard gave me that locket," she said. "It's not in the house any longer. I've looked and looked. It had a note inside. 'From Howard with love.' It's just a little pewter thing, but it's the little things you miss."

"Jenny, stay with me," I said cautiously. "Please? This is important."

She pulled her eyes away from the picture. "I'm with you, Abigail."

I plucked the photograph of the pale man off the top of the pile and held it up for her to see. It was grainy with a sepia tint, but the face was unmistakable. I had seen him watching my window from the street corner, and then again, lurking outside the train station. Now I had seen him up close through Jenny's memories, and not a hair on his head had changed in those ten years.

The pale man stood in the foreground of the picture, a smug smile on his face. He was not alone. In the background of the picture, five men stood around a worktable in what appeared to be an industrial factory. Bright lamp-light illuminated their faces and left hard shadows on the wall behind them. The men wore dark work aprons, thick gloves, and tinted goggles pushed up on their heads. The one in the center was Howard Carson.

There were no other pictures of Howard in the house–none hanging in Jenny's room nor propped up on her nightstand. She spoke of him fondly but rarely, and always with trepidation, as if feeling gingerly around a bruise.

Along the bottom of the picture had been inscribed five words in tight cursive: *For posterity. From humble beginnings . . .*

"He worked with my fiancé." Jenny's voice was quiet.

I tensed, the hairs on the back of my neck prickling up. "Jenny? Are you still with me?"

She pursed her lips, nodding. "I remember now." I held my tongue, not daring to tip the balance. When she spoke her voice was scarcely more than a breath. "He was called Pavel."

The photograph had been in her case file for years, but Jenny had never been able to identify the pale man before, nor anyone in the file save Howard Carson. There had been something about the image she responded to–an uneasy remnant of a feeling–but like Jenny herself, the memory remained frustratingly intangible. Looking at any of the photographs in her file for too long put her in a fragile state, but still she tried. When I had recognized the pale man as the same wretch whose trail of havoc we had followed across the valley, she had tried even harder, wrestling with the demons in her mind for anything–a detail–a name–but the effort had only triggered her to echo every time. Until now.

"Is he . . . ?" I whispered. "Is he the one who . . . ?" Jenny's eyes narrowed in concentration, and a cold breeze crept under my collar. My trip into her thoughts might have brought a flickering light to Jenny's memories, but those corridors were still shrouded in something darker than shadow. "Perhaps we should take a rest," I said.

"He was here. Why was he here?" Jenny's silver hair whipped in a sudden breeze, though the windows were latched tight. "I don't like him. I don't trust him."

"Neither do I, Jenny. I think we ought to stop."

"He came to the house. He's at the door. He knows that Howard is here."

"Jenny, stop."

"I don't like him." She blinked, her eyes drifting in and out of focus, and then her stare turned icy. "I know who you are. You work with my fiancé."

I stuffed all of the photographs and the loose clippings and notes back into the file and slammed it shut as a bitingly cold gust of wind pressed into my back. When I looked around Jenny was already gone.

"Jenny?" I called to the silence. The silence deepened.

"Give her time."

I jumped at the sound of a man's voice. "Mr. Jackaby!"

I gasped, clutching my heart. "I didn't hear you come in. How long have you . . . ?"

"I just got back. I won't be staying long. I wasn't expecting to find myself stepping into an icebox." He dropped his satchel with a thump and picked up Jenny's file as hc walked around the desk. "Be careful, Miss Rook. Our undeparted friend has a thorn buried deep in her metaphorical paw, and we find ourselves in the lion's den." He tucked the file into his desk and shut the drawer with a click. "I assure you, we will do everything in our power to remove the injury–but I have no intention of making it worse and getting torn to ribbons for our efforts. Patience and diligence are paramount."

"With all due respect, sir, ten years stretches the definition of patient. She is already a decade into her afterlife."

He stared at the old papers and receipts spread across his office floor. "Still, we must consider the possibility that the thorn and the lion are one."

"Sir?"

He met my gaze and sighed. "Ghosts are beings of discontent, Miss Rook. The undead remain bound to this earth by their unfinished business. Either we will not succeed because we cannot succeed–because her soul will never be content–"

"Or we will succeed," I said, realizing his implication. "And her business will be finished."

"And she will depart from us at long last." Jackaby

nodded. "That is her decision, though. She says she's ready. We will provide her with what few answers and what little peace we can, but there's no benefit in rushing the job." He slid into the chair and leaned heavily on his desk, his gray eyes gloomy.

"Sir?"

"I dislike the idea of being without Miss Cavanaugh."

"Have you told her that?"

"She has her own concerns to attend to right now."

"She really can handle more than you think, sir. She's making considerable progress."

"The state of my office says otherwise. I noticed the glass in the wastebasket, by the way. I take it this is not her first echo today. How long was she incorporeal for the last one?"

I hesitated. "Only an hour. Maybe two. It was just a little one." His gaze drifted to my cheek, and I could feel his eyes catching on the slender scar on my cheekbone. The mark was a trivial thing–already it had faded to a soft pink line–but it was a souvenir of a nearly catastrophic brush I'd had with a Stymphalian bird, another supernatural force I had woefully underestimated. Getting Jackaby to stop treating me like a fragile thing was difficult enough without having reminders of past close calls etched on my face. It didn't help that the injury in question had been inflicted by nothing more than the creature's feather. I redirected the conversation. "She had a revelation."

"A revelation." Jackaby nodded with a deep breath. "Splendid. Because nothing bad ever happens in Revelation."

"The pale man. His name is Pavel. She remembered him."

Jackaby's eyes darted up, but he quickly hid his interest. "Pavel? A given name only. Likely an alias."

"She can do more."

"But she should not. It's too dangerous, Miss Rook. In light of recent developments, I think it best we suspend Miss Cavanaugh's direct involvement altogether."

"What? That's absurd! This is her case!"

"Precisely my point! She is far too emotionally invested to handle the minutia of this investigation. With each new twist and turn we risk pushing her over the edge, and we cannot foresee what might lie beyond the next curve. Walking this path was hard enough on her when the trail was cold."

"She's stronger than ever!" In my frustration, I nearly told him about our secret practices, about our remarkable success with possession–but I bit my tongue. The secret was not mine alone to tell, and Jackaby was being especially bullheaded right now. A cog clicked in my mind. Something had happened. "Wait a moment. What recent developments?" I asked.

"See for yourself." Jackaby flipped open his satchel and passed a handful of papers across the desk to me. They were torn at the top, as though ripped out of a booklet.

"Lieutenant Dupin of the New Fiddleham Police Department very kindly lent me his notes on the matter."

"Does Lieutenant Dupin know that he very kindly lent you his notes?"

Jackaby shrugged. "I'm confident he'll piece it together sooner or later. Marlowe keeps him around for something."

I shook my head, but turned my attention to the notes.

The body of Mrs. Alice McCaffery was found early this morning by one Rosa Gaines, age 32, a maid in the McCaffery household. Mrs. McCaffery had been at my desk in the station house only the day before to file a missing persons report for her husband, Julian McCaffery. En route to investigate now.

I arrived at the McCaffery home just prior to 8 o'clock in the A.M. The scene within is as Ms. Gaines described it. Alice McCaffery lies on the floor of her chamber. Her dress is torn at the neck and signs of a struggle are evident. Cause of death is a single deep laceration to the chest. Blood has dried in a wide pool around the body. My word, but there is a lot of blood.

I stared numbly. I could see why Jackaby was hesitant to share the news. The missing person, the bedroom struggle, the body, the blood. I might as well have just read the police report in the file sitting beside me. It was Jenny's murder to the last detail.

"What do you make of it?" Jackaby asked.

"Eerily familiar, sir."

"More than you know," said Jackaby. "Julian McCaffery was a research scientist, not unlike Jenny's fiancé, Howard Carson. Carson and McCaffery both studied under Professor Lawrence Hoole at Glanville University, although years apart."

I swallowed. "That's an awful lot of coincidences. Hoole went missing, too, didn't he? Yes, I remember. It was in the *Chronicle* weeks ago."

Jackaby nodded. "He makes an appearance in the lieutenant's next entry, as well." He gestured to the papers in my hands. I flipped to the next page and read aloud:

It is not yet midday and I have been presented with my second corpse of the day. The discovery was made by Daniel & Benjamin Mudlark. The brothers, ages 7 and 9, disclosed the information in exchange for compensation. They agreed to 5¢ payment and escorted me to the scene.

The body appears to have washed up with sewage runoff on the northern bank of the Inky. Based on physical description and documents found on the body, the deceased is Lawrence Hoole, age 56, a professor at Glanville University. The corpse is waterlogged, but given the minimal state of decay, I estimate he is not more than two days deceased. The only visible injury is a puncture wound at the base of his neck, surrounded by a circular bruise.

The professor is survived by his wife, Cordelia. Glanville Police Department has responded to my inquiries, but inform me that the widow Hoole is . . .

I turned the page over, but that was the last of it. "The widow Hoole is what?"

"Bereaved?" suggested Jackaby. "Disconsolate? Something mournful, I imagine. Probably 'sad.' Lieutenant Dupin is nothing if not frugal with his adjectives."

"Those poor people," I said. "A single puncture wound and a rounded bruise–that's Pavel's dirty work and no mistake. There can be no question that this whole mess is connected, then."

"What about Cordelia Hoole?" Jenny's soft voice caught both of us by surprise. I spun to find that she had rematerialized by the window, the sunlight slipping in sparkling beams through her translucent figure.

"Jenny," I said. "How long have you–"

"I'm sorry, Miss Cavanaugh," Jackaby cut in. "We really ought to follow up on these leads more thoroughly before we trouble you with the details. I don't wish to–"

"Jackaby, ten years ago my fiancé vanished and I was murdered. Yesterday that McCaffery man vanished and

Alice McCaffery was murdered. Their mentor, Hoole, vanished, and now we know he was murdered as well, and you're–what? Waiting for the pattern to complete itself? You're ten years too late to save me, detective. You're a day too late for Alice McCaffery. The question is, what about Cordelia Hoole?"

Chapter Four

The afternoon air was thick and hot as Jackaby and I left Augur Lane and made our way into the center of town. I had been introduced to a snow-swept New Fiddleham earlier that year, a New Fiddleham where baroque buildings glistened with frost and chilly winds whispered through the alleyways. With the summer sun now beating down on the cobblestones, the city did not whisper so much as it panted heavily, its breath humid and cloying.

Jackaby, still draped in his bulky coat, swam through the mugginess with his usual alacrity, stubbornly unaffected by the swelter.

"Sir," I said. "With all due respect, I don't think that Lieutenant Dupin is likely to be very forthcoming about this case, our having stolen what little we already know from his blotter."

"Borrowed," corrected Jackaby. "We borrowed what little we know. But I agree. I doubt that Lieutenant Dupin will be of much further use to our side of this investigation. Dupin is merely an artery."

"He's a what?"

"An artery," said Jackaby. "And a good one. But he isn't the heart. No, we need to speak directly to Commissioner Marlowe. If anything unseemly has landed on the streets of this city, Marlowe will know of it."

It was still hard to believe that this was my life–murder and mystery in the gritty underbelly of New Fiddleham. Not all of it was as beguiling as it sounds on the page. Truthfully, for all of its intrigue and excitement, adventuring was a most unglamorous career. I grew up on the other side of the Atlantic, a proper English girl. By the time I was ten, I could tell with pinpoint accuracy where I was by the accents around me. I was beginning to develop a similar sensory map of New Fiddleham based on odor. It was not a map I enjoyed filling out.

The industrial districts to the west smelled of coal fires and wood pulp, and the docks to the east of salt spray and fish. In between lay the sprawling, pulsing heart of New Fiddleham, along with every aroma its inhabitants could make. Savory spices of frying, baking, and boiling food would mingle with the whiff of pig slop and chicken coops, only to be shoved aside by the thick, nearly tangible stench of outhouses and steaming sewer drains. A bucket of foul wash-water would evaporate in minutes on the hot paving stones, but its essence would linger for days, wandering the rows of the tenements like a stray cat.

Jackaby and I skirted past a street sweeper whose horse and cart took up most of the narrow alleyway. The man barked a few words at us that I don't care to record and made a rude gesture.

I loved New Fiddleham. I still do. New Fiddleham had been very kind to me since my arrival–it had only tried to kill me once–but there are two New Fiddlehams: one that knows the light and another that keeps to the shadows. Some corners of the city, I was coming to find, were always dark, as if to spite the sun. At the bottom of a steep hill, I saw a clothesline hung with wash that looked as though its ground-in stains might be the only things holding the tattered fabric together. Between the rags hung a little burlap dress sized for an infant. It was stitched with care, but the words "Gadston Golds" and a picture of a potato were still visible on the side of the skirt. The fabric looked itchy. A pang of sympathy ran through me. I had been raised in privilege, always looking up a little wistfully at the aristocracy, hardly aware that there were people lower down on the social ladder who did not know the bother of having a maid put too much starch on a day dress. I had never thought about the children born in the dark.

Jackaby pressed forward up the hill. He rarely took the same route twice, but I had come to know the landscape well enough to tell we were not bound for the police station.

"Sir," I called after him. "I thought you said we were going to talk to the commissioner."

"We are, though we will not find him behind his desk this afternoon. Commissioner Marlowe has scheduled an impromptu meeting with Mayor Spade. He has postponed all other matters and explicitly forbidden any of his subordinates to interrupt, so I gather their conference is of a sensitive and urgent nature."

"I don't suppose we're going to wait patiently for that meeting to conclude?"

"Given the news Lieutenant Dupin delivered him this morning, the news which I relieved the good lieutenant of before leaving the station, I think it is safe to assume we know the topic at hand. Our business is one and the same, so they will have to pardon the intrusion."

"I suppose it won't be the first time you've needed a pardon from the mayor."

"Some cases go more smoothly than others," he confirmed with a wink. "Not everyone appreciates my methods."

As we climbed the hill, the housing improved visibly

with each block. We came to neighborhoods whose properties were spaced more and more comfortably apart, until it became a bit of a misnomer to call them neighborhoods at all. Proud white houses–houses that looked as though they might prefer to be called *manors*–were bordered not by their neighbors' walls, but by sprawling, elegantly manicured gardens. Here we found the mayor's home, a stately colonial building. Marble pilasters framed his broad front door, and the whole structure was a testament to right angles and symmetry. It could not have been less like our abode on Augur Lane.

Jackaby rapped the knocker soundly. A long-faced man in a starched collar and black necktie opened the door. "Oh dear," the man moaned.

"Bertram!" Jackaby patted him on the arm affably as he bustled past him into the front hall. "It's been ages, how are the kids?"

"I remain unmarried, Mr. Jackaby, and I'm afraid you can't be seen just now."

"Nonsense. Miss Rook, can you see me?"

"Certainly, sir."

"Well, there you have it. You must have your eyes checked, Bertram. Now then, is our meeting in the drawing room? I hope I'm not late, I would hate to keep the commissioner waiting." Without giving the butler time to reply, Jackaby strode past him into the house.

Bertram hurried after, urgently trying to get ahead of Jackaby, but my employer spun gaily. I followed close on their heels.

"No, he is not, Mr. Jackaby. And you are not expected today. Please!"

"Ah, the study, then–of course. No need to bother yourself, I remember the way."

"Mr. Jackaby! This is a private estate, not the mayor's public offices. My lady, Mrs. Spade, is very particular about the sort of person she admits into her home."

"Come now, Bertram. I'm sure I'm just the sort of person your lady Spade would be happy to admit."

"Actually, you are the only person she has mentioned by name to refuse."

"Then she does remember me, after all these years–how sweet! And we were never even properly introduced. I guess I do tend to leave an impression."

"More of a smoldering crater," Bertram grumbled.

Jackaby quickstepped through a hall with a high arched ceiling and came to a mahogany door. "Please, Mr. Jackaby!" Bertram implored.

"Very well. If you insist," Jackaby said, throwing open the door. "I will. Thank you for the escort, Bertram. You've been too kind."

Bertram was red in the face. He looked as though he were about to object again when his master called from inside the room. "Don't bother, Bertram. It's fine." The man huffed and turned, giving me a disgruntled look as he trudged away. I shrugged apologetically and hurried after my employer.

The room was accented with rich woods and carpeted in tones of deep red and chocolate brown. The shelves were decorated with a collection of leather-bound books, all of which looked expensive and none of which looked as if they had ever been read. Mayor Spade and Commissioner Marlowe sat in high-backed chairs on opposite sides of a cherrywood desk whose ornate legs curved into elegant clawed feet. A third chair sat empty.

Marlowe wore his usual double-breasted uniform, with a silver eagle pinned to his lapel. He looked, as usual, tired but resolute.

"Jackaby," said Marlowe.

"Marlowe," said Jackaby. "Good morning, Mayor Spade."

Spade had doffed his jacket. It was draped over the back of his chair, and a coffee brown bow tie hung undone over his beige waistcoat. He had a full beard and a perfectly bald dome, and he wore a thick pair of spectacles. Spade was not an intimidating figure at his best, and today he looked like he was several rounds into a boxing match he had no aspirations of winning. He had seemed more vibrant the first time we met, and that had been at a funeral.

"I haven't been up here in years," continued Jackaby. "You've done something with the front garden, haven't you?"

"Yes," said Spade. "We've let it grow back. Mary still hasn't forgiven you."

"Is that why she's been avoiding me? Your eyebrows have filled in nicely, by the way, and you can tell your wife the roses look healthier than ever. I'm sure being rid of that nest of pesky brownies did wonders for the roots. I understand a little ash is good for the soil, too."

"I never saw any brownies, but there was certainly plenty of ash to go around," Spade mumbled. "That fire spread so quickly we're lucky we managed to snuff it out at all."

"You should try blowing up a dragon some time," I said. "No, scratch that. That went terribly. I don't recommend it."

"Impressive blast radius, though," Jackaby confirmed.

Mayor Spade looked from me to my employer and rubbed the bridge of his nose with one hand. "Good lord, one of you was quite enough. You had to recruit?"

"You know that I love wistful anecdotes about the destruction of property and endangerment of the public as much as the next man," Marlowe interjected, "but we're busy here."

"Then let us get to business." Jackaby slid into the remaining chair on Marlowe's side of the desk. I glanced around, finding myself standing awkwardly just outside the group.

"I'm afraid the commissioner and I have been discussing very sensitive matters, detective," Spade began. "We really are not at liberty to–"

"Yes, yes, yes. The McCafferys–the mister is missing and the missus is murdered. Lawrence Hoole also washed up, minus a heartbeat and plus one hole in the neck. We know all about that. We also know that these are not isolated instances, but part of a much larger and more nefarious plot. It is all connected. It goes back at least a decade, and we are keen to see that it does not continue for another one. Tell me, gentlemen, what do you know about Cordelia Hoole?"

Marlowe leaned back in his chair, watching Jackaby. Mayor Spade answered instead. "Cordelia is gone."

"Kidnapped? Another one?"

"Not kidnapped. No. The housekeeper saw her pack a suitcase. Nobody knows where she went."

"Then perhaps that's where we should begin," said Jackaby. "We're here to assist."

"The last time you assisted on this case," Marlowe said at last, "you spent a week investigating one body in the valley and managed to bring the tally up to five dead, one severed limb, and two leveled buildings. What you failed to do was bring back any viable leads whatsoever."

"It wasn't the entire limb," Jackaby replied. "It was just the hand. Hudson looks very smart in a hook, by the way. It suits him. And we did come back with a solid lead."

"Right. 'A man.' That was very helpful. Have you thought of anything to add to that? Let me guess–not human?"

"Well, I can't be certain of that until I've seen him in person, but I can give you his name and a precise description," Jackaby said. "He is called Petrov or some such, and he has an anathematic aura with distinctly lavender accents."

Marlowe scowled. Jackaby was not your average detective.

He was also a seer. I had come to find that he was not actually all that adept at making the sort of connections that Commissioner Marlowe could make, and frankly he missed a lot of clues that leapt out to even an untrained eye like my own. But Jackaby saw something else that no one else could. He saw auras and energies–the reality behind the mask, he called it. He saw the truth, no matter how improbable. Making sense of any of that truth to anyone else was another matter entirely.

"He's called Pavel, actually," I chimed in, leaning forward from behind my employer's chair. "Or at least he was ten years ago."

"Yes, that's right," Jackaby confirmed. "Pavel."

"He's not a tall man," I added. "He's close to my height, I would say, with thinning black hair and very pale skin. He looks about forty, forty-five years old at the most, but he looked the same age a decade ago. He tends to dress all in black. Does any of that help?"

Spade and Marlowe exchanged glances. Marlowe looked at me. "It's certainly a start, Miss Rook. You should lead with her next time, Jackaby. She's better at this than you are."

"Pavel is back," Jackaby said, ignoring him, "and what's more, he has been at his bloody business for a very long time. The McCaffery murder is not unique. You should know that there was a strikingly similar case, ten years ago. The woman's name was–"

"Jennifer Cavanaugh," Marlowe finished. "Unsolved."

"That's right!" I said. "You've read her file, then?"

"I helped write some of it," Marlowe grunted. "I was a probationary detective in eighty-two. My mentor sergeant was assigned to the Cavanaugh murder. I probably did more legwork on the case than he did. Safe money around the station had the fiancé for the killer. Howard Carson had just accepted a major payment before skipping town, and his colleagues all turned up dead or didn't turn up at all."

"No, Carson's wrong for it," said Jackaby. "The pale man, Pavel–"

"Has a very unique signature, I know. Single puncture wound to the neck. Exsanguination. Very clean. No witnesses. Cavanaugh's murder was nothing like it. It was a mess. Bloody. Neighbors reported screams. Alice McCaffery's case looks very much the same. Whoever killed Cavanaugh and McCaffery, he had a very different approach than your pale man."

"But you can't possibly think that the murders are unrelated!" I said.

"We do not, Miss Rook," Marlowe said, heavily. "There are patterns playing out with eerie familiarity here. The method of their deaths, their occupations and relationships, their preceding circumstances."

"Preceding circumstances?" I asked.

Again, the mayor and commissioner exchanged glances.

"Twelve years ago," Mayor Spade began, "my predecessor, Oslo Poplin, organized a council for the advancement of technology in New Fiddleham. The New Fiddleham Technological Center was going to be Mayor Poplin's legacy. He hired a team of experts to drive the construction and launch New Fiddleham into the forefront of innovation and industry."

"The future," I breathed. "They were building the future."

Jackaby nodded. "Not an unworthy goal."

"No, but it was an unpopular one," Spade continued. "For two years it diverted funds from every other facet of public works. Poplin let the parks become neglected and overgrown. Major roads were riddled with potholes. The future was everything to him, at great cost to the present. It might have all been worth it, except that the closer the project came to completion, the more things went wrong." Spade removed his glasses and polished them clumsily with one loose end of his bow tie. "In the spring of eighteen eighty-two, the lead architect and two chief engineers disappeared. Then a few scientists and inventors who had declined involvement went missing as well. There was a major investigation. For a time, Poplin managed to keep the newspapers quiet about it. The project was still inching forward, and his entire reelection platform was based on its success."

"But then there was Jenny," said Jackaby, soberly.

Spade nodded. "People liked Jenny. When the lovely Miss Cavanaugh was found dead and her fiancé was not found at all, word got out. No bribe was large enough to silence the journalists. There was public outrage. The whole project was rocked by scandal, spinning off the rails. And then it blew up entirely."

"What happened?" I asked.

"It blew up, quite literally. There was an explosion. The Technological Center was decimated. The observatory collapsed, walls came tumbling down. Years of work and thousands of dollars vanished. Poplin's bold new plan to change the world was suddenly a pile of scrap metal and cinders. I'm told the blast bent metal girders in half and melted the glass right out of the windows."

"Don't look at me," Jackaby said. "I didn't move in until eighty-seven."

"Don't think I didn't check," Marlowe said.

"Two of the bodies they uncovered were identified as scientists who had gone missing, Shea and Grawrock," Spade continued. "There were other remains, but they were too far gone. Carson was notably not identified among them."

"Then he might still be alive?" I said.

"And long gone by now if he is. He took his money and disappeared. Poplin was indicted, accused of everything the court could throw at him, from sabotaging his own project to kidnapping and killing his architects. None of it stuck, of course, because nothing could be proven. If anyone knew what really happened, they were either long gone or buried in the wreckage. Poplin's political career was over, obviously. He was completely ruined."

"I see," said Jackaby. "And now, ten years later, men of science are disappearing again, their loved ones slaughtered in their homes. The parallels are hard to ignore. It's a good thing you haven't rebuilt the Technological Center as well, or we should be watching the skyline for fireworks."

Mayor Spade swallowed hard.

"You haven't . . ." I said.

"Not exactly." The mayor took a deep breath. "Poplin mismanaged his affairs, but he wasn't wrong. We do need to keep above the current or we will flounder beneath it, so in the past few years I've made another push toward modernity in New Fiddleham. The city of Crowley is already phasing out gas lamps. The university district down in Glanville looks like something out of a Jules Verne novel. We've fallen behind. The people are ready. With all of the hubbub about the World's Fair coming to Chicago next year, the public is clamoring for innovation. The city council was unanimous. We installed electric lights in Seeley's Square, remodeled the Cavendish district, everything was going smoothly. But it's like some invisible force doesn't want New Fiddleham to move forward. I fear it's all happening again."

"Wait a moment," I said. "Cordelia and Professor Hoole lived in Glanville. It's a tragedy to be sure, and a most urgent case–but not a mark against New Fiddleham."

"Except that Lawrence Hoole was my chief architect." Spade sank in his chair. "I enlisted his help for the New Fiddleham project. He was a central part of my elite team. Together we were going to achieve what Poplin never could. But now . . ."

"Your team?"

Spade nodded, his complexion wan and his eyes unfocused. Marlowe spoke for him. "Professor Hoole was not the only member of the intellectual community whose expertise the mayor solicited, nor is he the only one to go missing."

Spade nodded his head in confirmation and pointed to a picture on the shelf behind him. It showed Mayor Spade beaming at the camera as he shook hands with a man I recognized from the newspapers as Professor Hoole. A third man stood proudly at their side. "Julian McCaffery," Spade said sadly, "–missing. Lawrence Hoole–dead. I brought them both into this, and now I'm the only one in that photograph whose corpse the police aren't either looking at or looking for. Lawrence was a good man. He told me last month that he was having misgivings about the project, that something felt wrong. I should have listened. Poor Cordelia wasn't even a part of this."

I stared at the picture. Lawrence Hoole was smiling in that way my father always had before an expedition. It was an eager smile, a smile of grossly misplaced optimism. I looked away and found my eyes drifting across the other portraits on his shelf. A beautiful woman with brunette curls stood beside Spade in several of them.

Spade must have followed my gaze. "Her name is Mary," he said softly. "My wife. I think the two of you would get along very well, Miss Rook–so involved and inquisitive." He took a deep breath. "Please, gentlemen, Miss Rook. Whoever is behind this didn't stop at Carson or McCaffery. The wretch went after their families. He killed Jennifer Cavanaugh and Alice McCaffery. Lord knows what's become of the widow Hoole. I'll put my own neck on the line for this town–but not Mary's. I would give anything to keep Mary out of this." Spade's jaw was set and his expression hard, but his eyes glistened in the warm light of the study.

"Don't worry, Mayor–" I began, but Jackaby cut in.

"Worry. It is worrisome indeed, and you're at the core. This all started up again precisely when you picked up where your predecessor left off. Is it possible our culprit is an economic vigilante who doesn't want another mayor playing in the public coffers?"

"I guess it's possible," Spade said. "But we've avoided making the same mistakes that Poplin made with the city's money. The whole project has been negotiated quietly and kept separate from public works. We held private fund-raising dinners and petitioned sponsors through the post. It was a very successful campaign. We found stable benefactors interested in supporting our work at a very early stage."

"I am so sorry," said Jackaby earnestly. "Your occupation sounds tedious. I mean, really, woefully dull. Politicking must be the most unstimulating job in existence. No wonder Poplin blew it all up."

"Hold on," I said. "Benefactors?" My mind lurched to the man in Jenny's memory with white-blond hair. *Our benefactors have provided us with very clear objectives*, the man had said. "What sort of benefactors?"

Marlowe smiled appreciatively. "You really are better at this than your boss. That was my first question, too. I've already got a few officers cross-referencing the donors to see if anything out of the ordinary turns up. If there's anything to find at the end of the money trail, we'll find it. For now it seems like that's about the only trail we've got. I'm getting very tired of my missing persons leading to nothing but dead ends and dead bodies."

"Well then. Perhaps it's best if you enlist our services after all, Commissioner," I said. "At least we can pursue the one missing person we know was still alive when she disappeared."

"Cordelia Hoole." Marlowe considered. His eye twitched involuntarily as he regarded Jackaby, but even he couldn't deny that, for better or worse, the detective had a way of making unexpected findings come out of the woodwork.

Jackaby flashed his best reassuring smile, which was never as reassuring as he thought it was. The commissioner heaved a heavy sigh, but nodded. "Send your expenses to my office, Miss Rook. You two are on the case."

Chapter Five

The train ride to Glanville was smooth, if a bit winding. The trolley was serving something that resembled tea, although I have come to realize that Americans are all too quick to bestow that title on any warm beverage that isn't coffee. My unfinished cup of brownish liquid had gone lukewarm by the time the train hissed to a stop, and our reception was equally tepid.

"R. F. Jackaby and companion?" A uniformed officer confronted my employer on the platform.

"That's me," Jackaby confirmed. "And this is Abigail Rook."

I offered my hand. "Pleased to make your acquaintance, Officer . . ."

"Moore," grunted Officer Moore, not returning the gesture. "I take it you're the specialists New Fiddleham sent because your commissioner doesn't think we can do our jobs." He sniffed. "You won't find anything we didn't."

"We've managed to make ourselves useful in the past," said Jackaby.

Yeah, we'll see." The officer gave a halfhearted shrug toward the exit. "Got a patrol wagon waiting. I guess I'm taking you to the professor's place." Without any further courtesy, he trudged through the gate, and we followed.

The Hoole house was an imperial-looking building, three stories tall with long, narrow windows and a prim mansard roof. Moore tied off his horse's reins and stalked up the front walk. A tall woman in a wide straw bonnet watched him from the neighboring garden, her watering can gradually drifting to water the paving stones instead of the foliage.

"Have you caught her yet, officer?" she called to him when he was nearly at the door.

"Please go about your business, ma'am." He gave a tug on the bellpull and leaned unceremoniously against an ornamental urn on the front porch to wait.

"Caught who, madam?" Jackaby asked the neighbor.

"That Cordelia woman," she said. "I knew she was bad news. I told Mr. Hoole–rest his soul–I told him that she was no good from the beginning."

"Cordelia was an unpleasant neighbor?"

"Oh, no. Not at all–she was nothing but sunshine and smiles." She narrowed her eyes. "That's how you can tell."

"Because she was nice to you?"

"All the time. It was very unsettling."

"I see. And how was she with Professor Hoole?"

"Oh, she doted on that man. She was always flattering and supportive. The perfect wife. Nobody's the perfect wife. She was the one that told him he should go and take that job in New Fiddleham, even though it meant he would be traveling all the time. Told him it was his chance to make a name for himself."

"How do you know she said that?"

"Well, she said it with the window open. Not really my fault, is it? Anyway, she said that after the science thing up north was done he could retire and spend time with the family. You see what I mean?"

"Not remotely. I infer you felt she was disingenuous and dangerous, though. Do you think she might have been a rusalka? Possibly a succubus? A siren? Did she ever seem to be all or part avian to you?"

"What?" said the woman

"What?" said Jackaby.

"Go about your business, ma'am," said Officer Moore. "This is an ongoing investigation. Go on. Thank you."

The woman eyed all of us with suspicion, but she took her watering can and shuffled off.

Moore gave the bellpull another tug.

"Pardon me, sir," I asked, "but with the professor and Mrs. Hoole both gone, who are we waiting for?"

"They've got a housekeeper," Moore grunted. "Live-in." He pounded on the door several times. "Hurry it up, Miss Wick! Police business!"

The door clicked open at last and a small woman with wide, round eyes gestured for us to come in.

"Good afternoon," I said.

"Show them around like you showed me," said Moore. Miss Wick looked out of sorts. "The house, woman." He gestured at the walls around us. "Show them the house."

She nodded but said nothing as she walked us through each room and up and down stairs. There were small scale replicas of steam engines and half-finished clockwork projects tucked all over, as well as schematics and sketches littering the professor's office. Aside from these myriad marvelous designs, it could have been any family home. There were no obvious skeletons in the Hoole closets, only linen sheets and neatly folded towels. There was something else, though–some detail that tripped into the back of my mind and hid. The silent tour was finished by the time I had fully worked out what it was.

"Pavel has been here," Jackaby whispered to me as we returned to the foyer. "I'm sure of it–although his aura has long faded. Some of the professor's projects are quite keen, but otherwise I've not seen anything extraordinary. The general atmosphere of the place is a mix of innocence and secrets, though. Not sure what to make of it. Did you notice anything?"

"Only that someone else seems to be missing," I said. He raised a meaningful eyebrow. "Diapers are folded neatly in the closet, little wooden blocks have fallen under the sofa . . ."

"Oh!" He nodded. "Yes, I see."

"Pardon me, officer," I said, "but did the Hooles have any children?"

"Nope," Moore answered flatly.

"Curious," I said.

"Not really. Only married about a year–which you would know if this were your investigation and not ours. All right. That's it. You've seen the whole house. Can I take you back to the train station now, or do you feel like wasting more of my time?"

"Just a moment," Jackaby said. He turned to Miss Wick. "Before we go, we would like to discuss with you the embarkation of your employer, if you don't mind."

Miss Wick nodded uncertainly.

"Could you expound upon the circumstances of the lady's departure?"

She nodded politely again, but her eyes bespoke total confusion. She did not reply.

"Miss Cordelia's departure?"

"Ah. Mrs. Cordelia, yes. Mrs. Cordelia is gone." Miss Wick nodded again.

"She doesn't speak much English," Moore said. "Do you, Miss Wick?"

The woman shook her head. "Not much English, no."

"Polish," said Moore.

"Hm." Jackaby looked to me. "How is your Polish, Miss Rook?"

"Nonexistent," I answered.

Jackaby turned back to the housekeeper. "There was a baby? A child?" He motioned holding an infant, rocking his arms back and forth. "Where is the baby?"

"*Przepraszam*," the woman said, looking helplessly to Officer Moore. "*Nie rozumiem.* I–I don't understand."

Jackaby scowled and leaned in very close, gazing into the woman's eyes. Miss Wick staggered back a step.

"Mrs. Cordelia is gone," Miss Wick repeated.

"Well, this is no help," he said, and then brightened. "Just a moment." Jackaby crossed the hall to the window, which stood ajar to let in the summer breeze. "Hello! Yes–you there. I can see your straw hat just beneath the hedge. What can you tell us about the child?"

Officer Moore and I hurried to join Jackaby at the window, outside which the nosy neighbor had been conveniently trimming an already immaculate bush. She swallowed and glanced around her garden.

"I'm sure it's none of my business to meddle–" she hedged.

"Please do, madam. You meddling would be greatly appreciated."

"Well"–she dropped the shears and leaned in–"the baby isn't Cordelia's. It came in with that maid, the foreign one. Anybody's guess who the father is. She is a woman of ill repute, make no mistake. The Hooles hired her on shortly after they got back from their honeymoon. I have no idea why poor Lawrence–rest his soul–why he let that woman into his house. Cordelia was always fraternizing with her, too. Talking–and laughing, even! It's not how you're supposed to interact with the help, let alone such a disreputable sort."

"If the baby is Miss Wick's, then where is it off to now?" I said. "We've been through every room in the house." I turned back to regard the Hooles' unassuming housekeeper, but Miss Wick was suddenly nowhere to be seen. "Miss Wick?" I said. Moore and Jackaby joined me in scanning the room. "Miss Wick?"

Officer Moore helped us search the house from top to bottom, but Miss Wick had vanished. "Her aura is stiflingly unremarkable and it's everywhere in this house," Jackaby griped as he hunted for a trail. "It's like searching for hay in a haystack." Eventually he caught a recent thread of panic and distress in the air, but it led out the back door and off into the bustling Glanville streets. "She's gone," he announced.

"Huh," grunted a baffled Officer Moore. "Miss Wick's

been around for every stage of the investigation. She never gave us any trouble. Her running off like that . . ." He took off his uniform cap and shook his head as he peered up and down the busy lane. "That's odd."

"Ycs," said Jackaby. His gray eyes sparkled and his lip began to pull into an involuntary smile in spite of the sudden turn the day had taken. "Yes, it is."

Chapter Six

"I really don't see what you're smiling about, sir," I said as the evening express to New Fiddleham chuffed to life beneath us. "We haven't come any closer to finding our killers or finding truth and justice for Jenny. We've found nothing but more questions." Glanville ambled lazily past our window, and the setting sun painted the marbled buildings outside our train car in shades of gentle reds and oranges.

"Questions are good," Jackaby said. "Questions are to the clever mind as coal is to the stoker. I will worry more when we run out of them."

"Be that as it may, I would be happier if we had at least a few satisfying answers to go with them when we report back to Commissioner Marlowe."

"Detective work is neither a happy nor a satisfying business, Miss Rook," said Jackaby, settling in as the amber buildings sailed past our window. "Marlowe will understand."

"I don't understand at all." Commissioner Marlowe kept his voice low and even as we sat across from him the following morning.

"What I mean to say," Jackaby explained, "is that our excursion yesterday was very instructive indeed."

"You found your missing woman?"

"Not exactly. Not remotely. No. We did manage to find a woman who was not missing." Jackaby's optimistic humor found little purchase on Marlowe's granite countenance. "And then we misplaced her," Jackaby admitted. "So now there are two missing women. Also there is a baby."

"What? A baby? Where did you find a baby?"

"We did not find a baby. The baby is also missing."

The commissioner's eye twitched as he set both palms on the table and took a deep breath.

"We're still looking into the matter, sir," I cut in. "We will be certain to keep you abreast of any developments, but in the meantime, my report should detail more clearly the results of our inquiry in Glanville." I passed the pages I had typed up that morning across the desk and Marlowe accepted them with a curt nod–high praise from the stoic commissioner.

"Hm," he said as he looked over the report.

"Strange and unsatisfying seem to be the tone of this case, sir, I know," I said.

"It's been no more satisfying on our end," Marlowe grunted. "My boys followed the money trail for Spade's project, like I told you. It seems his fund-raisers got a few donations from legitimate businesses, but the lion's share came from a corporation called Buhmann's Consolidated Interests. Turns out the exact same company bankrolled major portions of Poplin's project a decade ago."

"Buhmann?" Jackaby shook his head. "Not the most creative façade."

Marlowe rolled his eyes. "I know. German for *bogeyman.* I looked it up. The group is more than just children's stories and nursery rhymes, though. They own some legitimate real estate downtown, including an impressive-looking building in the Inkling District."

The bogeyman. Jackaby nodded sagely as though it were perfectly ordinary to hear that the bogeyman has been inconspicuously funding major municipal science projects. I shook my head. Every new clue just seemed to stir up the mud in the already murky waters of this case.

"It's a start," said Jackaby. "Chasing fresh leads has left us empty-handed. I would say it's definitely worth our while to pursue a much older one. We'll have to go and say hello to the mayor's mysterious benefactors."

"Good luck with that." Marlowe tucked my report into his desk and shut the drawer. "On paper the Buhmann building is their head of operations and the beating heart of another fine example of American industry. In reality—much less so."

"Empty?" Jackaby said.

Marlowe nodded. "The place is a dried-out husk. It's like a set from a vaudeville production about depressing old factories. There's nothing there."

"Sounds like somewhere we might find a few more questions," I said.

Jackaby grinned.

"Seriously," said Marlowe. "It's cobwebs and rats."

"We'll have a look around anyway," Jackaby declared, rising to his feet. "Miss Rook loves cobwebs and rats."

Chapter Seven

The sun beat down on us as we made our way across what felt like the entire length of the city before we came to the Inkling District. The Inkling was a channel that wound lazily eastward through New Fiddleham, looping north and south in wide arcs as though it were dodging the buildings that had grown up around it. When all of this had been farmland, the Inkling might have provided irrigation for row after row of healthy vegetables. Today it served the far less noble duty of rushing the city's waste out of sight and out of mind, and the townspeople had affectionately dubbed it the Inky—not an imprecise descriptor on its worst days. The Inkling District was a collection of businesses and factories tucked into the widest loop of the snake.

The air was thick and heavy, and it tasted like wet clay

and coal fires. The sky was cut with streaks of black from the smokestacks of the factories around us. It was already past noon by the time we had marched through the rows and rows of tall brick buildings and finally approached our destination. The Buhmann building had a gothic façade, broad and imposing with black spires running along the rooftop. Billowing steam from a street vent puffed whirling clouds into the air in front of it, giving the building a haunted atmosphere.

"That sewer line runs directly under the building," Jackaby observed as we passed through the steam cloud, "and I would wager it empties out very near to where the professor's body was found."

"I wouldn't bet against you, sir," I said, not feeling any better about entering the ominous building. It looked like precisely the sort of place where a living body might go if it wanted to become a dead one.

A fence ran along the perimeter, but the front gate hung ajar, and Jackaby and I stepped through without obstacle. The Buhmann building's double doors were ten feet tall and set with big brass handles in the shape of a double B. They were unlocked and weighted, swinging open with only a low creak at Jackaby's tug.

The inside of the structure was less than abandoned; it was barren. There were no old bookshelves or deserted desks. Granite floors lay bare from the front door to the far end of the building. Where one might have expected a broad foyer to give way to hallways and offices, the whole structure was simply hollow. Windows ran along the exterior at about the height one might expect a second floor to sit, but there was not so much as a landing to reach them. Through their dusty glass the afternoon sunlight seeped in, sickly and sallow by the time it spilled onto the floor below.

More eerie than its jaundiced light or staggering emptiness was the building's familiarity. "This is it!" I said, with a sudden realization. "Pavel was here, and Carson and all the rest. This is where they took that tintype of the pale man. 'For posterity,' it said. This is it, I'm sure of it! Look at those pillars against the wall, and the shape of the windows." I had pored over Jenny's file enough times to commit the photograph to memory.

"Interesting," said Jackaby.

"Well, sir?" I said. "Do you see anything I can't?"

"Constantly," said Jackaby. It wasn't exactly arrogance—but by the same token, it wasn't *not* arrogance. I waited for my employer to explain his paranormal perception of the cavernous room.

"Anything . . . supernatural?" I asked.

"No. Yes." Jackaby rubbed his eyes. "Everything. The walls, the floor, even the ceiling . . ."

"What?" I said.

"Ha!" He shook his head and spun in place, marveling at the dark, dusty cobwebs hanging over us. "It's been scrubbed clean, every inch."

I looked around. “This might be why you and Jenny rarely see eye to eye about housekeeping,” I said.

“Not scrubbed clean of dust or droppings,” he said. “There are plenty of those, of course.” I decided not to look too closely for confirmation about the droppings. “Scrubbed clean of magical residue. I can’t pick out any unique otherworldly auras in this space.”

“Couldn’t that just mean that this place doesn’t have any?”

“Hardly. When you were young, did you ever spill red wine on your parents’ carpet?”

I blinked. “Er–yes? I knocked a bottle of merlot off of the table once.”

“And what did your mother do to clean it up?”

“Nothing. My mother never did the cleaning. She always had a maid handle that sort of thing.”

“Precisely–white vinegar! Nothing better for a stain. Except that the carpet is never quite like it used to be, is it? Even if you can’t see the red anymore, there’s always something about that spot. It’s a little too clean for the rest of the rug, and it keeps that lingering vinegar smell, right? Now a healthy suspension of sodium bicarbonate might help with that, but there’s always something left behind.”

“You know a lot about cleaning carpets for someone whose floor looks like a topical map of the East Indies.”

“I know the Viennese waltz, too, but I don’t waste my

time doing it every day. Focus, Rook. Someone has layered this space with an essence of natural spirits."

"They cleaned the whole building with alcohol?" I said.

"Not that sort of spirits–actual spirits. There are countless varieties of fairy folk, oddlings, and minor deities residing in the world at any given time. Most are confined to the other side of the veil, but nature spirits are especially prevalent on our side. They are largely innocuous. I see them perpetually, so I tend to ignore them, the way you might take no notice of dandelions in a field or clouds in the sky–but in their simplicity they are also a pure source of magic."

He gazed around again, breathing in the dusty air. "There is no reason for an industrial building in the middle of the city to reek of nature spirits in exactly the same way that there is no reason for a carpet to reek of vinegar. Someone or something has been here, Miss Rook, and they went to great lengths to scrub themselves from my sight–which means they knew that I would come looking. Whoever was here, they are far more aware of me than I am of them."

I swallowed. The already meager sunlight drifting through the dirty windows seemed to dim as if responding to the mood. The hairs on the back of my neck stood up. I would not care to find myself back here after dark. "Perhaps we should be heading home, sir," I said. "It's getting rather late and we have a long walk ahead of us."

The streets of New Fiddleham were never empty, but by the time we had made our way out of the Inkling District, the usual bustle of afternoon traffic had ebbed, giving way to the quiet trickle of evening life. Our shadows grew longer and longer as we walked, and the tired sun leaned heavily on the rooftops. I tried to distract myself from my aching feet by running over the moving parts of the case in my mind. Jenny and Howard Carson, the McCafferys, the Hooles–Pavel was the one thread that seemed to tie all three couples together–but loose ends stuck out at every turn.

We passed through a neighborhood of tired old buildings, the sort that had once been big family estates, but whose ostentatious halls had long since been divided and repurposed into overflowing tenement apartments. Networks of creaking stairs and landings now hid most of the regal architecture. A man in an undershirt puffed cigar smoke from an open window and spat onto the pavement two stories below. Jackaby was striding past at his usual lightning pace when a sound caught our ears.

"Grab him. Grab his hands! Hold still, you little–"

My employer froze mid-stride. His head turned slowly. The voices were coming from a slim alleyway between the buildings.

"Yeah. That's what you get, freak!"

I have seen a monstrous dragon narrow its eyes to golden slits as it rounded on its prey. Jackaby's gaze as he spun toward the alley was slightly less friendly than that.

This was one of those neighborhoods that knew more shadows than light, without a doubt. I swallowed the lump that was climbing up my throat. We were walking the sort of streets my mother would not ride through at a gallop. So of course Jackaby was going in for a closer look. I bit my lip.

"Sir?"

Jackaby ignored me. The curtain of shadows within the alley welcomed him in, and I found myself suddenly alone on the sidewalk. "Sir?"

I took a deep breath. With all the willpower I could summon, I plunged after Jackaby into the dark.

"Hit him again! Hey! I said hold still, freak!"

Jackaby was not far ahead of me. He reached into his coat and produced three little red rocks as he stepped farther into the alleyway. "There is a story," he announced loudly to no one in particular, "that comes from the heart of the Chilean mountains."

Three men were leaning over a prone figure in the dark. "Who the hell are you?" said the largest, standing up straight. He was an inch or two shorter than my employer, but easily a hundred pounds heavier. His shirtsleeves were rolled up over thick muscles, and he cracked his neck as Jackaby approached.

"It tells of a monster," Jackaby continued, "a powerful elemental creature with a hide of dripping flames and bones of solid rock. It is said that this monster lives in the molten lava of an active volcano, and that it hungers for human flesh. Do you know what sort of human flesh it favors most?"

The men looked at one another, unsure how to respond to the uninvited storyteller. A whimper issued from the figure at their feet.

"Young women." Jackaby's voice was cold. "Virgins. Curious, isn't it? How the monsters always seem to prey on the innocent and the weak? Perhaps it's because goodness and love are so unlike monstrosity. It is the ugliest aspect of human nature that we fear what is most different from ourselves with such violent contempt."

The figure lying on the ground slapped away the men's hands and curled into a ball against the brick wall. My eyes were adjusting to the dark, and I saw that it was a woman. Her hair was pinned up in tight black curls and her skin was deep brown. She wore a pink, sleeveless dress with high-cut skirts, like a dancer from a burlesque show. Her dress was muddied, and just one pink shoe lay at her feet.

"What, you mean this filth?" The big man sneered. "Ain't nothing innocent about him."

"Her," Jackaby said evenly.

"Psst!" One of the other men nudged his comrade. "That's that detective. The one who sees things. They say he caught a werewolf who was pretending to be a policeman."

The third man swore derisively. "You believe that load of–"

"There were witnesses. Lots. He's the real thing. I hear he sees through walls and things."

"He can't see through much," said the first man, "if he can't see that's a damned boy. Freak show in a dress." The pink dress shuddered and the figure let out a whimper. "Sicko makes his money off walkin' the streets. Now he's learning a lesson about what happens when his kind walks down the wrong street–so why don't you two just keep walkin' before we teach you the same lesson?"

"The thing about the legend," Jackaby went on, seemingly oblivious of the scene before him, "is that monsters like the Chilean Cherufe are never satisfied. You can keep sacrificing young maidens until you've burned through them all, but the monster will still be there, will still be waiting, will still be a monster. I've ceased appeasing monsters. Young lady? Shall we?"

A face peered up in the darkness, eyes rimmed with red and full of fear and anger. The woman glanced between her attackers, and then pushed herself unsteadily to her feet. She left the shoe behind and limped forward on torn stockings. Her hands were shaking and she glared daggers at the big man. She was larger than I had expected, tall enough to look her attacker in the eye. I half expected her to lash out and strike him, but she gritted her teeth and walked away as steadily as she was able. Jackaby held out a hand as she approached, but she shied away and stepped past him.

As she reached me, I saw her face in the light at last.

Tears had streaked down her dark cheeks, and her lip was bloodied. She had a strong jaw and broad shoulders for a girl. She looked at me with suspicion as she drew near. I offered her a sympathetic smile. "It's all right," I said. "You can lean on me."

Her lips shook and fresh tears welled in her eyes, but she nodded and put an arm around my shoulder. She was a foot taller than I was, so I don't know how much support I actually provided, but she seemed to rally a fraction as she turned back to watch Jackaby and the other men.

"So you're a freak, too, huh?" sneered the big man.

I couldn't see Jackaby's face, but I could almost hear the broad grin in his answer. "I'm not generally one for titles, but that is one I'll embrace with pride."

"Whatever," the man spat. "You can have him. That sick bastard ain't the innocent virgin from your fairy tale, Mr. Detective Man. And we ain't the monsters here."

"Oh, you seem to have gotten the wrong impression," Jackaby replied. "The metaphor may be appropriate–but I wasn't simply speaking figuratively." He held up one of the little red rocks. "I was explaining what you're up against. Cherufe's tears are rare relics, and more than I care to waste tonight. When I packed I was anticipating more menacing monsters than the likes of you. I think we are both fortunate we could conclude our little encounter on reasonable terms. Good day, gentlemen."

Jackaby turned and walked away.

"You *are* a freak!" the man yelled after him.

Jackaby kept walking.

"Better not let me see that sicko around here again!" the man hollered. "His kind don't deserve to walk free! You should've let us finish teaching him a lesson! It was for his own good!"

Jackaby stopped. His fists were clenched.

"If I ever see him again, I'll–" The man never finished his taunt.

The first red rock hit the ground with an ardent blast. The cobblestones liquefied on contact, and, with a splash of flame, the alleyway in front of the thugs was suddenly glowing with heat, bubbles of bright orange spattering and sizzling as they popped.

The men fell backward, but Jackaby let fly another stone before they could rally. It arced over their heads and erupted on the other side of the thin alleyway, locking them between two glowing pools of magma. Terror danced across their faces in flickering reds and yellows.

"If you ever see *her* again," my employer growled, "you will remember that monsters pick on the weak and the harmless because it is the monsters who are afraid." He held the final stone in his fingers and stepped to the edge of the bubbling pool. "And they are right to be afraid."

The men cowered against the bare bricks as Jackaby raised his hand for a final throw. "No! Don't!" The ring-leader's voice cracked.

"Leave them be." The voice at my side startled me. It was soft and low.

Jackaby turned. His arm dropped slowly until it hung at his side. He was breathing heavily.

Behind him, the magma was already cooling, ruby red pools hardening to charred black rock. The three men scrambled, jumping over the patch on the far side and scampering off into the night.

"They would not have been merciful to you," said Jackaby.

"No," she agreed. "They wouldn't."

Jackaby's lips turned up ever so slightly. "Ah, I see. That's precisely the point, isn't it? Yes. I suppose you're right."

"I'd rather be the maiden than the monster any day," the woman said. "But you're wrong about me."

Jackaby raised his eyebrows. "Oh? I'm generally a very good judge of character."

"Weak and harmless?"

Jackaby paused. "I did not mean to imply . . . but fair enough. My apologies. Please allow me to introduce myself–"

"Detective Jackaby," she said. "I read the papers, too, mister. You had a hat in the picture."

Jackaby nodded with a pout. "I certainly did. A good hat, too. This is my associate, Miss Abigail Rook."

"My heroes," she said. "You can call me Lydia. Lydia Lee."

"Charmed, Miss Lee," I said. "I would rather our meeting had come under better circumstances."

She laughed weakly. It was a deep, husky laugh. "That's sweet, miss, but I don't see folks like you ever meeting someone like me under *better circumstances*."

I swallowed, not knowing how to respond. "We'll get you to a hospital straightaway," I said.

"Don't bother with any of that," she said, making an effort to straighten up. "I've been through worse. I'll be through worse again."

Jackaby stepped forward to take her other arm. "And still true to yourself. You are anything but weak, Miss Lee, I'll grant you that. If you won't accept our help, then please allow us the pleasure of your company as far as your front door?"

Miss Lee accepted Jackaby's arm and we escorted her a few blocks to the east, where she informed us that she shared a cramped apartment on the second floor. Lamps lit up in the windows as we approached, and a crowd of women soon came pouring out of the nearby doorways to help. An old woman with thick gray curls tied back in a tight bun pushed to the front. She rounded on Jackaby before we had even reached the stairs. "Is this your doing?" She menaced Jackaby with a prod from a hefty rolling pin.

Lydia waved her off. "It's okay, Mama Tilly. They're only helping."

"Are you sure you'll be all right?" I asked as one of Miss Lee's neighbors took my place at her side, nudging me out of the way.

"I'll be fine, miss," she said, wincing as she tested her weight on the first step. Jackaby spoke quietly with the woman called Mama Tilly, and then as quickly as we had gotten ourselves into the whole mess, we were out of it. Jackaby trod back up the road as if nothing had happened.

"What were you talking to Mama Tilly about?" I asked, keeping pace.

"Hm? Just making some arrangements. Miss Lee was not entirely truthful about her state of affairs. She is in tremendous pain. She has at least one fractured rib and serious bruising on her legs and arms, possibly more serious injuries beneath–she needs medical attention. We happen to know a capable nurse. This should be a perfectly simple house call for Mona O'Connor–at least compared to the last one she performed for us." Miss O'Connor's last patient had been only mostly human. "I gave Mama Tilly Mona's information and advised her to charge the services to me."

I nodded. "That was kind of you." We walked on for a few more paces. "Was Miss Lee really . . ." I hesitated.

"What?" Jackaby looked back at me.

"Miss Lee was really a boy, wasn't she? Underneath?"

He slowed and then came to a stop and looked me square in the eyes. "That's up to her to decide, I suppose, but it's not what I saw. Underneath, she was herself–as are we all. Lydia Lee is as much a lady as you or Jenny or anyone. I imagine the midwife or attending doctor probably had another opinion on the matter, but it only goes to show what doctors really know."

"Shouldn't a doctor be able to tell at least that much?"

Jackaby's expression clouded darkly. "I have great respect for the medical profession, Miss Rook," he said soberly, "but it is not for doctors to tell us who we are."

Chapter Eight

The sun slipped down to meet the horizon as we pressed on through New Fiddleham, the sky darkening like a dying ember. A lamplighter was making his way from streetlight to streetlight as we passed. My feet were beginning to ache and I had a stitch in my side, but Jackaby's inner fires seemed only to have been stoked by our encounter with the thugs. He marched forward briskly and I began to lag behind.

A hansom cab rolled past with rubber wheels that glided smoothly along the cobblestones behind its horse. The couple seated within looked impossibly, almost arrogantly comfortable. "Have you ever considered hiring a driver, sir?" I called ahead breathlessly. "It's just that we do seem to do quite a bit of traveling."

"There is a great deal to be experienced in this city," he answered, not looking back. "No reason to limit the scope of our vision."

"The scope of my vision," I said, panting, "is not quite the same as the scope of yours, Mr. Jackaby. And I have experienced blisters before."

He paused at the end of the street and waited for me to catch up. I half expected him to be cross with me, but he looked sympathetic. "There is quite a lot to miss," he said. "Do you know that long before it was ever called New Fiddleham, this area was already inhabited?"

"You mean by Indians?" I said.

He leaned against a wrought iron hitching post and nodded. "Do you see that?" He pointed at the empty road. At midday, this stretch of Mason Street would be a blur of carriages and pedestrians clamoring to and fro, but in the dwindling light of dusk it was abandoned. "Just there," Jackaby prompted, "in the middle of the lane."

Between the worn path of countless carriage wheels, a single weed had pushed up through the paving stones. "I see a little green plant, if that's what you mean" I said.

"And I see the spirit watching over it," he said. "The Algonquian peoples would call it a manitou. It is older than any of these buildings, older than the city, older even than the tribes who named it. I would wager it will be here long after all of these bricks have crumbled to dust."

He began to walk again, but slowly. "There is something

humbling about knowing that an entity capable of moving mountains and reshaping continents still takes the time to tend to the smallest patch of dirt. Little things matter. Footsteps matter." He stepped a little farther down the block and I followed. "There," he said. "The flower shop. Do you see the little alcove in the wall?"

"Yes," I answered. It was an inconspicuous break in the masonry, an indentation only a foot deep, topped by a simple awning of red stone. I might have taken it for a bricked-up window.

"This whole block had become home to predominantly Chinese immigrant families until about the 1880s, when the ungentle gentry saw potential in the neighborhood and bought the property out from under its denizens. Most of the Chinese inhabitants who stayed in New Fiddleham relocated to the burgeoning tenement district a few blocks south. But not everyone left."

He put his hands together and bowed respectfully to the hollow. "Tu Di Gong is a modest figure, but a noble one. He's there now, still looking over his village like a kindly grandfather. That was where they kept his shrine. He serves his little corner of New Fiddleham in whatever ways he can these days, though his influence is overlooked and misunderstood. I find it all too easy to sympathize."

We came to the end of the block, where the city opened to accommodate a broad park bordered by streetlights. The sun was setting on us–it was no time to be wandering in the darkest quarters of the city, but the shadows were not so intimidating here. The lamps shone brighter around the park than they did in the rest of the city, and the whole park hummed with pleasant energy.

"This is Seeley's Square," said Jackaby. "Mayor Spade's only successful foray into his grand electrical city. Do you know for whom the park is named?"

"Erm, Mr. Seeley, I presume?"

Jackaby shook his head. "Not for a Mr. Seeley, nor for any man. The Seelies are kindly fae. They arrived with the city's founders, long ago, and I do believe they like it here. They and the native manitous might be more kindred spirits than the humans who tell their tales. This park is a haven for benevolent beings of all kinds."

He looked out across the open space, and I followed his gaze. I could almost convince myself that I could see what he was seeing. Flickers of light seemed to dance through the greenery–although it might have been nothing more than the bright streetlamps reflecting on the leaves. "People often feel more alone than ever when they first arrive in a new place," Jackaby continued, "but we are never alone. We bring with us the spirits of our ancestors. We are haunted by their demons and protected by their deities."

He took a deep breath and turned to me. "I prefer to walk, Miss Rook, because I appreciate this city–and all the more when it's being threatened. I like to see the lights all around me and feel the ground beneath my feet. This city is alive. It has a soul, and that soul is a glorious mess of beliefs and cultures all swirling together into something precious and strange and new."

"Like Monet," I said.

"Nothing like Monet," said Jackaby. "What's a Monet?"

"A painter. He's French. My mother met him once at a gala in Paris. They had a few of his works in the museum back home. He uses a hundred little daubs of color, and then from a distance they all melt into one big lovely picture. When you're right up close, though, it's just beautiful madness."

"Oh. Yes." Jackaby smiled. "Just like Monet. Exactly like that. I prefer to walk because I like to be right up close to the beautiful madness."

The museum back home also had cushioned chairs you could take a rest in whenever your feet were sore, I remembered, but I kept that thought to myself. A figure was marching across the park now, making a beeline right for us. "I do believe one of your more colorful daubs is coming to see you, sir."

"Hm?" Jackaby locked on to her and smiled. "Oh, Hatun! Auspicious timing."

Hatun could have been the queen of her own kingdom in some far-off land, had the streets of New Fiddleham not needed her more. She was an elderly woman, poor, but with a naturally regal air about her and a domineering presence. As much as she stood out, she seemed equally able to do the opposite, melting instantly into the scenery in that subtle way that made it hard to remember if she had ever been there at all. She wore several layers of faded petticoats, and her pale gray hair was tied up in a handkerchief.

"Good evening, Hatun," I said.

"Hammett's cat," she replied.

"Come again?" I said. "Hammett the troll?"

She nodded. "Yes, yes, of course the troll. He has an orange tabby, only it's gone missing, and now Hammett's in a terrible state."

"Not to put too fine a point on the matter," Jackaby said, "but isn't being in a terrible state Hammett's natural state? He may be diminutive, but he's still a bridge troll. How many times has he threatened to eat your toes?"

"Pardon me, Detective Knows-So-Much, but which one of us spent all season looking after him? I know my troll, Mr. Jackaby, and he's off."

"Fair enough. Still, he can't have expected the thing to stick around forever," Jackaby said. "You've seen the way he abuses the poor creature. Cats were not bred for riding."

Hatun squinted her eyes at my employer. "Those two were nigh inseparable, thank you very much. Should've seen them hunting voles together at night. Two halves of a whole. It was like watching music by moonlight. Music played on a miniature saddle made from gopher leather."

"I'm sure we can help find Hammett's friend," I said. "Only right now we're already on a rather pressing case,

Hatun. People have gone missing and lives are once more at stake in New Fiddleham."

Hatun looked at me for several long seconds, until I began to feel a little uncomfortable under her gaze. Her eyes swam out of focus, and I could tell that she was leaving lucidity and falling into something else. Hatun, like my employer, saw visions the rest of us could not perceive. Unlike my employer, whose sight was constant, invading even his dreams, Hatun's visions were unreliable. She oscillated from normalcy to profound insight to absolute gibberish. Her inscrutable predictions included the coming insurrection of the city's united weathercocks, a strong chance of a mild rain on Thursday, and the approach of my imminent and inescapable death–a fate which thus far I had escaped. Twice. "What is it, Hatun?"

"This is the one," she whispered. She was squinting at me as though gazing into the sun. "Oh my. Oh dear. You're already so far down the path, aren't you? I told you not to follow him. I told you."

"Yes, you did, Hatun. Thank you for the warnings, truly. I do promise to be watchful."

"I see a hound," Hatun continued. She had screwed her eyes shut while she spoke. "And a man with red eyes at the end of a long, dark hallway . . ."

Jackaby went ashen. "What did you say?"

"Death. Death is waiting for you on the other side of

Rosemary's Green. This is the one, Miss Rook. This is the path."

"Of course there's death on the other side of Rosemary's Green," Jackaby said. "There's a cemetery on the other side of Rosemary's Green. What about the man–the hallway? What do you see? Hatun!" His sudden intensity seemed to rattle the woman. She opened her eyes. Dilated pupils contracted and she blinked up at him.

"What? Yes, rosemary's always green. It's an herb, isn't it? What's got you so bothered?"

Jackaby deflated. "Nothing. We will look into the matter of Hammett's cat at our earliest convenience, Hatun. Come along, Miss Rook."

"Take care of yourself," I said.

Hatun smiled weakly back at me, her eyes hung with quiet sadness. She patted my arm gently. "Good-bye, Miss Rook." She spoke the words heavily.

Jackaby was already halfway up the block when I turned to hurry after him. He said nothing. His shoulders were stiff and his face was clouded with dark thoughts as he rounded the corner ahead of me.

My feet still ached and, beautiful or not, New Fiddleham's labyrinthine streets were a shade of madness I would be hard pressed to appreciate even in full daylight. I froze as I reached the turn. The street was empty. I silently cursed Jackaby and hurried toward the next crossing. The alleyways to the left and right were dark. There was no sign of my employer in either direction. Children giggled somewhere nearby, and I could hear footfalls and the distant clop of hooves. A leaden feeling hit my stomach as I realized I was alone in the middle of the night with a murderer on the loose.

"Sir?" I called, trying not to sound too timid. "Mr. Jackaby?"

"This way, Miss Rook."

The voice crept in a whisper out of the shadows to my left. "Oh, my word!" I jumped and then collected myself, stepping out of the glow of the gaslights and into the gloom of the alleyway. "I lost you for a moment, sir. You nearly startled me out of my–"

My voice caught in my throat.

The face in the darkness was not Jackaby's. "Your skin?" The face was round and deathly pale, tinted with a bluish shadow along the chin. The pale man smiled and tipped his hat, and the grin etched wrinkles from his brow up into his jet-black hair. "Hello, Miss Rook. I'm so glad we could meet face-to-face at last. Please, call me Pavel."

Chapter Nine

My breath was coming in shallow gasps. I tried to steady my nerves. How far could I run before he caught me? Would I even reach the light? Would he kill me more quickly if I screamed? "You–"

"Me," the pale man confirmed with a wink. "Do calm down. I can hear your blood pumping from here. If I wanted you dead, you'd be dead, Miss Rook."

"You're . . ." I panted. "You're . . ."

He nodded. "Monstrously underdressed for our first business meeting, I know. I'm rather fond of this coat, though. It's older than you are–you'd never guess to look at it, but that's craftsmanship for you. Tailors today just aren't what they used to be. The scarf is new, at least. I do like a nice scarf."

I blinked.

Pavel shrugged. "I know. You were going to say *a vampire*, yes? This is also true."

"Y-You admit it?"

"Honesty is essential if we are to forge a functional working relationship, my dear girl."

"What are you talking about? We're not working together. You–You murdered all those people!"

"Yes, I did. More than you know. Lots more. That's honesty, right there. We've already discussed how I'm not killing you. So, let's call that compassion. See? I'm full of good qualities." He flashed a winning smile and I saw that he was missing a canine on one side. He caught my gaze and closed his lips self-consciously. "Never mind about that," he said. His tongue brushed over the gap. "I ate something that disagreed with me."

"Eating something that disagreed with you dislodged a tooth?" I asked.

"Well, he disagreed with my decision to eat him," Pavel said, "and he disagreed rather firmly. Bitter blood, that one."

I swallowed. "What have you done with Mr. Jackaby?"

"I haven't done anything with him, Miss Rook. As it happens, my benefactors have use for your master's unique services. That is why we're talking."

"Did you have use for Mr. Jackaby's services when you set him up against a fifty-foot, man-eating dragon?"

Pavel flinched. "Mistakes were made in Gad's Valley," he admitted. "Events escalated further than I intended."

"My friend is dead!" I yelled at him. His mistake had murdered the indomitable Nellie Fuller right in front of me.

"All of my friends are dead," he spat curtly. "Every last human being who walked this stinking earth when my heart still beat is dead. If it makes you feel any better, though . . ." He drew his chalk white hand gingerly from the pocket of his coat and held it up for me to see, flexing his fingers in the dim light. His pinkie had been severed just above the knuckle, leaving only a short nub. "My superiors were not pleased about the affair, either."

I looked away from the disfigured hand and focused on his eyes. They were hung with sickly blue shadows. "If you're just the big bad attack dog," I said, "then who's holding the leash?"

"Not so big and bad, Miss Rook." Pavel chuckled. "But I understand you have a special fondness for dogs, don't you?"

My hands clenched into fists and I gritted my teeth.

"Oh yes," he went on, reading me easily. "I know all about your little beau on the police force. Charlie Cane and I aren't so different, really. Oh, it's Charlie Howler or some such nonesense now, isn't it?"

My blood was pumping again. Charlie was sweet and noble and good. This cretin had no business knowing his deepest secret. "It's Barker. And you're nothing alike."

"Barker, right. A dog by any other name would bite as deep. I'm rather fond of him, actually. A fellow monster from the old country. You know, I camped with a pack of Om Caini for a while in Bulgaria. Do you think one of them might have been your little pup's grandfather? We're practically family!"

I glared. "Why are you here?"

"I'm not hunting tonight, if that's what you're afraid of—at least not the way you think."

"Then what do you want? Why are you doing this? Who are you working for?"

"My, my—you're looking for a lot of answers, young lady. Information is expensive in my line of work, but I would be happy to arrange a trade."

"Jenny Cavanaugh and Howard Carson. Ten years ago. I want to know what happened."

Pavel cocked his head ever so slightly. "I can tell you everything you want to know about Carson and his girl—but it won't come free."

"What do you want from us?"

"I understand Mr. Jackaby has a talent for finding things. We're looking for a man. An inventor." He reached into his waistcoat with his good hand and withdrew a folded slip of paper. "He's called Owen Finstern. My superiors believe he's a genius, and I'm inclined to believe whatever my superiors tell me to believe. Genius or not, he is, shall we say, less than stable. He needs a nourishing environment for his special talents to thrive, and regrettably he's gone astray."

"One of the scientists you kidnapped has escaped, and you think Jackaby and I are going to just round him up for you?"

"Kidnapped? Miss Rook, I'm offended. We have only the man's best interest at heart. And our own interests, of course. There's that honesty again. Here." He held out the paper and, against my better judgment, I took it. "Keep the sketch. Think about our offer."

I felt something cold in my hand and looked down to see that, along with the paper, he had passed me a small, round stone. "What is this?" I asked, but I was speaking only to the empty shadows of the alleyway. The pale man was gone.

Chapter Ten

I found my way back to the house on Augur Lane, chills crawling up and down my back with every step. Jackaby was not in the library when I arrived, nor in his laboratory or office. Even Jenny was conspicuously absent. By the state of her bedchamber, I could see she had had another echo. They were coming more and more often.

I climbed the spiral staircase to the third floor. This was, perhaps, my favorite space in all of Jackaby's property—a magical oasis that defied logic and geometric reality. A quiet pond stretched across most of the floor, both deeper and wider than the house logically should have been able to accommodate. Beside it stretched a mossy indoor hillside speckled with wildflowers and sweet grasses. Usually this was the perfect place to calm my nerves, but in the silent darkness I found little comfort. I called out until my words bounced back at me over the midnight black waters of the pond. My own voice was my sole companion.

At length, I trudged back down the stairs alone to my employer's office. My fingers were shaking as I lit the lamp at Jackaby's desk and took the stone and paper out of my pocket to inspect them properly.

The stone was smooth on one side, but the other was etched with a series of concentric ovals, like a crude carving of an eye. A warning, perhaps? Pavel's calling card? I unfolded the paper to find a man with wild hair staring back at me. His eyes were unsettling. The left was set a bit wider and a fraction higher than the right, and together they gave him a frantic, manic expression. He did not look like any of the men on Mayor Spade's mantel, nor like any from the photograph with Howard Carson.

I refolded the paper and slid both artifacts back into my pocket. The sketch would have to wait until morning. Jackaby was still not home, and my brief history in his service had taught me that when he latched on to something of interest, I might not see him until a late tea the following day. I stood up from the desk and stepped toward the door when the blood all rushed from my head. I shook the sensation away, blinking. My head was suddenly aching.

The day must have taken more out of me than I realized. I leaned against the heavy office safe until the dizziness subsided. As I shifted my weight, the thick iron door squeaked open a crack.

Of all the doors, cabinets, and cupboards in the entire house, I had only ever found one that Jackaby kept locked at all times. He stored a fat old jar plainly labeled "Bail Money" with hundreds of dollars on the shelf right across from me. Every spare nook and cranny in the building housed lavish payments and mementos from past adventures, opulent heirlooms and eldritch artifacts so unique they made the London Museum's Cabinet of Curiosities look like a collection of knickknacks. I had often wondered what a man such as Jackaby–a man who regarded gold candelabras and strangely luminescent gemstones with as little care as I might afford an incomplete deck of playing cards–saw fit to keep under lock and key behind a solid inch of iron. Blinking back my disbelief, I gave the safe another nudge and the door swung open.

A worn leather file lay within, several inches thick with papers. I glanced over my shoulder, but the house was still and silent. Quietly I lifted the hefty dossier and set it on the desk. A thin leather strap was wrapped loosely around the bundle, and this I unwound tenderly. Only a peek, I told myself, and then I would put it back.

The collection was subdivided into smaller files, and I recognized the one at the top as the same sort Jackaby often used for his general records. I had organized enough case files to know. Farther down, the papers were yellowed and much older than any stationery we kept about the house.

When I flipped open the first file, newspaper clippings and lithographs stared up at me. Among them I was startled to find my own face. My cheek was not yet marred by the little scar, but the images were recent. In one photograph, torn from a newspaper, I marched sullenly through the lobby of a building. My hands were locked in handcuffs, and Jackaby was at my side looking unperturbed by the matching pair around his own wrists. I remembered the scene. It was the Emerald Arch Apartments. Our first case together.

I picked up the next photograph. A fire-damaged cabinet card showed Jackaby and me on either side of a tree in a forest clearing. Hank Hudson, the burly trapper, stood just behind me, and a fourth figure hung upside down above us, his legs wrapped awkwardly around a tree branch and his face shrouded and blurred by his flopping coat. I smiled. Beneath that coat was Charlie Barker. The moment seemed funny out of context, cast in sepia hues, without the grisly red of a slaughtered animal painting the forest around us. It had not been such an amusing sight in person. The woman behind the camera, Nellie Fuller, had lost her life reaching the bottom of that mystery. Our second case.

Not a single portrait hung on Jackaby's walls. Unlike the mayor, who adorned his study with images of his wife and dear friends, Jackaby had no one. The closest he came were busts of Shakespeare and paintings of old folktales. I was oddly touched. These were not the most flattering pictures, but they were pictures of me–pictures of us–and hidden away or not, he had saved them.

I dug further. There were newspaper articles detailing other grim cases Jackaby had worked on, a blurry photograph of the house in which we sat, and a tattered wanted poster featuring Jackaby's smiling face. One of the images was of a pleasant if somewhat stuffy-looking man in a prim waistcoat standing proudly beside Jackaby. Something about him was vaguely familiar, but I couldn't place the face. An unnerving sensation that I was not alone tickled across my brain.

I closed the file and glanced guiltily behind me. Douglas had waddled into the doorway. He acknowledged me with a bob of his feathered head and then flapped up into the armchair across the room, where he settled to rest with his bill under one wing.

Taking a deep breath, I picked up the next file. This one contained comparatively little–a slim notebook and a few creased papers. I held them up to read the writing at the top. They were formal documents. PSYCHIATRIC EVALUATION was printed in large face across the top, but the patient's name was not Jackaby's. "'Eleanor Clark,'" I read aloud. As if in answer to my whisper, a little brown envelope slid out from behind the documents and off the desk. I made a futile grab for it, but it swooped through my fingers and came to land on the carpet.

"Miss Rook?"

Jackaby dropped his satchel in the doorway with a thump. I froze. He looked at the dossier on the desk. He looked at me. His face grew cold. Without another word, he knelt and retrieved the envelope, holding it as gingerly as if it were made of fine glass. He placed it back into the file very deliberately.

"I'm so sorry, Mr. Jackaby. I didn't mean to–"

"Then put it back."

I nodded and closed the dossier.

"I have given you free rein to my home and offices with very few exceptions, Miss Rook."

"Yes, sir. I'm sorry, sir. I–"

"I could, perhaps, have been more explicit, but I felt that several inches of solid metal and a rotary combination lock implied my intentions clearly enough."

"Of course, sir. It won't happen again, sir."

"How did you open it?" he demanded.

"I didn't mean to. It was unlocked. I just–"

"It is never unlocked! I have taken great pains to ensure–" His eyes sunk into dark shadows beneath a sober brow. "You are not lying," he said at last. "I don't know if I find that more troubling or less so." He stepped forward and took the bundle out of my hands. "How much did you see?"

"I only just picked it up when you came in, really."

He walked slowly around his desk. I held my breath. He placed the dossier back onto the desktop and settled into his chair to lean heavily on his elbows. "You should have left it alone."

"What is this, sir? Is it a case? I recognized the photograph from Gad's Valley. I didn't know any of those survived the fire. If they're connected . . ."

"It's not a case," he breathed, and I could see that he was deciding how much more to explain. He placed a hand gently on the leather. "I am a steward to something much older than myself, Miss Rook, and that role comes with responsibilities."

"You mean your sight?"

"I do." He brushed the dossier with his fingertips. "This collection is a perpetual record of the Seer."

"A record of–of you? Why would you need a massive file about yourself?"

"My own addition is very small, Miss Rook. I've told you before that there is only ever a single Seer alive in the world at any given time. That's me right now, but I am not the first and I will not be the last. The power is like a living thing. It transfers to a new vessel every time the Seer passes away. There are certain organizations–exceedingly ancient groups–who take an interest in my unique lineage. One of these organizations came to me many years ago. I was just a boy, confused and alone and beset by questions. They had very few answers to give me"–he tapped the pile–"but what they did have to offer was this."

He opened the folder again and flipped through the top file. "This is me. All of me that the future need know. I have included a few of my fondest memories and defining moments. It is my humble addition to an immeasurable legacy."

He closed the first file, then opened the next, the one with the psychiatric papers, and tenderly ran his hand along the cover of the slim notebook. With an unsteady hand, he once more retrieved the envelope I had dropped. He passed it to me. As I reached for it, he pulled back–just an involuntary flinch, as if caught by instinct, and then he shook his head and released it to my grasp. "Do be careful, Miss Rook."

I nodded, more curious than ever, and opened the envelope. Inside was a tintype. A man and woman in shades of gray occupied the foreground of the picture, well dressed and smiling. Beneath them stood a girl and boy, neither more than ten years old, and behind them were tents and banners. The girl looked very much like her mother, fair-haired with a heart-shaped face, but even in the grainy tintype her eyes were wrong–wide and wild, and much too old for a girl in grammar school. The boy looked out of place, as well. His hair was messy and much darker than the adults'. He wore scuffed knee-length knickers, and one sock had slid down to his ankle. Although the child was youthful, his cheekbones were already hard, and he looked thin and wiry.

"Wait a moment. Is this . . ." I looked between my employer and the picture. "Is this you?"

Jackaby nodded.

"You're so young! Oh my goodness, you're adorable. You've never told me anything about your life before New Fiddleham. Are those your parents?"

"No." Jackaby leaned in and reached a finger very delicately toward the girl. It quavered slightly. "They are hers, but they were kind enough to bring me with them to the fair that day." His voice cracked as he spoke. "She didn't have many friends."

"Please, sir," I said. "Tell me about her."

"It is not a happy story."

"Who is she?"

My employer closed his eyes and breathed in deeply. "Eleanor."

Chapter Eleven

The picture quivered in Jackaby's hands. He said nothing else for several seconds. Finally his eyes opened, but they were worlds away.

"Eleanor was my only friend," he said, "and I was hers. I read a lot of books. I scored well in the sciences, but even then I was more enthralled by myths and legends. I had no idea how much I did not know. The sight had not yet come to me. Other children were more interested in . . . well, in whatever it is that schoolchildren are interested in. Teasing bookish boys like me was high on the list, apparently. I kept my interests hidden, kept quiet, and kept to myself.

"Until Eleanor. She came in halfway through the year. Eleanor never said a word in class, and she preferred to play alone. The other children gossiped that she was mad.

They said she made up stories and got angry when people didn't believe her. They said she had been expelled from her last school for attacking another student. They said a lot of things. Eleanor, as a rule, said nothing.

"One day I was in the library and I saw her sketching a little fairy in her notebook. I asked her what sort it was, and she scowled and said what did it matter to me? I told her I was only wondering if it was a brownie or a pixie or what, because it looked a lot like the pixies in one of my favorite books, *Mendel's Magical Menagerie.*

"I shared my book with her, and she shared her secret with me, and we shared the day together–growing fonder of each other by the hour. For many months after, we were each other's sole companions. We collected special charms and wards and hid our artifacts in matching cigar boxes tied shut with twine beneath our beds. They were nothing more than chicken bones and salt and children's scribbles, but they were our most precious secrets. Eleanor would tell me about the impossible things she could see, and I made a game of finding examples of them in lore to remind her that other people had seen them, too–that she couldn't be mad–or perhaps just that she didn't have to be mad alone.

"It was wonderful at first, but her parents grew concerned. Their little girl was hallucinating–and worse, she was hallucinating unrepentantly and without shame. They had Eleanor committed to an institution."

Jackaby's tone as he said the word *institution* could have soured milk.

"After several months she was released, looking very thin and hollow. She told them the visions had stopped—that she was cured. There were no creatures in the leaves or sprites in the sunbeams. The long, dark hallway was just a long, dark hallway. There was no man at the end of it with eyes like glowing embers, always waiting—always watching.

"Her parents were so happy. They took us to the fair and allowed themselves to pretend that everything was better. Eleanor kept up her charade for nearly a month, pretending to be normal for parents who would lock her away for telling them the truth. But then the stranger came.

"He told her that she was in danger, that he was part of a society that was interested in her gifts. He told her there were others who would want to take her away, and that they had found her. He told her that her family was in great peril. Eleanor's mother returned home and saw the stranger talking to Eleanor. She chased the man away, threatening to call the police.

"When the clouds boiled red the next day, Eleanor saw death in the sky and she let it out, all of it. She traced the house with salt, said every incantation she could find, hung makeshift wards of chicken bones and twine around the property. It was every protection we had collected in our little cigar boxes and more. She was so afraid, my poor, sweet Eleanor. She only wanted to protect them, to keep them safe. She did everything she could.

"They saw it as a terrible relapse, of course. Eleanor knew that they were going to send her back, so she hid. She pulled me into the neighbor's run-down shed and begged me to stay with her. I didn't know what to do. I was afraid. We should have run. We should have run away and never stopped running. I should have kept her safe, but I was a stupid, frightened little boy, and I did nothing. I told her to think how it would look if they found us. She scowled and told me I shouldn't concern myself with how things look to others. Others are generally wrong."

"That's what you said to me," I said, "the first day we met." My interruption seemed to draw him out of his trance, and he blinked up at me.

"And so you shouldn't."

"What happened next, sir? How did you get away?"

Jackaby swallowed. "We didn't. They came. They took her. It was *for her own good*, they said. Three months passed, and they finally let me see her again. She was bone-thin and shaking. She barely registered that I was there. She was terrified of those red eyes at the end of the hallway. The long, dark hallway–she kept repeating it. Only there was no hallway. Her room opened into a commons. Nobody understood what she meant. She wouldn't tell me any more, or she couldn't. During her fourth month in the asylum"–Jackaby cleared his throat–"she died. There was no medical explanation; she was simply gone." His eyes were glossy as he stared at the tintype.

"I knew that it had happened before they told me. I knew it before they found her. I didn't understand it, but I knew. I knew the precise moment her life was snuffed out, because in that same instant a blaze was lit behind my eyes. It was as though I had been stumbling in the darkness my entire life and someone had just flicked on a light. It was precisely as she had described it. All of it. The auras, the images, the fairies, the monsters. I don't know why the sight chose me. The power has never passed to anyone so close to the previous steward. I like to think it was her will, though–Eleanor's final gift to a stupid, frightened boy."

His eyes were rimmed with red. He pushed back his chair and stared mutely at the dossier for several seconds. "Please put it away, Miss Rook."

I slid the tintype delicately back into its envelope and closed the file. I wound the leather strap around the heavy parcel again and tucked the whole thing back inside the safe. The door clanked shut and I spun the lock. The tumblers clicked to a stop, and this time the door did not budge when I tested it.

"Mr. Jackaby–" I began.

"It's irrelevant." He swallowed his emotions and stood up. "There are more pressing matters at hand. I paid a visit to the Mudlark boys on the way home. Ran into them with a group of their young associates. Daniel is the boy who stumbled across Professor Hoole's body in the sewage runoff. He and his brother, Benjamin, are enterprising boys. They apparently make a tidy living selling what they find to local jewelers or merchants. Quite a lot of worthwhile things find their way down the drain, for those who are willing to sort through the muck to find them."

"That is both intriguing and nauseating."

"I think you might have enjoyed meeting them. By the way, I wish you had let me know that you were planning on returning to the house directly rather than following me. I know that you are a capable young woman, but I would prefer you not wander off unescorted."

"It wasn't really my choice, sir."

"All is forgiven. Anyway, the Mudlarks are well established among the assembled youngsters of the area, and there's apparently a lot of talk recently about strange goings-on."

"The street gangs are talking about our killer?"

"They're talking about rats."

"Rats?"

"And cats and dogs. It seems Hammett is not the only one whose furry friend has gone astray. The city pays for the extermination of rats, did you know? There seems to be a whole sewer-based system of commerce I knew nothing about. They pay by the head, and so several of the young gentlemen in the Mudlark's company keep traps in convenient, inconspicuous locations. They can count on a fairly regular supply, except the traps keep turning up empty. Nearly started a few heated fights, as I understand, with one rat-catcher accusing the other, but then other animals began disappearing as well, particularly around the fringes of the city. One of the boys lost a spaniel."

"Chameleomorphs?" I speculated. The last time cats had gone missing around town, it had been due to the nightly snacking of a little shape-shifting creature posing as a house pet.

"I don't think so." Jackaby smiled. "This is where it gets interesting. The boys have seen lights in the forest–nothing constant like a campfire or a torch–strange lights, blue and flickering. I've never encountered one in person, but I am prone to suspect we're dealing with a hinkypunk, or maybe even a will-o'-the-wisp."

The gloom had lifted and Jackaby was himself again, enamored with the prospect of pursuing another nefarious fairy tale.

"Obviously a wisp isn't solely responsible for Jenny's murder, but their presence could explain what happened to Mr. Carson and the other kidnapping victims. Wisps are not physically intimidating, per se, but they are known for confounding their victims and leading them astray."

"Jackaby," I said. "I ran into someone on the way home as well."

"Speaking of victims," he rambled on, "I've also had a notion about Mrs. Beaumont's killer."

"It was the pale man, Jackaby. Pavel."

"Yes, exactly. I believe our pale man may be a creature called a lilu. They're mentioned in early Akkadian and Sumerian myths. Considered children of Lilith in some Hebrew texts. Gilgamesh was said to be the son of a lilu."

"He's a vampire."

"No, I know that was your first inclination," Jackaby said, "but it's much too obvious. I have a lot of experience with this sort of thing, and the obvious answer is never the right one. You see, a lilu, while much more obscure, is actually far more entrenched in–"

"He's a vampire. He told me."

"–entrenched in the history of..." Jackaby's gears ground to a halt. "Who told you?"

"Pavel. The pale man. The vampire. We talked. He didn't murder me horribly, no thanks to you. You were chasing after children at the time."

Jackaby opened his mouth, but, failing to find anything to say for once, he closed it again.

"He's not what I expected a vampire to be," I said. "We used to tell stories when I was younger, and vampires were always, I don't know, sort of elegant and refined in a dark, mysterious way. Pavel was just a shabby man in a black coat. His skin is even more unsettling up close. More than just pale, it's sort of blue around his chin and eyes."

"Suggillation. Not unexpected in the undead. Livor mortis sets in when the heart stops beating. You spoke?"

"Yes. And he's our man, no mistake. He's missing a fang on the left side."

"That accounts for the single puncture wounds on his victims."

I nodded. "He's working for someone, and they're not finished. They're after another scientist." I pulled out the sketch of Owen Finstern and handed it to him. The man was as unfamiliar to Jackaby as he was to me. I explained the vampire's sordid business proposition and his promise to reveal everything that had happened to Jenny and her fiancé if we complied.

Jackaby absorbed the information with a heavy scowl. "Jenny can't know about this," he whispered.

"What? Sir, you can't hide her case from her forever," I said.

"This is the first solid lead anyone has uncovered in a decade and we cannot follow it. Informing Miss Cavanaugh would be a meaningless torment."

I sighed. He wasn't wrong.

This was Jenny's case, at least it was supposed to be—but each thread seemed to burst into more threads, and it was becoming a challenge to keep them all sorted, let alone follow them to their conclusions. Howard Carson and the missing scientists were mystery enough, but then had come Cordelia Hoole and Miss Wick and her baby—not to mention Hammett's cat and the sewer rats—and now whomever this Owen Finstern was that Pavel wanted us to find.

It didn't even feel like following threads at all anymore; it felt like tugging at one great tangled knot. "This is not how cases are supposed to go," I said aloud. I had read enough mysteries by candlelight to have developed a sense of these things. Where were the puzzle pieces, sliding smoothly into place? Where was the hidden narrative gradually becoming clear?

"Oh?" said Jackaby. "How are cases supposed to go?"

"I don't know. Logically. This feels like madness."

Jackaby chuckled. "Beautiful madness," he reminded me with a wink. "We're still in the middle of our Monet, remember? Just wait. The picture is there around us. We will find our answers for Miss Cavanaugh." He swallowed.

"I know you care about her," I said.

"Of course I care about her."

"You really should tell her that once in a while. Or just once, at least. Before it's too late." Jackaby glowered at me, and I let the matter drop. "What's our next move, sir?"

"Get some rest," said Jackaby. "Tomorrow evening we follow our own clues and investigate the woods to the west. It will have to be after dark if we hope to see the lights."

Perfect. The city after dark wasn't eerie enough. Of course our next step would be directly into the deep, dark woods.

Chapter Twelve

In the morning I awoke to a rhythmic pounding in my skull. The spot behind my temples was throbbing, and it felt like someone was hammering on the walls with a sledgehammer. I sat up and blinked into the light. It wasn't just in my head. Someone was hammering on the walls with a sledgehammer.

I dressed hastily and, as an afterthought, tucked the strange stone and the sketch of the inventor back into my pocket before I made my way down the spiral staircase. We would not be pursuing the villain's quarry, but somehow I felt better keeping them on hand. The pounding noise had stopped as I descended to the ground floor, but I could hear the sound of frustrated voices coming from the laboratory.

"You can't just expect me to stay sealed in my room while you do whatever you like whenever you like. This is still my house!"

"Exactly the point!" Jackaby countered.

I pushed open the door and peeked inside. There was plaster dust in the air and Jackaby was leaning on a long-handled hammer. Jenny hovered between him and a crumbling hole in the plaster about a foot in diameter. The bare bricks that now showed were chipped and fracturing, with daylight beginning to shine through their cracks. Another blow or two and we would be looking at the garden.

"You can go anywhere in this whole wide world, you insufferable man. This house is all I have! Are you actually trying to push me over the edge?" Jenny demanded.

"In a manner of speaking, yes, I am. Please step aside. Well, float aside. Drift."

"Augh!" Jenny spotted me and threw up her hands. "He's impossible! Abigail, will you please tell this man to stop demolishing my house! At least when I destroy my things it's not on purpose!"

"Sir?" I said. "What *are* you doing?"

"I changed my mind, Miss Rook. I had been against Miss Cavanaugh working to expand her sphere of influence, but that may be just the sort of exercise she needs. You and I are going to be increasingly busy, so I thought it might be prudent and practical to provide Miss Cavanaugh with a little homework to keep her mind occupied while we're away.

No sense sitting idle. We never know when she may need to flex those metaphysical muscles. Can't be too prepared."

"And just how is punching a hole in the wall meant to flex anything but my patience? Wait. Have you learned something?" Jenny looked at Jackaby, and then at me. My expression must have betrayed that I was withholding something, because she drifted off the wall and toward me.

"No, not really," I bluffed unconvincingly. "Just chasing shadows."

She looked skeptical, but Jackaby punctured the moment with an opportunistic swing of the hammer. With a crash, light poured across the dusty carpet, and he dropped the hammer behind him. "There we are!" He knelt and reached through the hole.

"Oh, for the love of–Jackaby, this is my house!" Jenny stamped her foot, which might have had a greater effect if it hadn't been floating several inches off the floor.

"Every last brick," my employer agreed, illustrating the point by plucking one from the flower bed into which it had fallen and pulling it back inside the house. He held it up triumphantly.

"What is that supposed to be?" Jenny asked.

"You said it yourself," said Jackaby. "Your house. The very core of the structure. You can quibble about draperies and wallpaper, but it's hard to argue with a brick."

"You have no idea," said Jenny, shaking her head. "And yet after all these years I keep trying."

"Hold this," he said. He passed the brick to Jenny, who managed to catch it with both translucent hands. She looked uncertain for a moment, but her grip held firm. "Why?" he asked her.

"Shouldn't I be asking you that?" Jenny raised an eyebrow.

"Why does it work?" Jackaby asked, more gently. "You've never seen that brick, never touched it before, it's been inside the wall. Why are you able to affect it?"

"Because I'm connected to it, I assume? It's a part of my house, after all!"

"Your house–the only place on earth you seem able to exist–floating around in the palm of your hand."

Her eyes suddenly widened. "Do you think?"

Jackaby raised his eyebrows encouragingly. "Do you?"

Jenny held the brick close to her chest and swept out of the room. We followed hurriedly down the crooked hallway and into the foyer. She passed fluidly through the still-closed front door, and the brick, in the manner of most bricks, did not. It thudded hard against the cheery red paint and fell, cracking cleanly in two on the hardwood. In a moment the handle turned and the door opened. Jenny stood on the other side looking sheepish. "Old habits. I got a little excited."

I set half of the brick on the shelf and handed her the other. "Here," I said. "Go ahead. Be a little excited."

Jenny concentrated as she carried the half brick toward the sidewalk. She faded further out of sight with each step, all of her energy focused on the rust red cube. By the time we were halfway to the street, she had vanished completely, and the brick appeared to be hovering under its own power. When she reached the end of the walk, the brick froze in midair. It swiveled, and I could tell that Jenny had turned back.

"I can't do it," she said.

Jackaby put a single finger on the chunk of masonry, blocking her before she could retreat back toward the house. "Just look at me," he said tenderly and took a step forward. The brick drifted forward with him. "This is your brick, Jenny Cavanaugh." Step. "Your house." Step. "Your street. Your city. Your whole wide world." Step. Step. Step.

Jackaby was now in the middle of Augur Lane, talking to a broken brick that hung weightlessly at the end of his finger. A kid in a ragged flat cap and suspenders had stopped to watch the spectacle from across the street, and a carriage whipped around the corner at speed. The driver cursed and shook his fist as he swerved around Jackaby, but Jackaby ignored them all.

He leaned in toward the hollow space I knew was Jenny. He took a deep breath, and then his lips moved ever so slightly as he whispered something to the empty air. A moment later, the brick dropped away from his finger and clattered against the cobblestones. Jackaby's shoulders fell. He stooped and collected the chunk of masonry.

"That was a pretty good trick, mister!" yelled the raga-muffin on the corner. "But I could see the string the whole time!"

Jackaby nodded unenthusiastically and trudged back toward the house.

"That was marvelous!" I said. "It worked! Jenny hasn't been that far in a decade!"

"Hurrah." Jackaby looked underwhelmed.

"What were you saying to her, out there in the street?"

"I'm sure I don't know what you mean," said Jackaby. "I'll be going out, Miss Rook."

"Out?"

"Marlowe has asked that I keep him abreast of our investigation, and I suppose I should pick up some plaster from that shop on Mason Street. Please see to things around the office while I'm gone. Also, please watch for Miss Cavanaugh. With any luck she should reappear soon."

"Did you tell her?" I asked. "Did you finally tell her how you feel?"

"Make yourself ready, as well." He started off down the lane. "Busy night ahead. We make for the western woods at dusk."

Chapter Thirteen

The contents of Chapter Thirteen have been omitted by the request of my employer.

Relevant and related notes are now filed in the Seer's private dossier.

Chapter Fourteen

The western woods looked even more ominous than I remembered. The horizon had warmed to a dull orange as we reached the outskirts of New Fiddleham's old industrial district, and faint stars were already beginning to sparkle above us. The darkness of the forest ahead was profound, but in the glow of the factory lights and the crescent moon, the landscape was not entirely foreign. A half a mile north or so, Hammett's bridge climbed over a trickling creek. This was the forest in which I had squared off against a bloodthirsty redcap only a few short months ago. I had been armed then with only a handful of books. This time I had come better prepared.

A ring of rosary beads hung around my neck, and my pockets were stuffed with fresh garlic. Jackaby had lent me a tin flask of holy water and a silver knife with an ivory handle. He had also sprinkled mustard seed in my hair before we left the house, a timeless safeguard I suspected he had just made up, but I wasn't about to decline any help I could get.

Jackaby wore a crucifix made of silver, a Star of David forged from hammered brass, and a little tin pentagram. Every pocket of his coat was stuffed with herbs, odd relics, and handy artifacts. A rhythmic clinking and jingling accompanied our walk, and together we smelled like the inside of an Italian spice shop. I felt ready for a second encounter with a paranormal predator like Pavel, but I had to admit that to an ordinary bear or wolf, we were mostly just well-seasoned.

I also had no idea what to expect from the blue lights. "What exactly is a will-o'-the-wisp?" I asked.

"Will was a man," he answered. "A simple smith, or so the story goes, who made a deal with the devil himself. He bartered away his immortal soul in exchange for paying off a paltry bar tab or some meager gambling debt, and the devil took him for a fool."

We climbed over a grassy ridge and began picking our way into the dense forest as Jackaby continued. "By and by the smith's time came due, but when the devil came to collect, he found Will twenty feet up in the branches of a tree. 'You'll have to come up to me if you want to bring me back down with you,' called Will. Well, the devil was not impressed, and he shimmied up after him as quick as you please."

The black trunks of tall trees behind us were beginning to conceal the glow of the factory lights as we pushed forward into the woods. "What the devil failed to notice was a horizontal notch about halfway up the trunk, which Will had carved that very morning. The moment the devil crossed that line, old Will dropped right down, dragging his blade into the bark in a straight line as he fell. In one quick motion, he had carved the sign of the cross into the wood, and the devil could not cross it to get back down. He was trapped."

We stepped across a fallen fir tree and I realized my eyes were already adjusting to the darkness, at least to the point that I could discern where one black shape ended and the next black shape began. "So, with the devil at his mercy, Will struck a second deal. He would cut the symbol off the tree if the prince of darkness would leave him be and never bother him again. The devil knew he had been outwitted, and so he had no choice but to accept."

"Couldn't he have just climbed down the other side?" I asked. "Or turned himself into a bat or something and flown off? He's the devil. He does that sort of thing literally all the time."

"That isn't how this sort of story works. Anyway, when Will arrived at the Pearly Gates, Saint Peter shook his head. Will had veered off the path of righteousness with all his drinking, his gambling, and his dealing with the devil. There was no place in heaven for the likes of him. Forlorn, Will made his way down to the dark gates, but the devil, true to his word and wary of another trick, wanted nothing to do with him, either. Out of respect for a fellow deceiver, the prince of darkness did offer him a single coal from the fires of Hell to keep him warm as he wandered the earth for eternity. With that little glowing ember, Will has contented himself to trick travelers forever after, leading them from their paths, just as he veered from his own."

"So, we're looking for a moderately clever tradesman with a lump of coal? That's actually a bit disappointing."

"You have no appreciation for the classics. That's just one of the stories, anyway. Others attribute the phenomenon to fairy fire or elemental spirits. One of them involves gourds. All I know is that general consensus places them in the Unseelie Court, the branch of fairy taxonomy encompassing most of the more malevolent and malcontent of magical creatures. I told you, I've never seen a wisp in person. I have no idea what we're actually looking for."

A sudden flash of white-blue light lit the forest not twenty meters from where we were standing. It was accompanied by a loud, fizzing hum, and blinked out as quickly as it had started with a sharp snap like the crack of a whip.

"I take it we're looking for that," I whispered.

Jackaby nodded his agreement, and we crouched low as we moved toward the source of the light. "That wasn't remotely what the legends suggest," he said in a hushed tone. "In the accounts I've read, the fire is usually a feeble, elusive thing. Generally just a little hovering orb, like a bubble of flame."

"So we're up against a really enormous wisp?" I asked.

Jackaby took very deliberate steps as we neared a clearing. A dull, yellow glow lay beyond the line of trees, more like lantern light than the ribbon of white we had just seen. "There are living things ahead, but the aura isn't like any magic I've ever seen. I don't think it's a wisp at all. Or any kind of fairy folk. The energy is all wrong."

I could hear small, frantic animal squeaks, and there was movement on the far side of the bushes right in front of us. Jackaby put a finger to his lips, not that I needed the caution. Something whirred and clicked, and an instant later the forest burst into light with another arc of electric blue. It was as though lightning had struck the clearing directly ahead. For three or four seconds a snake of brilliant energy writhed just beyond the foliage, and then, with another crack, the forest was even darker than before.

I might as well have been staring at the sun. The afterimage of the coil of light floating in front of me was all I could see for several seconds. I dropped and pressed myself into the ground, hoping whatever lay beyond those bushes was as blind as I was for the moment.

A high, shrill whine cut the silence, followed by a chorus of squeals and squeaks. "No, no, no, no," someone grumbled. It was a male voice. "Output circuits still coupling. Damn! Need to recalibrate for diffraction."

Jackaby stood. "You're not doing magic," he said aloud, cheerfully. "You're doing science."

And then a spanner hit him in the face.

Chapter Fifteen

The sketch of Owen Finstern turned out to be very true to life. The inventor's hair was coarse and wild, and it drifted off behind him in tangled red-orange tufts like flames. His eyes were emerald green and ever so slightly offset. They moved constantly, darting between my employer, the surrounding woods, and me. He had been wearing a pair of perfectly round goggles with ink-black lenses, but he pulled them down to hang loose around his neck as Jackaby and I revealed ourselves.

The man was short and slight. He wore a dark waistcoat and a white shirt with the sleeves un-cuffed and pushed halfway up his thin arms. One sleeve had fallen back down and flapped loose as he moved about the little campsite, but he didn't seem to notice. I wasn't sure if he was wearing an overly large bow tie or a very short, thin ascot—and judging by the crooked knot at his throat, Finstern wasn't sure, either. He raised a second spanner over his head, preparing to launch another hand tool assault.

"Wait! At ease! Cease fire! We're not with those hooligans, Mr. Finstern!" Jackaby insisted, rubbing the bridge of his nose gingerly. "You have nothing to fear from us."

The man looked skeptical, although something told me paranoia was one of his principal expressions. "You can't have my rabbits."

"We're not here for your rabbits. For goodness' sake, we're not even here for you! Miss Rook, why is it the one time we seem able to find something straightaway it's when we've actively decided not to look for it?"

"That does seem to be the way of things, sir," I said.

"What do you want? How do you know my name?" The man's accent was distinctly Welsh.

"It's all right," I said. "My name is Abigail Rook and this is Detective Jackaby. We're not going turn you over, but the men who kidnapped you are looking for you. I think you may be in terrible danger."

"You can't fool me," the man said. "I would've known if I had ever been kidnapped."

"You weren't . . ." I faltered. "You're not hiding out from a cadre of villains?"

Jackaby had stepped around the man and was now looking at the assorted items in his campsite.

"I live here now. I work here. Don't touch anything!"

Finstern yelped as Jackaby knelt down beside a curious contraption in the center of the clearing.

Finstern's machine sat atop a sort of folding wooden platform. By the light of the dim lantern, it looked like the collapsible booths that street vendors sometimes used with three wooden legs all set with hinges for quick travel. There was a row of copper cylinders to one side, all capped with brass fittings and strung with coiled wires. The wires ran to an apparatus composed of thick pipes and slim copper tubes, all carefully fitted and joined in a fixture of wood and brass until something not unlike an enormous sidelong microscope took shape. The contraption had myriad revolving lenses and knobs of every size for making meticulous adjustments, and symbols I did not recognized were etched into the metal casings.

From crates stacked in the clearing just beyond it came several piteous mewls and squeaks. I stepped closer.

"What is it?" Jackaby asked, circling the machine with his nose practically inside the works.

"It is my invention," answered Finstern. "My life's work."

"You're using a modified Daniell cell for your condensers," Jackaby observed.

"That's right," Finstern confirmed, watching Jackaby closely.

"It's effective but rudimentary. I don't understand. There's no way you produced that burst of energy with a generator like this."

"Additional input is not necessary to initiate the process.

The battery of capacitors function only to prime the transference. They are the engine's spark, Detective, not its fuel." The strange little man was breathing heavily. At least he did not seem inclined to throw any more tools.

I crossed over to peek into the crates. Tiny furry whiskers and glistening eyes peered out at me. There were squirrels in the first box. Rats in another. A pair of tawny cat's paws clawed helplessly at a thin gap in the slats of the bottom container. We might have found Hammett's feline companion after all, I realized, although what Finstern was doing with all of these animals was more than I wanted to guess. The smell was horrible.

"So, what is the fuel?" Jackaby asked.

Finstern was now fidgeting excitedly. "With the right focus and proper channeling, transvigoration provides its own momentum." He chuckled with the giddy joy of his own work. A queasy feeling crept through me. Something about that man turned my stomach. The cat in the crate beside me mewled piteously.

"What does *transvigoration* do, exactly?" Jackaby asked.

I caught sight of a row of open containers back behind the rest. Stepping forward gingerly, I peered inside and immediately reeled at the horrid sight. I was going to be sick. The boxes were heaped with piles of lifeless chipmunks, rabbits, and mice. A big black hound dog, too large for any of the boxes, lay sprawled beside them. He wasn't breathing.

"Let me show you," Finstern said darkly. I heard a whir and a click and spun around to find myself staring directly down the bulging central lens of the inventor's apparatus. For a moment my vision swam and the forest darkened—and then just as suddenly the shadows all fled and the whole world went white.

Chapter Sixteen

I sat slumped against the base of an old tree as feeling gradually returned to my extremities. My lips still felt numb and a taste like iron lingered on my tongue. Jackaby was pulling open the last of the crates and releasing the frightened animals into the wild. An orange tabby bounded across the clearing, pausing to look back just once before vanishing into the underbrush. I hoped Hammett would be pleased to have her back. When Jackaby had finished, there remained a grim collection of beasts who would not be returning to their homes. I sat up stiffly.

Owen Finstern lay motionless on the earth across the clearing. I rubbed my temples with both hands and breathed in slowly. "Is he dead?" I asked.

"He's unconscious, but still alive," Jackaby answered. It was coming back to me. The whole experience had taken only a matter of seconds. With the flick of a switch, the apparatus had hummed to life. I had felt a jolt in my chest like the snap of static electricity, and then all at once it was as though a dam had burst and a massive current was rushing through me–not *at* me, but *through* me. And then it just stopped. The machine crackled. The light blinked out. It was over, and Finstern was on his back in the moss.

Jackaby stepped over to him, surveying the inventor. "He's human–at least, he appears to be–but I think there's something more. It's deep. Dormant. Latent potential at the core of him. I didn't even see it at first."

"He's a creep." I pushed off the ground and tried to shake off the tingling sensation rippling through my skin.

"You should sit down, Miss Rook. You're lucky to be alive."

"I'm fine, Mr. Jackaby, really. I'm just glad his awful machine went wrong."

"I'm not sure that it did."

I raised an eyebrow.

"I could see energy flowing out of you and into Mr. Finstern. The transference of energies–transvigoration–that's the purpose of this device. I don't think it went wrong, I think it functioned perfectly. You really shouldn't be standing."

"Stop looking at me like I'm about to crumble into dust,"

I said. "I feel fine." It was true. The tingling was fading away and, if anything, I felt curiously invigorated.

"You lost a lot of energy."

"I'm fine."

"A *lot* of energy." He had his head cocked to the side, regarding me with the same intensity with which he had examined the machine a few minutes ago.

"What do you mean? How much is a lot?"

He pursed his lips. "Hard to articulate. I've never seen this happen before. It shouldn't happen. I've seen death, Miss Rook. I've seen what happens when vitality leaves a body. It is difficult to quantify, but human life is finite. Did you know that the average human body can lose about half a gallon of blood and still survive?" said Jackaby.

"I'm not bleeding."

"No, but this may provide some context. Half a gallon of blood is roughly one third of one's liquid life force, and that is enough to throw the most virile subject into shock and eventually death."

"How much of my energy went into Finstern?"

"If your life force were liquid, I would say you hemorrhaged at least three gallons before you overloaded the mechanism. It went rushing back to you when the machine gave out."

"Mathematics was never my favorite subject, sir, but that sounds like you're saying I lost more of my . . . my *whatever* than I had to begin with."

"Yes," he said. "It does sound like that."

"Well, I can't explain it, but I'm fine!" I insisted. "Really. What are we going to do about him?"

Jackaby reluctantly let it drop and turned back to the inventor. "We can't leave him here. After that naughty little display, I'm less concerned about leaving him at the mercy of our vampire friend and more concerned about why Pavel and his benefactors want Finstern in the first place. A mind like his in the wrong hands could be disastrous."

With care, we collapsed Finstern's device. It had been designed with a quick getaway in mind, which was not surprising, given the tasteless nature of the inventor's field of study. The sides of the device folded up neatly, and the whole thing latched tight with a few simple brass fixtures. The capacitors were even affixed to a rotating hinge, so they angled themselves upright as the box tilted.

With some difficulty I hefted the device and slung it over my back. It was relatively compact, but heavier than it looked. Jackaby threw the inventor over his shoulder like a sack of grain, and we made our way through the forest back toward town.

"There is definitely something unnatural about that contraption," Jackaby said when we had almost reached the edge of the city. "The spirit of the forest is reacting to it. Can you feel it?"

I paused and listened. The woods had become eerily calm. We emerged from the forest a little north of where we had entered it, and I veered toward the footbridge just ahead. My bulky burden would definitely be easier to haul over a flat path than through the rugged wilderness.

I glanced back. "Aren't you worried someone might notice you carrying a body through town in the middle of the night?" I called.

"Not generally," Jackaby replied. "Surprisingly, it's never been a problem in the past."

Before I could reach the end of the bridge, a greenish shape whipped up from beneath it and hit the boards with a squelching slap. I stared down at the mauled carcass of a half-eaten carp. I blinked.

"You're welcome, Hammett!" Jackaby called cheerfully over the side. He nodded to the mutilated fish. "See that you record a new payment rendered in the ledger, Miss Rook. Clients of all sorts appreciate careful and accurate accounts."

We reached Augur Lane without further incident, but as we approached the bright red front door of number 926, the uneasy sensation of being watched crept over me. The hairs on the back of my neck stood on end. I glanced down the lane behind us, but only empty cobblestones and dark windows met my gaze. I had just managed to swallow my apprehension when a woman stepped suddenly out of the shadows and in our path to the doorway.

I started backward and nearly dropped the machine. My heart was hammering against my ribs. With willful control,

I found my nerve and managed to keep my feet beneath me. The woman wore a checkered dress and a dark bonnet pulled low over her eyes.

"Hello, detectives. My name is Cordelia Hoole," she said. "I got your message."

"Hello, Mrs. Hoole. My name is Jackaby," said Jackaby. "I've got the unconscious body of an unpleasant stranger. Would you mind holding the door?"

Chapter Seventeen

A few minutes later Cordelia Hoole was sipping her tea with trembling hands. She and Jackaby sat on either side of the front desk, with Owen Finstern lying motionless on the bench beside them. I had deposited Finstern's bulky machine in the laboratory and brewed a quick pot of tea before rejoining them. Jenny Cavanaugh did not reveal herself, and I wondered if she was just keeping out of sight because of our visitor, or if my ghostly friend still had not rematerialized since the incident in the street.

"You know that you're in danger?" Jackaby asked the widow Hoole as I took up a position beside him at the desk.

"Yes. Yes, of course," she replied. "That's why I've been in hiding." Her cup rattled against the saucer. "After what happened to Alice . . . I–I knew her."

"Alice McCaffery?"

She nodded. "She and Julian were so nice to me. I didn't know very many people in my husband's social circles—but the McCafferys were always so kind. It was bad enough when Lawrence didn't come home that night, but then I heard about Julian disappearing and—and about what they did to Alice . . ." She trailed off, her breath coming in shallow gulps.

"It's all right, Mrs. Hoole," I said. "You're safe here."

"How did you hear about them?" Jackaby asked. "Our contact in the police department said you were gone before word could reach you about the grisly state of your husband's corpse."

"Sir," I said, "some sensitivity."

"Excuse me," he said. "The grisly state of your *late* husband's corpse. Alice McCaffery's body was discovered the same day—how did you hear about it before police could reach you?"

"Miss W-W-Wick." Mrs. Hoole sniffed and set her cup and saucer down on the desk. "Our housekeeper. She tells me everything. I think she heard it from the McCaffery's maid. She was worried for me. I packed a bag and left at once. Miss Wick stayed to put things in order before joining me."

"Hm," Jackaby said. "Miss Wick was still at the house when we came to call on you. Until she wasn't. She was not as forthright as I might have hoped about our investigation."

"You speak Polish?" I asked Mrs. Hoole.

She shook her head. "No, but I've known Miss Wick for many years. She speaks more English than she lets on. It's sort of her little secret."

"Indeed," said Jackaby. "Your housekeeper is good at keeping secrets. Her baby, for example. Was the child with you when we came calling on her?"

Mrs. Hoole bit her lip. "Please, detective. Leave them alone. They've been through enough. I came here to help you. I want to put a stop to this before anyone else gets hurt. I'll tell you anything you want to know, but just leave them out of this. It's my fault they're involved at all."

"Hm," said Jackaby again. He looked unsatisfied, but he moved on. "Tell me about your husband's work."

Mrs. Hoole took a slow sip of tea before she spoke. "My Lawrence was a genius," she said at last. "He designed locomotives that could run on half the fuel for twice the distance and adding machines that could solve complex equations in a matter of minutes. He contrived such wonderful inventions."

"Which of them was he working on when he died?"

"None of them. He wasn't building anything of his own design–he was rebuilding someone else's. He said it was a brilliant but broken concept. He was very excited at first. It had something to do with electricity and conduction, but it was all Greek to me when he got talking about the details. Oh, it's my fault, I know it. He was content just tinkering away on his own projects. I pushed him to take the job. I just thought it w-w-would be his chance to be r-r-recognized."

"Can you tell us anything more specific about what he was constructing?" Jackaby urged. "Think hard now."

Cordelia shook her head. "Lawrence never spoke at length about his machines with me. Sometimes he would try, but he would get frustrated trying to simplify it all—or else he would get distracted by an idea and just start tinkering away at it right then and there and forget we were speaking. I used to tease him that I would have to register for one of his classes if I hoped to hear the end of a sentence. All of those clever ideas. It's s-s-such a waste. He never wrote half of them down. It was like his pen couldn't keep up with his brain. Whatever he was working on, he t-t-took it with him, I'm afraid."

Jackaby grimaced with dissatisfaction.

"And now he's gone and they're probably going to k-k-kill me, and I don't even know why!" Cordelia Hoole's shoulders shook as she finally broke. I hurried to offer her a handkerchief and she took it gratefully, burying her face in it as she sobbed.

"Mrs. Hoole," said Jackaby in an even tone, "if we are to keep you safe, you will need to be completely honest with us."

"Honest?" she wiped her eyes and sniffled. "I have been honest with you, detective."

"Honest–but not completely. I have a talent that allows me to see certain truths, and the truth is that you are concealing something. I can see willful obfuscation spread over you like marmalade on toast. I do not care for marmalade, madam, and I care less for secrets."

"Of course there are things about me you don't know." She sniffed and her brow furrowed indignantly. "I don't know anything about you, but I came, didn't I?"

"I suppose you did."

"And I c-c-came inside when you bade me, even after I found you carrying that man into your house. I've put more than my share of trust on the table, thank you very much, Mr. Jackaby. I think I'm entitled to my privacy where I see fit." She glanced back at the figure occupying the bench. Owen Finstern was breathing evenly. Every once in a while his cheek twitched as he slept off the effects of the jolt his machine had given him. "Who is he, anyway?"

"He is an inventor, like your late husband," Jackaby answered. "He's called Finstern. He is wanted by some thoroughly unpleasant individuals, the same individuals responsible for Lawrence's death. Beyond that we know very little." He shook his head, eying the prone figure. "There's something about him I don't like," he added.

"Could it be the fact that he tried to suck the life out of your steadfast and lovely assistant?" I suggested.

Jackaby glanced in my direction. "The question is: why didn't he succeed?"

"Your concern is overwhelming," I said.

"It just doesn't make sense," Jackaby groused. "Your vital energies should have been completely–" He stopped, staring straight ahead.

"This is madness!" Mrs. Hoole's eyes were pink and puffy. "I should never have come."

"Please, Mrs. Hoole," I soothed, "you're safe here."

"No," said Jackaby, his gray eyes locked on the front door. "She's not." A moment later the horseshoe knocker rapped out three loud clacks from the other side. "It's him." Jackaby's voice was grave. "I know that aura. A foul, anathematic shade with a faint halo of lavender. It's him. It's Pavel. The wretch is on our doorstep."

My eyes shot between the widow Hoole and the dormant Finstern. Of course Pavel was here. We could not have painted the house with two larger targets. "What do we do?"

"The polite thing"–Pavel's voice came muffled through the wood–"would be to stop acting as though I can't hear you and invite me in. Maybe put the kettle on?"

Chapter Eighteen

"Don't open it!" I said.

Jackaby crossed the room. "It's all right. There are rules about this sort of thing and safeguards in place. Stay back, ladies. I think it is high time I met Mr. Pavel face to face."

The pale man looked exactly as before. He smiled his crooked, arrogant smile up at Jackaby as the door swung open, and I could see the dark gap of his missing fang. I heard a gasp from Mrs. Hoole.

"Detective Jackaby. An honor to meet you at last. I am a big fan of your work," the vampire said. "I must admit, I was not expecting such quick results. And what's this?" He waggled a finger at Mrs. Hoole. "You caught the slippery little fish that got away from us, as well! You truly have a gift, my friend. We're all very impressed."

"I take it you've come to make good on your agreement with my assistant?" Jackaby said. I swallowed.

"That's right. Be a chum and invite me in, would you? I'll take the wandering woman and sleeping beauty off your hands before you can say boo, and then you two can get back to your relaxing evening."

"That was not the deal you struck." Jackaby stood up a little straighter. "It is my understanding–and Miss Rook is very good about conveying all the pertinent details–that your arrangement was that Miss Rook would receive information from you regarding certain persons of interest in exchange for our finding Mr. Finstern, is that correct?"

"That's right."

"Well, we found Mr. Finstern. Our end of the bargain is complete. Delivery of the gentleman into your custody was never stipulated. Now then, I believe you have something to share?"

Pavel's eyes narrowed and his expression turned icy. "You don't know me very well," he said softly, "and you *really* don't know my superiors, if you think I'll be leaving this house empty-handed." He cracked his neck and composed himself. "I'll tell you what, Detective. In the interest of keeping our relationship professional, why don't you just turn them both over to me, and I will consider not murdering your pretty little assistant in her sleep."

"You're right, I don't know you," said Jackaby. "But I do know stories, and that's not how yours works. That thing at your feet? That's a threshold. You are a vampire. Huff and puff all you like, you may not come in."

Pavel stared daggers at Jackaby through narrow, powder-white eyelids. "Hold on," he said at length. "I've seen your face somewhere before, haven't I?"

Jackaby stood his ground, glaring back at the pale man. "I expect you've seen quite a lot of me. You seem to be doing more than your fair share of lurking."

Pavel shook his head. "No. Not the famous R. F. Jackaby. You're right, I have been watching. I know a great deal about R. F. Jackaby. I know, for instance, that R. F. Jackaby did not exist twenty years ago. You look older than twenty, detective. Twenty-seven? Thirty? Forty-two? Years are difficult to judge when you start counting in centuries."

Jackaby said nothing.

"No. Wait a moment. Now that I see you closer, I do remember. Yes, I have seen that face, long before this ridiculous character that you invented. Helpless scrap of a thing, weren't you? What did they call you back then? It's on the tip of my tongue."

Jackaby's fists were clenched tight. His knuckles were turning white.

Pavel smiled. "Oh, that's an interesting thought, now, isn't it? Clever little boy hides his true name from the world because words have power, is that right? They do, of course. You were right to hide your name. The thing is, sometimes you need that power."

He slid closer until the scuffed leather tips of his shoes were right on the edge of the threshold. "I wonder, Detective, whose name is on the deed to this old place?" His milky white hands felt the air in front of him as if he were brushing an invisible curtain. "R. F. Jackaby owns this place, doesn't he? Only–and here's where it gets interesting–we both know that R. F. Jackaby does not exist." He planted one foot and then the other inside the door, and Jackaby staggered backward a step.

"You're still just a helpless scrap of a thing. Now then, if you don't mind–" Pavel swept past Jackaby and toward Cordelia Hoole. His movements were effortless and inhumanly fluid. Mrs. Hoole threw herself backward with a squeak, but her checkered dress got caught up in her chair, and she toppled to the ground.

I fumbled a rosary off of the hook beside the desk and leapt over to her, holding it up like a shield. The little wooden cross danced as my hand trembled.

"That's cute," Pavel said. "I'm Jewish–at least I was a very long time ago. I must admit, I haven't exactly been keeping kosher." He winked and then batted my hand away. My wrist instantly stung, as though I had been bitten. "The thing about faith is that it only works when you have it. Now, you're beginning to make me grumpy. Are you going to get out of my way, or will I have the distinct pleasure of going through you?" His eyes were rimmed with red.

"Y-You can't!" I stammered. "Your benefactors!" Pavel flinched. "They want us alive! Remember? What do you think they'll do to you if–"

"First of all, my benefactors want *him* alive." Pavel nodded at Jackaby. "So don't get too full of yourself, girlie. Second, there are oh-so-many creative things I can make the detective watch me do to you"–his expression darkened–"if either of you decides to be difficult."

He made a sudden motion as if to lunge at me, but then drew up short. His sickly white hand, the one with just a stump of a pinky, slowed to a crawl as it extended toward me. Far from his fluid, effortless actions a moment ago, his whole body was now moving as if through heavy syrup–and then he froze completely, his face contorted in a mask of confusion and anger.

"How are you doing this?" he snapped. His eyes darted toward Jackaby, although my employer looked as baffled as he was. "You have no power over me! This is not your house!"

"No." A shimmer of light rippled in the air between Jackaby and the vampire. "But it is mine." Jenny's eyes were ice and her glare was iron as she coalesced. She was fury incarnate, her long silvery hair whipping around her. "You," she said. "You worked with my fiancé." The temperature in the room plummeted and Pavel's body abruptly stiffened. He made a strangled wheezing sound as though he were suddenly being squeezed very tightly. His feet lifted off the ground until just the tips of his brogues scraped the floorboards. "You shouldn't be here," Jenny whispered darkly.

With a mad vampire frozen in midair and a vengeful ghost hovering in front of her, I fully expected Mrs. Hoole to bid farewell to her last nerve and collapse at my feet as unconscious as Owen Finstern, but the widow proved surprisingly more resolute. She made thc sensible and reasonable decision, instead, to clamber frantically behind the desk, hug her knees to her chest, and huddle in a tight ball taking very deep breaths. I could not fault her. In fact, I considered joining her.

"You're a dead thing!" Pavel croaked. He spun slowly in place an inch off the ground. "You're like me! You shouldn't be able–grkk!"

"I have been feeling much more *able* of late." Jenny's voice was cold. "I don't like being told what I can't do. My brick. My house. My whole wide world."

Paper spun off the desk in a sudden flurry, but Jenny remained solid and composed. Crystals had begun to form on the windowsill and Ogden the frog was burying himself into a pile of shredded newspaper in the corner of his terrarium.

Jackaby righted the chair that Mrs. Hoole had toppled. He planted it next to the captive vampire and plopped casually into it. “Words do have power,” he said, “and my dear friend Jenny keeps hers. She made me a promise once, right here in this very room. I asked her never to give up on the place. She never has. You crossed a line, Mr. Pavel, and now you’re in her world. I believe you were about to tell us a story?”

Chapter Nineteen

"You already know I didn't kill you, Miss Cavanaugh." Pavel's voice was much less confident now that he was stuck hanging, suspended by Jenny's will, in the center of our foyer. "You died while I was sleeping."

"That's true," Jackaby said, thoughtfully. "Alice McCaffery, too. They were both attacked in the daylight. You work with an accomplice, then? Who is it?"

"Their lives were insignificant." Pavel sneered. "But just thinking about all that blood just draining across the floor." He turned his eyes to Jenny. "Such a waste. She's sloppy. I would have savored you." A windowpane cracked behind Jenny, and Pavel winced painfully.

"*She?*" Jackaby said. "Your associate is a woman, then?"

"There's always a woman." The vampire chuckled wetly. "Hell of a woman, too. Worlds better than any human doxy. Your boy Howard Carson certainly thought so."

"You're lying," Jenny snapped. For a moment I thought

I saw her face flutter into a double-image, just a hint of an oncoming echo, but then her chest rose and fell as she maintained control. She was stronger than I would have been. It wasn't even me he was taunting and I wanted to knock the rest of Pavel's teeth in.

"So, Jenny's killer is a woman, and not human," Jackaby pressed calmly. "Is she your benefactor?"

"Good effort. Ribbon for trying, Detective, but you're off the mark."

"Then who are you working for?"

"Not a chance. Hell hath no fury and all that, but the most your ghost girl can do is kill me. I've been through that. I can handle death. *They* would do far worse. They're downright visionary in that way."

"You're underestimating me again," said Jenny. "How well did that work for you last time?" Pavel said nothing.

"You may not have killed those women," Jackaby interjected, "but you have plenty of blood on your hands."

"Not at all," Pavel said, attempting to sound casual, although his throat was tight. "I always wash up after meals."

"Mrs. Beaumont?"

"She thought I was a dignitary. A count from Romania. She was useful for a time. Her blood was surprisingly sweet."

"Mrs. Brisbee. Mr. Denson. Professor Hoole." Jackaby rattled off victims.

"Yes, yes. I remember last week's menu. Do you have a point?"

At the sound of her husband's name, Cordelia Hoole stopped rocking. She peered over the desk, and I could see waves of emotions washing over her. Her hands were trembling.

Pavel noticed her, too. "Your husband didn't put up much of a fight," he said. "In case you were wondering."

Cordelia Hoole swallowed. "Why?" she managed.

"Call it professional dissidence. Your darling Lawrence was a promising architect, but he found the nature of our work distasteful toward the end. I found his lack of cooperation equally distasteful–although I liked his carotid artery well enough." He sneered smugly at the widow and licked his lips.

The words struck Cordelia Hoole with physical force. She buckled, but caught herself with one hand on the desk. She looked as though she might need to be sick.

"What was Hoole working on?" demanded Jackaby. "What did your benefactors want him to build?"

"Let me go and I'll send you to ask him yourself," Pavel snarled. I could see his muscles straining against Jenny's will, but his invisible bonds held fast. He breathed heavily. "Better yet, why don't you tell them, Miss Cavanaugh? You helped your busy little beau build it the first time. Tell them what you helped us create."

Jenny's scowl deepened. "I don't–I don't know."

"So many things forgotten. The future, Miss Cavanaugh.

Don't you remember? Well, not your future, of course. Yours ended years ago. You're just one of the forgotten things now, like the rest of us."

"Tell me what happened that night."

The pale man twisted abruptly and squawked in surprise and pain.

"Miss Cavanaugh . . ." Jackaby said.

"Tell me what happened the night I died." Jenny's voice was hollow. Pavel's back was beginning to curve in an unnatural backward arc. The wind whipped and the windows rattled. A piece of plaster chipped off from the wall and spun across the room.

"Jenny." Jackaby's voice was soft. "We have time. He does not."

Jenny's shoulders relaxed a fraction and the cold eased up a few degrees. She nodded. "Make yourself comfortable, Pavel," she said, although her captive looked anything but. He revolved slowly like a grotesque ornament from an invisible string. "You have about three hours to sunrise."

Pavel continued to evade our questions for the rest of the night, although he was far from silent. He goaded Jenny at every chance, but she refused to rise to any more lurid implications about her fiancé and the mysterious murderess.

Eventually he turned his venom on Jackaby.

"The last Seer was much more fun," he said.

I froze. There was no way this monster knew about Eleanor, I thought. I watched Jackaby's face, but he did not give Pavel the satisfaction of a response.

"The two of you were friends, weren't you?" Pavel continued. "What a pair. I don't remember seeing you the day they sent the legion. You weren't there, were you? You should have seen her. There was none of this standing around for hours nonsense. She was a firecracker, that one. What was her name? Ellen? Ella? Eleanor. That's it."

"Miss Rook," Jackaby said with forced calm. "Does that window look smudged to you? It would be a shame to miss even the smallest bit of a beautiful sunrise."

"I cleaned them just last week, sir," I said.

The sky was already beginning to glow. Pavel strained against his invisible bonds. "Your little Eleanor wasn't so fiery by the end," he continued. "She broke. My benefactors saw to that."

Jackaby set his jaw and did not respond.

"They had such high hopes for her. In the end she was just another disappointment."

Jackaby took measured breaths.

He knew. Pavel knew. Jenny's past and Jackaby's—both of my dearest friends' darkest hours were somehow tied to this awful man. I was reeling. He knew, and time was running out. The sky was ripening to a soft orange as the sun prepared to breach the horizon.

"Eleanor spoke of a man with red eyes and a long, dark hallway," Jackaby said at last. "What was it? Where was it?"

Pavel chuckled. "Is that how she described it? A child's mind is a beautiful, tender little thing, isn't it?"

The chair slammed backward onto the floor as Jackaby stood up. He stepped forward until he was inches away, face-to-face with the pale man. "Time's up."

The sky was growing lighter by the second. Pavel was breathing heavily. An unhealthy slate gray was darkening his pallid complexion. "You want to know about Howard Carson? He's dead!" Pavel grunted. "Carson is long dead."

Jackaby looked at Jenny, and then back to Pavel. "Howard Carson is dead? You're certain?"

"Yes, damn it! Howard Carson is dead!"

"You're running out of shadows, Pavel, and I don't think Miss Cavanaugh is satisfied with that answer, do you?"

"I did it myself!" he roared. "I ripped out his throat and I drained him. The bastard had it coming." Sores were beginning to break his skin, and the room smelled of sulfur. "You should thank me!" His head lolled at a sickening angle toward Jenny. "He abandoned you to go trotting after that strumpet, and he never looked back. She cut you open the very next day while the disloyal rake stayed on with us."

Jackaby closed the curtain, and in the sudden darkness Pavel sagged like a broken marionette. Jenny flickered. "No. Y-You're lying. That's not what happened." Her voice shook. She was upright, chin held high, but then in the same moment she was on the ground. Her contours flickered. Her elegant pearlescent dress was now torn and darkness was spreading across her chest. The anger had left her. She looked sad. She looked confused. She looked like she was dying and she did not know why.

"The council doesn't leave loose ends," Pavel panted. "That's all you ever were. A loose end." Wheezing breaths became a ragged laugh.

I felt the blood rising to my head. I wanted to hit him. I wanted to wipe that wretched half grin off his face. Suddenly the room was spinning. I felt a hand on my shoulder, but whose I could not say. The edges of my vision darkened and I leaned against the shelf, my fingers stumbling over the broken half-brick. I blinked.

Wind whipped through the torn curtains in front of me and I found myself kneeling on the floor. There was glass everywhere. Where had it come from? I felt nauseous.

"Abigail?" Jenny's voice sounded muffled and distant.

Hands shook my shoulders and I looked up into Jackaby's cloud gray eyes. "Rook. Rook!"

I whipped around. Cordelia Hoole was still crouched behind the desk. Finstern lay on the bench, but Pavel was gone.

Panic shot through me. "What happened?" I managed to say.

Jackaby's expression was furious. "Hold still," he said,

staring into my eyes intensely. At length he stood and helped me into the chair. "She is herself again," he said. "What do you remember, Miss Rook?"

I tried to make sense of what was happening. "I don't know! I just–he was talking about Jenny and I was furious, and then I felt dizzy and . . ." I took a deep breath. "Where is Pavel? What happened?"

Jackaby and Jenny looked at each other. Their expressions were not reassuring. Jackaby stepped over to the window. Glass crunched under his shoes as he looked through the broken frame into the garden. "He's gone," he said.

"What was that?" Jenny asked, looking at me nervously.

"She shows signs of a phrenic mutuality. The aftereffects of possession."

I glanced at Jenny. "There are aftereffects?"

"Of course there are aftereffects!" Jackaby pulled the curtain shut again over the shattered hole and crunched back across the room. "Two spirits are not meant to occupy the same mind. If you and I were to wear the same pair of trousers at once, what do you think would happen?"

I swallowed. "They would stretch out all wrong?"

"That's an optimistic outcome. How do you feel?"

"A little weak about the seams, now that you mention it." I took a deep breath. "Jenny, we need to tell him."

Jenny nodded. "Tell me what?" Jackaby looked back and forth between us. "You wouldn't. You didn't. Of course you did. What were you thinking?!"

"Oh, Abigail! I'm so sorry! I had no idea," said Jenny.

"We only tried it once," I said. "Well, a couple of times, but not for very long. She was making such marvelous progress, sir!"

"Have you felt any other dizzy spells? Blackouts?"

"No, I–" I caught myself. "Well, yes, actually. Right before Finstern turned on his machine, and maybe once earlier, in the office."

"This is all my fault." Jenny looked mortified.

"And how did you feel, right before it came over you?"

"I was angry," I said. "He was laughing, and it just made me furious."

Jackaby considered. "You may be experiencing Jenny's emotions alongside your own. If she entered your mind, then she may have left a part of herself behind. Argh! How could you be so foolish? Both of you! Spiritual possession is inexpressibly risky and unpredictable. This is absolutely unacceptable!"

"It won't happen again," I said. "But I still don't fully understand it. I had a dizzy spell–but that doesn't explain how Pavel broke free."

Jenny answered gently. "Pavel didn't, sweetheart."

I shook my head. "What? Me? I pushed him out?"

"I don't think *push* fully expresses it. You were"–Jackaby paused to choose his words carefully–"forceful."

I wracked my brain to recall my own actions, but all I came up with was a headache. I stood slowly and crossed to the window. The morning light stung my eyes as I brushed aside the drapes. The sun was beating down and there wasn't a cloud in the sky. Glass and scraps of wood from the window frame littered the front lawn. A rough patch of grass had been singed in the middle of the debris, and in the dead center lay a broken red brick.

"Is he dead?" I asked. It felt like the brick was in the pit of my stomach.

"If he isn't dead, he is in exceedingly poor shape," Jackaby replied. "He's not the one we need to worry about right now."

"I'll worry just a little bit, if you don't mind," I said. "I don't make a habit of making enemies out of creatures inclined to murder me horribly in my sleep."

"Pavel mentioned a council," said Jackaby. "His benefactors. Now, there are countless factions within the otherworldly courts, but the Unseelie have never been well organized. Dangerous, yes, but historically unruly and wild as lightning. The collective races have never coexisted, which may be the only reason the human race has survived this long. Now they're organizing. And what's worse, they're good at it."

I didn't know what to say. A splinter of glass freed itself from the ruined frame and tinkled to the ground. The tiny clink resonated in the silence of the room.

"I don't know who this council is," Jackaby said, "but they're organized, they're effective, and they're powerful enough to make a self-serving monster like Pavel risk death before disloyalty. If you're going to worry, Miss Rook, worry about them. They are architects of chaos, and now they have the creative genius of some of the most powerful scientific minds of our age engineering their evil. Whatever they're building, it isn't good."

"The future," Jenny breathed.

Jackaby turned to the broken window. "Not if we can help it."

Chapter Twenty

"They're going to kill me." Cordelia Hoole's voice broke the tense silence. Her eyes were glassy.

"They're going to try," confirmed Jackaby without emotion. "But if you–"

"They killed you," the widow said. She was staring at Jenny.

Jenny nodded. "Yes, they did. A long time ago. And we're going to find out who did it, and we're going to stop her from ever doing it again."

Mrs. Hoole just stared blankly. "They're going to kill me."

"That isn't going to happen, Mrs. Hoole," I said. "We're here to protect you."

"Yes," Jackaby confirmed. "You're safe here. Well, not

right here, obviously." Glass crunched beneath his feet. "The cellar is the most secure chamber on the property, and given the circumstances, probably the best place to put you up for the evening. Or down for the morning, I suppose."

"We have a cellar?" I said.

Jenny nodded. "It's just a little root cellar. There's a trapdoor in the back garden."

"You're going to make me sleep in a cellar?" Mrs. Hoole asked shakily.

"It is ideally suited to your needs," said Jackaby. "My home is warded, but I would prefer to exercise special caution for you, given the circumstances. The forces pursuing you are not common criminals, as you've just witnessed firsthand. We face foes of an eldritch and unearthly ilk. The doors of my cellar are reinforced with iron plates, soldered with silver, and etched with apotropaic charms. The walls are coated in a lacquer derived from wolfsbane, sage, and Irish white heather, and there are several significant reliquaries buried not far beneath the surface to discourage tunneling. You will find that it is a stronghold unlike any other, madam, and quite possibly the only place in the world where I can guarantee your safety right now." Jackaby swallowed the last of his tea in one gulp and gazed gloomily at the leaves in the bottom of his cup. "Also, there are pickles and jam down there," he said absently. "You are welcome to the pickles and jam."

The cellar was slim with an arched ceiling that made it feel a bit like the inside of an empty barrel. The air was cold but dry, and it smelled not unpleasantly like earth and incense. In the light of a little oil lamp, I could see that the walls were inscribed from floor to ceiling with symbols ranging from simple runes to sprawling, elegant patterns. A few wooden shelves toward the back housed, as promised, jars of preserves and pickled vegetables.

Jackaby assembled a simple cot and showed Mrs. Hoole how to secure the door from the inside. Three heavy bolts made of silver, iron, and stone could be thrown and released only from inside the room. I brought down fresh linens and a good heavy quilt, and she thanked me for my kindness. As I left, I heard the three bolts click firmly into place.

"Do you really think she'll be safe in there?" I asked as we reentered the house.

"There is no safer chamber in all of New England. I have come a long way since collecting lucky herbs in a cigar box. Besides, I prefer keeping the lady close but not too close."

"You don't like her?" I said.

"I don't like secrets." He paused at the spiral staircase. "Get some rest, Miss Rook. You've had a long day and a longer night, and I need you sharp."

I managed a few fitful hours of sleep while the day was still young, but by late morning I found myself staring at the ceiling feeling more anxious and discontent with each passing minute. I had attacked Pavel. It felt wrong. It wasn't just that I could not remember it–I could not fathom initiating such a violent assault, even against someone so loathsome.

Hearing the faint murmur of voices downstairs, I abandoned my bed and dressed for the day. Owen Finstern was awake.

"Magic, Detective?" I heard him say as I slid down the hallway.

"Yes." Jackaby's voice. "I know you're a man of science, but please keep an open mind. This is important."

I stepped into the room. Finstern was sitting up on the bench and Jackaby had pulled up the chair next to him. If Jenny was around, she had not made herself visible. The inventor glanced up as I entered. "Hello again, miss," he said without a modicum of remorse, although not with any ill will, either. His eyes continued to dart about.

"Good morning," I said. "No, actually, rather awful morning. You tried to shoot me with some sort of energy thing!"

"I did shoot you. You survived. Mr. Jackaby informs me you carried my machine out of the woods. Where is it now? Were you very careful?"

"Did Mr. Jackaby also inform you that you're a cad?"

"He mentioned something along those lines, yes. Subjective. Hard to quantify. He also tells me that I am the target of paranormal kidnappers." He still had a slight twitch just under one eye, which only added to his naturally manic look.

"It's true," I said. "One of them came by and tried to bully us into turning you over while you were sleeping. I'm beginning to wish we had let him have you."

"I think perhaps you should have. I would be very interested to meet a council of magical creatures."

It was hard to tell if Finstern was mocking my employer or if he was speaking in earnest. He showed little emotion and seemed as unfazed by talk of fairies as he was unapologetic about attempted murder.

"I noticed the markings on your device," Jackaby said. "Alchemical symbols and arcane invocations. You've made a study of the occult?"

Finstern nodded.

"Curious hobby for a man of science, isn't it?"

"Mother used to tell me that my father was a magic man," Finstern said, his eyes wandering around the cluttered artifacts on the shelves. "He knew my mother for only one night, but she spoke of him as if he were the sun and the moon. She also told me that when I was born I had a twin, a sister. The girl could walk before I could crawl, and swam like a fish while I cried in the shallow bathwater. Her hair changed colors in the moonlight, Mother said. Not a child in the world was as precious or perfect. I certainly was not. Sometimes I think I can almost remember my sister. We were only infants when my father came back."

Finstern fidgeted a splinter of wood off of the bench and flicked it away. "He came back for the girl child only. I was of no significance. Mother told me this. Often." He twitched.

"No one believed the stories about my father, of course. They said my mother was that sort of woman. Unwed. Unfit. They said such terrible things. Mother pressed me to prove them wrong. She needed me to be exceptional–she needed me to be powerful."

"That's a lot of pressure to heap on a little boy," Jackaby said.

"Pressure. Perpendicular force per unit area. Quantifiable. Yes, it was a lot of pressure. Spending my life as a disappointment proved to be an instructional childhood, though. I learned a great deal about power, Detective. I learned a great deal about how to control it, about how to make it, and about how to take it."

He met my employer's eye, and for the length of a slow breath he was eerily still. The moment passed and he went back to assessing the layout of the room around him with darting glances.

"That's your life's work?" said Jackaby. "Your machine?"

"Transvigoration."

"How does it work?"

Finstern scratched his neck. "Manipulation of currents."

"Electrical currents?"

"Vital currents," corrected Finstern. "Electrical would be easier. Volts. Electromotive force. Quantifiable."

"You've created a lightning rod for vital energies?"

"No, no, no, no. Too primitive. A vital life force has no inclination toward conduction through grounded wires. Won't do. Fields are a better analogy. My latest prototype actually built on some of the principals of Nikola Tesla's study last year. Radio frequency resonant transformers excited to induce coupling. Tesla has vision."

"That's all very technical and impressive," I said, "but you're not doing anything new. People have been taking lives for a lot longer than they've been playing with frequencies and volts. You've just put a shiny brass casing on a very old wickedness."

"It's not about taking life." Finstern twitched. "It's about controlling life. It's about transferring vital energies from one host to another. It's about power, Miss Rook. It's always about power. About who has it, and who gets left behind."

"You've reduced all living things to power cells?" Jackaby asked.

"No, no, no, no, you're still not seeing it. It's not just power, it's *powers*. Skills, proclivities, inborn talents. Why is one child a prodigy and the next a foundering cretin? Vitality! My machine doesn't just absorb raw energy, it absorbs the essence, the spirit, the soul!"

"That's spiritualism," I said. "Not science. How can you quantify a soul?"

Finstern twitched again and bit his lip. "The nature of

vital energies is problematic," he said. "But everything is science. Life is science. Magic is science. I've devoted my life to a subject I can't see or touch or measure, but I know it's there, and I know my device works."

"How can you be so sure?" said Jackaby.

"Have you ever seen a crow attempt to walk on all fours?"

"Crows don't have four legs," Jackaby said.

"No. But the rabbit inside of its head didn't know that, did he?" His eyes widened and his mouth crept into a zealous smile. "It works. I've seen it work. The only thing left is the fine-tuning."

"You have interesting taste in laboratory space," Jackaby said.

Finstern sneered. "I was invited."

"You were invited to the middle of a forest?"

"I was invited to New Fiddleham." Finstern scrabbled about in his pockets and produced a crumpled letter. Jackaby took it and glanced it over, then passed it to me. It was written on official-looking letterhead and read as follows:

CITY OF NEW FIDDLEHAM

FROM THE OFFICE OF THE MAYOR

March 13, 1892

Mr. Owen Finstern,

We are pleased to extend this offer of employment. Your exemplary efforts in the field of experimental energy are precisely the sort of innovation we seek in modernizing and revitalizing our burgeoning metropolis. Should you accept, you will be working with some of the finest minds in the country as a member of New Fiddleham's Technological Committee, and will be furnished with any and all resources necessary to continue your important work. We look forward to working with you very soon.

Mayor Philip Spade

"That's Spade's signature," Jackaby said. "It's authentic."

"Tell that to him. I have poured everything into my work. Everything. There is nothing left but my machine. I thought I would be funded at last, thought that I would have a chance to finish my research–but Spade turned me away the day I arrived. He said he had never heard of me, and that he certainly hadn't sent for me. He had already assembled his crack team. I was superfluous. It's fine. It is not the first time my talents have been overlooked. Perhaps this Unseelie council of yours will have a finer appreciation for visionary science."

Jackaby took a deep breath. "That was unkind of the mayor. You have done amazing work. A device like yours has immeasurable potential." Finstern acknowledged the compliment with a nod. "With the right research and application you could really help a lot of people, Owen. You need to know that the people who came for you–the council–they want to harness that potential for their own means."

"What means?"

"We don't know yet, but you can be certain that it's nothing good."

Finstern shrugged, his green eyes flickering from the glass on the floor to the fluttering shade. "Good. Bad. Subjective," he said flatly. "I don't need lectures about ethics, Detective. What I need are benefactors."

His choice of words sent a shiver up my neck. The man was a creep, but an invention like his given seemingly limitless funding in the hands of a sinister council of monsters—that was something far worse. It was bad enough to know that Pavel's mysterious benefactors were looking for Owen Finstern without Finstern also looking for them.

I excused myself politely. I needed to not be in the same room with that man any longer. Within the span of forty-eight hours I had been possessed by a ghost, had been shot by an energy ray, had done battle with a vampire, and had borne witness to the ravings of a real-life mad scientist. I was officially living out the pages of the penny dreadfuls I used to hide under my mattress from my mother. The heroes in those battered novels, I could not help but recall with a knot in my throat, did not always make it to the final page.

I was glad for the sunlight streaming in through the windows as I made my way to the back of the house. I did not relish the coming night, knowing that a furious vampire with a compelling reason to be angry at me might only be biding his time for sundown.

I took a deep breath and patted the dusty bust of Shakespeare on the head as I wound down the twists and turns of Jackaby's crooked hallway. I had these few daylight hours, at least, before I had to worry for my life.

That was when I heard footsteps in the library.

Chapter Twenty-One

I held my breath. I dared not scream or call out for Jackaby.

"Jenny," I squeaked as quietly as I could. "Jenny, can you hear me?"

More footsteps issued from behind the library door, and with them a scraping as of claws against the hardwood floor.

I gave a start as Jenny melted through the ceiling directly above me. "Abigail? Have you two finished interviewing that unpleasant man?" she asked. "I almost preferred the vampire. Why, what's the matter with you?"

"Shh!" I gestured frantically and mouthed the words *in there.*

Jenny nodded, suddenly alert, and swept to the library

to investigate. As she neared the door she faded away until she was entirely invisible. I strained to hear anything, but even the skitter of claws had stopped. I leaned closer and nearly flipped backward as Jenny's face popped back out of the wood in front of me.

"On second thought," she said with a playful smile, "this one is all yours." In another moment she was gone and I was left alone in the hallway again, more bewildered than before.

I opened the door cautiously and found myself overwhelmed by a wave of emotion. A trim young man with dark, curly hair was seated on the floor by the open alcove window. He was out of his policeman's blues, and in his lap flopped a scrappy, black-and-white sheepdog. It was licking his face mercilessly as he attempted to keep the thing still. I put my hands over my mouth and almost cried.

"Charlie?"

Charlie Barker looked abashed and quickly stood, letting his furry companion hop onto the floor. The dog's paws clicked across the wood until he reached the carpet at my feet. He butted his head into my legs affectionately and wound around me, sniffing eagerly.

"Yes–hello, Toby. I missed you, too." Toby had survived the incident in Gad's Valley when his owners had not, and Charlie had not the heart to leave him. "Charlie, what on earth are you doing here? You're a wanted man! There are posters! People talk about the Werewolf of the West End now like it's a real thing! You're a bona fide legend! If you had been seen . . ."

"People see what they want to see," Charlie said, shuffling his feet. "And if they cannot see the difference between a wolf and a hound, I think perhaps they might not notice little old me. Marlowe sent a telegram. Jackaby has been keeping him abreast of new developments. He told me about the pale man–about you. There was no way I could sit in Gad's Valley waiting for the next post to arrive telling me you were dead."

"Charlie!" I wanted to kick him for being so rash and to kiss him for being here. There was no one I wanted closer and no one I wanted less to join me in harm's way.

"It's good to see you, Miss Abigail." He smiled shyly, his deep brown eyes full of real and unapologetic relief. I gave in.

I crossed the library and wrapped myself around him. His arms were warm and strong and he smelled of cedar. Our first kiss had been a parting kiss. This one, our second, was all the more satisfying. It was like honey in hot tea.

I pulled away, breathing him in. "You shouldn't have come," I sighed.

"I know." He tucked a lock of hair behind my ear, his hand brushing my neck softly. "I was careful. I slipped in from the back streets. Apparently I am not the only legend lurking in the alleyways, though. Is it true? The pale man?"

"Yes. It's true. He's called Pavel. He's a vampire, and a despicable cad. I'm all right, really, although Pavel can't say the same. Wooden stakes and holy water might be preferable, but it turns out a sturdy brick to the face is not entirely ineffective against the dark scourge of the night. I'm a bit hazy on the details, though."

Charlie pulled away, his eyebrows knit in concern. "What? Marlowe's message only said that he spoke to you–something about a slip of paper . . . A brick?"

"Oh," I said. "Oh, yes–you're a bit behind."

I recalled to him the details of the past few nights, and Charlie listened dutifully, nodding silently until I was done.

". . . and that's all of it," I finished. "Mr. Jackaby is speaking with Finstern now. They're in the other room. Would you like to say hello?"

He held my hand as we slid down the hallway. It was a small gesture, but it made me feel sweet and warm and not so alone.

Toby bounded through the door before us, and Jackaby stood up, surprised. "I need to seriously reexamine my perimeter defenses. Is there anyone else in my house that I'm not aware of?"

"My house," came Jenny's voice softly, and Owen Finstern spun his eyes suspiciously around the room.

"I'm very sorry to arrive unannounced," Charlie said. "Under the circumstances–"

Jackaby waved him off. "No explanation needed. We can

use any help we can get, to be honest. Miss Rook filled you in on the pertinent details?"

Charlie nodded.

"Then you know that our most immediate threat is Pavel's daylight accomplice, a female foe employed by the same base and brutal benefactors who bankrolled Pavel."

"How do we find her?"

Jackaby sighed. "Unfortunately, anyone who knows anything about the mystery murderess or her shadowy council is either missing or dead." Jackaby scowled at the inventor. "Which you would do well to remember before you go running off to meet them."

"Then perhaps we should focus on the people who are dead," came Jenny's voice from the air above the desk. "Professor Hoole was closer to this device than anyone."

Finstern spun around on the bench. "Is everybody hearing that?" he asked.

Jackaby nodded. "Yes, and it's impolite to interrupt while others are communing with the departed, or didn't your research into the occult teach you that much?"

Finstern's face lit up. "You're the dead woman?" he said to the room. "Can you hear me?"

"I can hear you. I don't like you." Jenny's voice was flat.

Finstern clapped like a toddler at a puppet show. "Brilliant! I told Edison it was possible! I told him communication with the other side could only be a matter of calibration and sensitivity. He scoffed at my designs for a spirit phone–of course he didn't let me keep them, either. This is marvelous, though. How are you speaking?"

"I don't know. How are you speaking?" Jenny did not sound amused.

"Practiced modulation of the vocal chords. Do you have a larynx? Is there a frequency you need to employ to become audible? Can you see frequencies? Tell me, how many spirits like yourself reside in a city of, say, a hundred thousand?"

"I don't know!" Jenny said. "I'm not an expert on ghosts, I just am one."

"Of course," Jackaby said.

"What's that?" I asked.

"If our answers lie with the dead–then perhaps we should speak with someone who is an expert on ghosts. You're brilliant, Miss Cavanaugh, and absolutely right. Nobody knows what Hoole was building better than Hoole. All we need is a means of communicating with him from beyond the grave."

"Oh, is that all," I said.

"There are a handful of mediums operating in New Fiddleham," Jackaby continued. "Lieutenant Dupin used to see one every month to have his cards read."

"Mediums lie," Finstern said. "Misrepresentation of observable phenomena. It's not real."

"It's called showmanship," Jackaby said.

"It is invalid data."

"Not everything needs validation to be real. Charlie may be onto something. It's worth a try, anyway."

Jackaby set Charlie to watching Mr. Finstern and sent me to check on Mrs. Hoole while he darted into his laboratory to make the necessary preparations. I slipped outside and knocked on the door to the cellar.

The bolts click, click, clicked and the door swung open. The widow was in one piece, but she did not look as though she had slept a wink.

"You really shouldn't open the door straightaway," I said. "I could have been anyone."

Mrs. Hoole nodded. "Of course you could. That was stupid of me."

"Are you all right?" I said. "We're going out to see if we can find some answers. It's probably best that you keep yourself sealed in. Do you need anything, though?"

She shook her head. "Why did you protect me?" she asked. "Last night when that monster attacked me, you jumped in front of him. You don't know me. As you say, I could have been anyone."

"Oh. It was just the right thing to do, I suppose."

"How do you know if you're doing the right thing?" she asked. "I keep trying, but sometimes I feel as though I've done nothing but the wrong thing all my life."

"I'm sure that isn't true," I said. "You keep trying–and in the end I think maybe that's the only right thing anybody can do."

She nodded, although she did not seem bolstered by the advice. "Thank you, Miss Rook. You have been far too kind."

Mrs. Hoole pulled the cellar door gently closed and I heard the locks click, click, click back in place.

I hastened back into the house, where I met Jackaby emerging from his laboratory with his satchel slung over his shoulder and a long brown cord in his hand. The bag on his arm looked even heavier than usual, but he didn't seem to be bothered. "Ready?" he asked.

"As ever, sir."

We returned to the foyer, and Jackaby held out the cord to Charlie.

"A leash?" Charlie said. "Toby is really very well trained, sir. I don't know that that's necessary."

"Toby's staying here," Jackaby said. "Don't worry, Douglas is a reliable custodian."

"Douglas is a duck."

"Yes, well, he wasn't always!" Jackaby was still a little sensitive on the subject of Douglas's transformation. He blamed himself for allowing his former assistant to blunder into harm's way in the first place. To his credit, Jackaby had long since found the means to reverse the curse. It was Douglas who chose to remain in fowl form, which frustrated my employer to no end. "The bullheaded bird is more than capable of looking after your mutt for a few hours. The leash is for you."

Charlie glanced at Finstern, who was pacing the room. The inventor didn't seem to be listening. He leaned down to look into Ogden's terrarium, about to tap the glass with his finger.

"I wouldn't do that if I were you," Jenny's voice chided. Finstern looked up and all around him.

"You can't mean to suggest that I wear . . ." Charlie whispered to Jackaby.

"You can't very well go walking down the street in broad daylight, can you? And as much fun as it sounds to travel through New Fiddleham exclusively through back gardens and over hedges, we are a bit short on time. We can go without you, if you prefer?"

Charlie took the leash without enthusiasm. "I'll be right back."

"No," said Jackaby loudly, so that the inventor could hear. "You won't. Do release the hound, though. We'll be taking our guard dog with us."

Chapter Twenty-Two

Charlie was an impressive hound. His ancestors, the Om Caini, had roamed as nomads for generations, always on the move due to the unique nature of their bloodline. Like werewolves, the House of Caine were half men and half beasts, but unlike their monstrous cousins, the Om Caini were not ruled by their animal instincts or by the lunar cycle. They could transform at will, although the phases of the moon still pulled at their deepest sensibilities. They were mighty hounds in their animal form; less powerful than the wolves, but still proud and noble and more fiercely loyal. Also—although I had not told Charlie this—they were impossibly adorable.

His coat was full and soft as he padded out, patterned in light caramels and chocolate browns blending to rich, silky blacks. His paws were wide and fluffy, and his ears were like thick velvet. I knelt to fasten the leash loosely around his neck. He watched me, embarrassment playing across his dark eyes. "It's just for show," I reminded him. He pressed his forehead against mine and I leaned in to hug him around the neck. "Goodness, but you're soft. When this is over, we are curling up in the library to read a quiet book together," I told him. "I could cuddle up against you for hours." I realized what I had just said and felt my ears go all hot. I could never have said something like that to Charlie as a human. Charlie just wagged his tail.

"Ready?" Jackaby called.

We received the occasional stare as we took to the streets of New Fiddleham. Charlie was a big dog. He had a wide muzzle, and his back came up nearly to my waist. Even padding peacefully down the lane in his role as the harmless house pet, he inspired more than a few passersby to favor the opposite sidewalk.

Finstern had agreed to come along. Jackaby did not feel comfortable letting him out of our sight for too long, and the inventor seemed to be interested in seeing what our investigation might uncover anyway. He also regarded the hound with a level of interest I did not like.

"Powerful beast," he said. "Charlie? Wasn't that also the name of the young man–?"

"The one is named for the other," Jackaby answered curtly.

"Which is named for which?"

"That," Jackaby replied, "is an excellent question. Oh, look–here's the first place, just ahead."

The medium had a sign hung from her window, an outstretched hand with an eye in the center. The sign read:

MME VOILE–CLAIRVOYANT
PALMS. LEAVES. SÉANCES.

Jackaby strode inside first, and the rest of us followed. A bell chimed, and from somewhere inside the building a chair squeaked against the floor. The cramped lobby was thick with the aromas of rosewater and sage. A curtain behind the counter whipped aside and a woman emerged dressed in flowing purple robes, a silk head scarf, and a lace shawl. She wore heavy makeup, her eyelids smoky blue and her eyes framed by thick black lashes. As she surveyed us, she adjusted a bronze tiara just above her hairline. It was strung with delicate, dangling chains that swayed hypnotically across her forehead.

"Greetings, weary travelers," she said. "I sense that you–"

"Nope," Jackaby said and pushed past us back out of the shop.

Back on the street Finstern caught up with him.

"What was that?"

"A charlatan," Jackaby replied frankly. "To be expected. We'll hope for better luck at our next stop."

"How will you know?"

"I will know," said Jackaby. "This way. There's a whole shop dedicated to the occult about two blocks down on

Prospect Lane. Mostly artificial relics and harmless trinkets, but several Lwa of the Vodou pantheon used to manifest there on Saturdays."

Finstern narrowed his eyes at Jackaby. There was skepticism in his gaze, but also something else—something far more unsettling—like a deep and insatiable hunger.

"Come along," called Jackaby. "It's just ahead and to the right."

Charlie made a small growling noise.

"Hm? Oh—to the left, I mean. Ahead and to the left."

We wound our way around the city for an hour or two, stopping in at various esoteric little parlors. Some were little more than kitchen nooks hung with spare bedsheets, and others were richly decorated rooms with warm lighting and cloying incense.

Most of these Jackaby passed over with little more than a casual glance, although a few had apparently incorporated some legitimately supernatural set dressing or authentically arcane accoutrements. One of the frauds, Jackaby was amused to report, was not remotely gifted in extramortal communication, but was a budding telekinetic. The trembling table and rattling windows bespoke a genuine and admirable talent, although not one that would help us find the answers we sought.

Finstern caught sight of a posting on a public board as we moved on up the street. "Does that look like your Charlie boy to you?" he asked. I looked.

Sure enough, he had spotted one of the wanted posters featuring Charlie's human likeness. Charlie's ears flattened. "No," I said. "No, not so much. I mean, similar features, to be sure–but they have very different, erm, noses. And the eyebrows are all wrong."

Jackaby glanced back to see why we had stalled. He followed our gaze and grunted in annoyance. He had already given Marlowe an earful when the posters first appeared, but the commissioner could not seem to stop his district chiefs from papering the town with the confounded things. Beneath Charlie's face it read:

WANTED

FOR MURDER, DEVILRY, LYCANTHROPY

$1,000 REWARD

CHARLIE CANE

"Hrm," said Jackaby. "I'm almost impressed one of those simpletons bothered to look up the term lycanthropy, although they've got it wrong on all three accounts, of course." He tore down the paper and stuffed it in the bin a half a block down the road. "Different Charlie," he added over his shoulder for good measure, and then continued on his way without further explanation.

Jackaby knew of just one more medium operating out of New Fiddleham, and I held out hope that our last stop might make the whole trip worthwhile. A row of brick buildings with tattered awnings stretched before us, and at the end of the block I could see a banner with suns and moons circling a crystal ball. As we neared my hope dried up. The Glorious Galvani had long since closed up shop. His door was boarded up, and mischievous scoundrels had broken several windowpanes. I peered inside and sighed. It was very empty.

"You looking to see the future?" a voice called out weakly from across the street.

"We're actually more interested in the past," Jackaby replied. "Specifically we're interested in *those* passed. Hello, Miss Lee–shouldn't you be resting?"

Lydia Lee, the same Lydia Lee Jackaby had rescued in the alleyway, stood in the darkened doorway of a building across the street. I had gotten a bit mixed up with all of the twists and turns, but we couldn't have been more than a few blocks from the neighborhood where we had dropped her off. Her tight black curls were tied up with a red ribbon, and she wore a sleeveless white chemise with lace fringe and a corset of black and red. She had a black mantle draped over her broad shoulders, but it provided little in the way of concealment.

"It wasn't as bad as it looked," she said. Her auburn lips were still marred with a dark cut, around which a ring of purple had blossomed.

"It was exactly as bad as it looked," Jackaby said. "You have a cracked rib, Miss Lee, and if you're not careful with that corset you'll make it worse."

"The corset makes it feel better."

"The corset restricts air flow. You're going to give yourself pneumonia. I went to the trouble of saving your life; the least you could do is keep it saved."

"Mr. Jackaby." Miss Lee spoke softly but firmly. "I appreciate your help, and that O'Connor lady you sent to check up on me was sweet—but don't confuse saving a life with owning it. No one owns my life but me. I'm not staying cooped up forever."

Jackaby shook his head but relented.

"I *am* in your debt, though," Miss Lee said. "And I hate that. You're looking for a real psychic? I tell you what, how about I take you to Little Miss?"

"Little Miss?"

"All Mama Tilly's girls know Little Miss. She's a special one."

We wound our way back up through the streets slowly. Miss Lee moved stiffly and took shallow breaths. Every time Jackaby cautioned that she not push herself or suggested she take a rest, she only pressed on harder, as if to spite him. Eventually he stopped trying to help.

Finstern turned to me as Miss Lee led the way. "Why are we following a man in a dress?"

"She's not . . ." I began, feeling defensive, but out of my depth to explain. "She's just different from other girls. She's really quite lovely."

Charlie slid over to stand between the inventor and me,

eyeing the man from under a furry brow as we plodded forward.

"She has an Adam's apple."

"You're awfully judgmental for someone who's been keeping company with dead rodents," I said. "Look, I don't know that I fully understand her, either, but that doesn't matter. I don't need to understand someone to respect them. I think she's very brave."

"How is she brave?"

"How?" I considered. "There are lots of people out there who are terribly hateful. She could avoid a whole lot of trouble and dress and act as they want her to, but she chooses to be herself. That's brave. Also–the last time we met she stopped Jackaby from hurting the men who hurt her. They might have killed her. Kindness is an act of bravery, I think, just as hatred is an act of fear. I'm sure you can appreciate that not all strength is muscle, Mr. Finstern. She has a strong spirit, and I believe she is very brave about the way she chooses to use it."

Finstern seemed to accept my explanation without further argument, or else he had simply stopped paying attention. It was hard to tell with a man whose eyes never sat for two seconds on the same thing. "Your employer," he said. "Why is he so certain of which mediums have powers and which do not?"

"Don't you know?" I said. "Jackaby is a Seer. He calls it looking past the veil. He sees the truth of things."

Finstern's cheek twitched. "What sort of things?"

"Anything, really. He sees magical creatures when they're trying to hide. He can see traces of people after they have gone like he's looking at footprints in the air, especially if there is something supernatural about them. He sees auras, which I think are sort of like people's characters–their past, present, and potential–manifested as colors all around them. It's not always clear how it works, but he says he sees the true nature of things."

Finstern nodded thoughtfully and fell silent. The hungry look had crept back into his eyes, and he watched Jackaby like a dog might watch the edge of his master's plate.

Soon we came to a familiar wooden sign–an outstretched hand with a simple eye in the center.

Jackaby pinched the bridge of his nose and shifted the heavy satchel on his shoulder. "Miss Lee, thank you ever so much for your assistance, but we have already met Madame Voile. I'm afraid she is not quite the clairvoyant her advertisement indicates. I appreciate your help all the same. Please, now–do get some rest. Repay your debt to us by spending just a little time on the mend."

"You don't want to meet Madame," Miss Lee said. "I told you. You want to meet Little Miss."

Jackaby cocked his head to one side, and Miss Lee gave him a wry smile.

"Tell her Mama Tilly's girls say hi. We all look out for Little Miss. It was a pleasure to see you again, Mr. Jackaby."

She gave a little wave and Jackaby tipped his head courteously before stepping back into the shop with a little chime. Finstern followed close on his heels.

I hesitated. "Miss Lee," I said. "Do be careful."

Miss Lee gave me a smile. "Careful, Miss Abigail?"

"Yes, of course. Those men might have . . . you could have . . . just be careful."

"Don't go down the wrong streets, you mean?"

"Yes, exactly."

"You're a sweet girl," she said in a kind tone that made me feel less *sweet* and more *woefully naive*. "But open up those pretty eyes. For me, they're *all* the wrong streets." Her voice broke just a little and she swallowed and straightened, pushing past the moment by force of will. "I don't want to be careful, Miss Abigail. I want to be Lydia Lee."

And then she was off again, marching down the sidewalk with her chin up and her shoulders back. Charlie nudged my hand with his head, and I realized I had been staring after her. "I'm coming," I said. "Let's go meet Little Miss, shall we?"

Chapter Twenty-Three

We slipped back into Madame Voile's cramped little lobby just as the curtain swept aside and the clairvoyant reappeared. "Greetings, weary travelers," she said. "I see you have been drawn once more toward my door by the inexorable pull of fate."

"Something like that," said Jackaby. "Anyway, *fate* sounds more impressive than *a lack of other options*. Either way, here we are."

Madame Voile hesitated.

"Pardon me, ma'am," I said. "We were wondering if we might talk to Little Miss?"

Madame Voile scanned our faces suspiciously. "No one here called Little Miss," she said. Her accent, I couldn't help but notice, had suddenly lost its theatrical cadence.

"You're quite sure?" I asked.

Jackaby was staring at her intently.

"Am I sure? Of course I'm sure. Now, if you are not here for a reading–"

"You are lying," Jackaby said, happily. "Marvelous. Who is Little Miss, then? A niece? A sister? A daughter?"

Madame Voile glared at my employer.

"A daughter, then. I understand she has taken to the family trade rather exceptionally. I'm sure you're very proud. We will be happy to offer remuneration for her services, of course. Just a few minutes of her time."

The curtain behind Madame Voile wiggled, and a wide pair of dark brown eyes peeped out.

"Remuneration?" The woman crossed her arms at Jackaby.

Jackaby answered by plucking a handful of crumpled banknotes out of his satchel. "For her trouble, and for yours," he said.

Madame Voile's eyes widened as the money tumbled onto the counter in front of her.

"Well," she said, "I don't know. She's only five, my Little Miss. She's a sweet, precious little thing. What kind of mother would I be if I let strangers harass her for a mere . . . how much was that?"

"Half," answered Jackaby. "That is half. The rest after we've had our consultation."

The woman stared at the money hungrily. "Irina!" she

called over her shoulder. The girl emerged, her bright eyes barely able to see over the top of the counter. She wore a head scarf, but she was dressed without any of her mother's rich fabrics or ostentatious bangles. "These people want to talk to you, Irina."

"I'm seven," she whispered. "I'm not five."

"Oh, hush up, now. Take them around back, there's a good girl."

The girl looked up, and then she stared at the window behind us for several seconds. I glanced out to see what she was looking at, but the street was empty. "They won't all fit in the booth," the girl murmured.

Madame Voile grunted. "Hm. That's true. Well, they're not paying me for the show, anyway. The kitchen table will have to do. Show them the way."

We filed past the curtain and through a slim, dark room, which held a round table draped in black cloth with a crystal ball in the center. On the other side of the room sat a jarringly ordinary kitchen. There were pots and pans hung on the wall and dirty dishes soaking in the sink. A wide wooden table occupied the center of the room, and we shuffled in and sat around it. Charlie padded in last and lay down against the wall behind my chair.

The door chimes sounded and Madame Voile glanced at the clock. "Oh, that'll be Mrs. Howell. I'll be back to check on you all shortly. Be a good girl, Irina." She plucked a deck of cards from the mantel and bustled off back through the curtains. We could hear her voice pronouncing a muffled, "Greetings, Mrs. Howell. Oh! I sense fate has much in store for you!"

The girl sat down at the head of the table. She was very small, and she hunched nervously as she looked at us. She seemed to look past Jackaby as though she were staring at the wallpaper behind him rather than at the detective directly.

Jackaby deposited his satchel on the floor with a thud. He smiled reassuringly. "Good afternoon, Irina," he said.

She nodded, still not quite meeting his gaze. She looked as though she might recede completely into her head scarf at any moment.

"A friend of mine told me you were very clever," he said. "One of Mama Tilly's girls? She told me that you're a bit like me, actually."

Irina looked up at him for a moment.

"I also see things that other people can't see," said Jackaby. "And I know about things that are sometimes hard to explain."

Irina nodded.

"We're not exactly the same," he continued. "I can see there's something extra special about you."

"Can you see her?" the girl asked.

Finstern swiveled in his chair to look around the room, and I felt the hairs on my neck prickle up. *Her?*

Jackaby smiled. "Yes. I can see her. Don't worry, she's

very nice." He reached into his heavy satchel and pulled out a familiar cracked brick. He set it on the table. "She's my friend, and she came along just to meet you."

The air just over his shoulder shimmered, although Jenny did not materialize completely. She had been there all along, I realized, right where the girl had been watching. I shook my head, astonished and proud of Jenny's progress. How long had we been walking around town? This was a far cry from taking a few steps onto the sidewalk.

"Hello, sweetie," Jenny said softly. "You don't need to be nervous." Her voice was gentle and kind. "It's an honor to meet you. You have a marvelous gift. Not many people can see me unless I really want them to. Do you see many other people who are . . . like me?" Jenny asked.

The girl was quiet.

"It's just that we were hoping to find someone," Jenny's voice continued. "Someone who was dead."

"I see them." Irina's voice was barely a whisper. We all leaned in to listen.

"That's fantastic," Jenny said. "Have you seen anyone recently? Can you describe them?"

The girl took a deep breath. "I see all of them."

Jackaby cleared his throat gently. "All of them?" he asked.

"Everyone that's dead," she said. "Your friend is pretty."

Jackaby nodded. "She is that. You see everyone that's dead? Do you mean *everyone*, or just the ghostly ones, like her, who have stayed around?"

"Everyone. Forever. There are lots and lots. Too many. Lots more of them than there are of us. Most of them are on the other side. I can't see them as well as the ones on this side, like her–but I can still see them. I can always see them."

Jackaby's eyes were alive with enthusiasm. "My word. She's telling the truth."

The girl nodded, meekly.

"You are very special indeed, Little Miss," said Jackaby.

The girl said nothing, but climbed down from her chair and over to a rolltop desk in the corner. She retrieved a map and brought it over to the table, where she unfolded it. It was a street map of New Fiddleham. "Want to see the trick?" she asked.

Jackaby nodded, intrigued, and the girl reached across the table toward him. "Hold my hand. Think of a dead person. I can find them. If they're on this side, I can tell you where."

Jackaby took the girl's hand and said aloud, "Jenny Cavanaugh."

Irina shut her eyes tight. Her little pointer finger hovered over the map and landed squarely on the address where we sat.

"Oh! That's you, isn't it?" she said, looking up.

"Very keen," Jenny's voice replied.

"Do you want to try another?" Irina asked.

"Mayor Philip Spade," Jackaby suggested.

Her finger hovered for a moment and then she shook her head. "I don't see him."

"No, you shouldn't," Jackaby confirmed. "The mayor is very much alive. Well done. Let's try Lawrence Hoole."

Irina concentrated and shook her head again. "I can see him, but he's on the other side. He passed on."

"Let's try another," Jackaby said. "He's undead, but he's not like Jenny. He calls himself Pavel. I don't know his last name."

"Just hold on to him in your mind," Irina instructed. She let her hand hover over the map again and closed her eyes. Her finger landed in the Inkling District. "He's there," she said. "But he's not. He's underneath, I think."

"The sewers." Jackaby nodded. "Well, I guess it was too much to hope that he had passed on to the other side as well."

"What about Julian McCaffery?" I suggested.

"Yes. Julian McCaffery," Jackaby repeated.

Irina concentrated. "I don't see him."

"McCaffery's alive? Well, that's interesting, but not much help until we know where they're keeping him. Who else might know about the council?"

"Howard Carson," Jenny said. The room went quiet.

"Jenny . . ." Jackaby began.

"She can tell me if Pavel was lying. She can tell me if Howard is alive or dead. She can tell me if he's a ghost like me, or if he's gone forever. Show me Howard Carson."

Jackaby nodded solemnly. "Howard Carson."

Irina closed her eyes and concentrated. After a few pregnant moments her hands dropped into her lap.

"He's alive?" Jenny's voice trembled, as though speaking too loudly might shatter the fragile hope.

"No," said Irina. "He's passed on. He's on the other side."

I could feel the air chill by several degrees, and Irina looked nervous. Finstern, who had been watching all of this with rapt interest, shuddered. Jackaby's eyes were curiously alight.

"Sir?" I said.

"They're beyond the veil, but you can sense them?" Jackaby pressed the young lady. "You sense them the same as you sense Jenny?"

Irina nodded. "They're just farther away."

"The afterlife," said Jackaby. "The underworld. Whatever you'd like to call it. The other side. It's a place?"

Irina nodded again. "I guess so."

"Can you show us how to get there?"

Irina looked startled. "You . . . die."

"I mean aside from the usual way. There are countless doors or bridges in the old stories. Is there a gate near here, a tunnel, the roots of a massive tree?"

She shook her head. "I don't see places. I don't see doors. I only see the people."

My employer nodded, thoughtfully. "Let's do it again," he said.

Irina took his hand. Her finger hovered over the map. "Who would you like to find?" she asked.

"Charon."

"Charon, sir?" I said. "Really?"

"Who's Charon?" Finstern asked.

"He's not a real person," I said. "Charon is the mythical Greek ferryman to Hades, he's not–"

I swallowed my words as Irina's finger jabbed down on the map. Every head around the table leaned in.

"Charon," said Jackaby quietly, "is on the other side of Rosemary's Green."

Chapter Twenty-Four

Rosemary's Green was on the opposite side of town. Augur Lane was on the way, so Jackaby opted to take a detour to collect a few things at the house before we visited the rolling fields.

"You mean to say there's something you haven't already packed in that big bag of yours?" I asked as we rounded the corner. Number 926 Augur Lane was just ahead.

"Good things come to those who bring them along in the first place," said Jackaby. "I prefer to be prepared."

"Prepared for what, though?" I said. "Do we have any idea what we're getting ourselves into?"

"I have many ideas. The afterlife is a popular subject in every major religion around the world. Countless descriptions have been written chronicling the descent into the hereafter, from Hades to Heaven to the Happy Hunting Ground. Yes, Miss Rook, I have a limitless supply of–" He froze. We had just reached 926 Augur Lane. Charlie began to growl, low and menacing.

"What is it?" Finstern asked before I could.

"Someone has been here," Jackaby said. "Fae. Unseelie. Very strong. Something else, too. Something large . . ."

Charlie padded past the gate, sniffing the path. "Oh my word. Sir," I said. "Take a look." Several of the flagstones leading up to the bright red front door were cracked, and in the grass to either side were massive footprints. It looked as though an elephant had come calling in our absence.

"Trolls?" said Jackaby. "No. Elementals! This makes no sense–elementals can be brutes, but they're neutral. They don't cavort with fairies. There's no reason for this–it's all wrong!"

The beautiful red door was now riddled with cracks and hanging open, the frame splintered to bits. It was senselessly violent–it wasn't as though Jackaby ever locked the thing, anyway. The center of the door was bare, and I realized the horseshoe doorknocker had been torn off entirely.

The wind whipped through the trees and the skies darkened. "Wait here," said Jackaby, pushing the abused door open the rest of the way with a creak.

"No." Jenny's voice was a low boil. "My house. You wait here."

Jackaby, uncharacteristically, did what he was told. A

few anxious minutes later the winds died down and Jenny reappeared in the entryway. "They're gone," she said. "But they've been all through the house."

My skin crawled as I stepped inside. The drawers of my desk had been pulled out and emptied on the floor. Papers were everywhere. A swampy stink lingered in the air, and I could tell that Ogden had defended the place as only he knew how. The pungent little frog's terrarium lay shattered on the floor. There was no sign of its amphibian occupant. I felt sick and angry.

"Was this room different when we left?" Finstern asked. "Something seems different." I glared at him. Jackaby continued on through the hallway, and I followed. The bust of Shakespeare had been knocked roughly aside, leaving a hole in the plaster of the wall and cracking the bard's cranium in two.

Jackaby stalked straight out the back door as I paused to survey the damage in each room. Jackaby's office was in no better shape than the front room. The heavy safe appeared to have been thrown directly through the standing blackboard, leaving the former upside-down on the floor and reducing the latter to shards of chalky slate and broken wood. The laboratory across the hall was strewn with bits of broken beakers and bottles, and steam whistled steadily from two or three bent pipes no longer connected to their big brass boiler.

The back door slammed shut so violently it rattled the

broken glassware at my feet. I stepped out in the hallway to intercept Jackaby as he stormed back inside. "She's gone!"

"Mrs. Hoole? No!" I felt dizzy. We had promised the widow our protection and we had failed her. "But I thought the cellar was safeguarded! How did they–"

"They didn't," Jackaby snarled. "The wards are still active. There's not a jam jar out of place. The cellar wasn't breached. *They* didn't do anything–she did. The bolts were thrown from the inside."

"She opened it herself? But why?"

Jackaby was fuming. "This," he said through gritted teeth, "is why I don't like secrets!"

I followed him as he tramped up the stairs. We emerged on the second floor. A cabinet toward the far end of the hall had toppled. It stood wedged diagonally against the opposite wall, its doors hanging open and its contents spilled on the floor.

"Argh. Stay on this side of the house," Jackaby warned as he trod forward angrily. "Some of those artifacts are highly unstable. I'll set it right myself." His fists were clenched as he went to see to it.

My room was first on the right. It had been ransacked as well. The chest of drawers had been emptied and my dresses and shirtwaists lay all over. Directly in the center of my bed lay the sketch of Owen Finstern with the little carved stone resting on top of it. It was hard not to take their placement as a sign. They had sent Pavel to collect, and he had come back worse for wear and without their quarry.

As I scooped them up angrily, the door to my armoire rattled. I tensed, holding my breath. It rattled again, this time accompanied by a bark and a muffled quack. "Oh! Douglas!" I relaxed and stuffed Pavel's little mementos in my pocket as I opened the door. Douglas burst out, flapping across the room and squawking. He perched on my headboard and shook out his feathers. Toby was cowering in the back of the armoire, and I patted his head. "It's all right, boy," I said.

Across the hall, Jenny's door hung open, as well. I tiptoed over. Her room looked untouched at first glance, and I almost dared to imagine the perpetrators had spared her the indignity of trespassing there. Then my eyes fell to the floor.

A shape had been carved into the wood. It was just a silhouette etched in crude, jagged lines, but the image was clear. The rough cuts outlined the body of a woman in a flowing dress, lying sprawled in the center of the room. There, in the center, where the woman's heart should be, lay a tarnished pewter locket. I did not need to open it to know it was the locket from the photograph, the locket *from Howard with love.*

"Abigail?" Jenny said behind me. "What are you looking at?"

I spun around. "Oh, Jenny–don't . . ." but she was already past me.

Jenny stooped, and her fingers traced the rough gashes in the wood. With trembling slowness she reached out and took hold of the locket. She clutched it so tightly her fist shook, and she pulled it to her chest. Her whole body fluttered like a moving picture in a broken penny arcade machine. Her hair whipped behind her and the windows shook. The wind stole my breath and sent shivers down my neck.

"Jenny, she's gone. It's over. She can't hurt you anymore. She's just trying to–"

Without warning the windows exploded. I held an arm in front of my face as tiny bits of glass spun around the room.

"Jenny!"

Jackaby was behind me at once. The wind was deafening, but he stepped past me and spoke quietly, earnestly. "You're not alone, Miss Cavanaugh. Not this time. Not now. Not ever, ever again."

The wind died down as quickly as it had started, glass skittering along the ground and coming to a rest with a million little tinkles. Jenny blinked into view in front of Jackaby, fluttering in and out of sight. Her eyes were sad and desperate as she reached a hand toward him. Her lip quivered. Her translucent fingers brushed his stubbled jaw and then she flickered again. In the same instant, her body lay motionless in the center of the room, a perfect fit within the lines of the grisly silhouette. Her eyes stared blankly ahead, and the darkness that saturated her dress was beginning to spread like a grim shadow on the floor.

And then the room was silent and Jenny was gone.

"Too far." Jackaby's eyes were steel as he slid a long bronze knife and a little red pouch into the inner pockets of his coat. He had blown into his laboratory like a savage gale, and I knew his moods well enough to know I should stay out of his way. A broken test tube crunched under his shoes. He ignored it, picking over what was left of his work space as he stocked up for the journey ahead. I watched from the doorway as he pulled drawers out of a damaged storage rack, throwing them on the floor one after another as they failed to produce whatever artifact he was looking for. "Too far."

Charlie came around the corner. He was dressed again, and standing on his own two human feet. Toby stuck close to him, leaning into Charlie's legs for comfort. Charlie put a hand on my shoulder, and I leaned into him, too.

"Are you all right?" he asked.

"I don't know," I said. "I don't even know what they were looking for. I haven't found anything actually missing, as far as I can tell. It all just seems malicious. It was her–the woman–Pavel's accomplice. It had to be. She came back just to taunt Jenny."

"Mrs. Hoole," Charlie said. "She's been taken."

"Not taken," I said. "She left. I don't know what to think

about the widow Hoole anymore! I have a hard time believing she's a part of this madness, but frankly I'm having a hard time believing any of this madness is happening at all!"

Owen Finstern pushed his head in the doorway. "My machine is what's missing," he said. He pressed past us and paced an uneven circle around the ravaged laboratory. "They took my machine!"

"They don't have your machine," said Jackaby, his back to the inventor.

"And you know that for certain?" He squinted at Jackaby.

Jackaby turned and glared. "They don't have your machine," he repeated.

"Where were you during all this?" Finstern asked, turning back to Charlie. "Hiding from them?" He narrowed his eyes. "Helping them?"

Charlie kept his composure. "I was out."

"You're a wanted man. I saw the posters. Where did you–?"

"Shut up." Jackaby pushed past the inventor and out toward the front of the house. "We're leaving. All of us. Now."

"Sir?" I said. "What's the plan?"

"Lawrence Hoole is the plan. He's our freshest corpse and the most likely to know who made him into one. We are getting answers for Miss Cavanaugh if we have to drag them back from the depths of Hell to do it."

Chapter Twenty-Five

Rosemary's Green was two or three acres of rolling fields dotted with trees and bushes. A few humble houses stood nearby, a quiet neighborhood toward the outskirts of town. One wide stretch of the perimeter shared a fence with the churchyard and its rows and rows of granite gravestones. On the far side of the expanse rose untamed hills. I was unsure how anyone knew exactly where Rosemary's Green ended and the wilds began. This place was on a threshold of its own, with the world of men behind us and proper nature ahead–singing birds and buzzing bees to the right, and a stony, silent boneyard to the left.

There was something quietly stoic and important about Rosemary's Green, as if the whole expanse were one giant mossy cathedral. Jackaby pressed forward over the grass. He moved with focus and purpose.

"Do you know what we're looking for, sir?" I asked.

"I think so. I've been here before," he said. These were the first words he had spoken since leaving the house. "I investigated this field the month I arrived in New Fiddleham. Lines of force for miles around intersect near the southwest corner, but I could never discern anything further. Having come together, the channels of power simply stopped. I've always suspected something of significance lay just beyond my reach here, but I've never had the means to penetrate the barrier. There are very few things in this world I cannot see. I suspect, Miss Rook, that we are approaching a portal to the Annwyn."

"The Annwyn?" Finstern perked up. "I know the Annwyn. Welsh?"

Jackaby looked back over his shoulder, surprised. "That's right."

"I know all the stories," Finstern said. "And about the sídhe mounds in Ireland, too."

"Huh." Jackaby looked legitimately impressed. "That's a rather unexpected facet of your education."

"I am a skeptic, but I am a scientist first. Never dismiss the possibility of forces beyond our comprehension. I've read the Mabinogion and the old Arthurian legends. I've been to Stonehenge. You can never exclude that which has not yet been proven. That's the essence of inquiry. The Annwyn is an intriguing theory. Interdimensional overlap, a converging of realities." His darting eyes lost focus for a moment as he stared at the trees in front of him. "If you had lived my childhood, Detective, you might have sought for other worlds as well."

"My childhood brought the other worlds to me," Jackaby replied. "Whether I wanted them or not. You may have had the better end of that deal."

"Pardon me, sirs," I piped up. "There are those of us present who have not spent our lives developing a lexicon of obscure mythologies."

"The Annwyn is one of many names for the infamous *other side*," Jackaby said.

"So, the afterlife?"

"No. Not exactly. But I believe that our entryway to the underworld might lie behind a barrier of another sort. There are worlds beyond ours—the domains of creatures who once shared the earth openly with us. There are places where the veil is thin and a few places where it has been rent clean through, but it stretches to all corners of the globe."

Finstern twitched. "Globes are spherical. No corners."

Jackaby ignored him and continued. "The Annwyn exists all around us, but it is one of very few things that even I have never seen."

"Then how can you be certain?"

"If a native Parisian told you that France was a real place, would you doubt him? I've met residents of the Annwyn, Miss Rook, many times. Call them immigrants or visitors or whatever you like–there are a great many beings in our world who hail from the Annwyn. The craftsmen who reconstructed my third floor were from a domain of the Annwyn that the Norse call Alfheim. Here we know them as elves."

I blinked. "You had elves do your remodeling?"

"Can you think of a more practical way to fit an entire functional ecosystem in a single story of a New England colonial?"

"I really can't."

"The duck pond on the third floor is much deeper than the ceiling on the second," he said. "They overlap without either losing any space. It's a neat trick."

"Yes, I've noticed that."

"Well then. The Annwyn works in a similar way," Jackaby said. "It's here, all around us, but mere mortals like us can never pierce it. The Seelie Court has taken it upon themselves to maintain the barrier at all times. The portals are theirs alone to open."

"What exactly are they protecting behind their barrier?" Finstern asked.

Jackaby came to a stop at last. We were looking at a great grassy mound in the earth. It was nothing more than a rather geometrical hill, as though an oversized globe had been half buried and then covered in sod. "Us," Jackaby replied, setting down the satchel. "They're protecting us."

"How are they protecting us," Charlie asked, "if they're the ones who can come and go as they like and we're the ones locked out?"

"Not every creature can come and go," Jackaby answered. "The Seelie Court are peacekeepers by nature. The *Unseelie* Court are . . . not." He glanced to Owen Finstern, who was circling the mound, transfixed. Lowering his voice, he added: "Your own ancestors, Mr. Barker, were born of a marriage between humans and Seelie fae. Werewolves, in contrast, were born of a marriage between humans and the Unseelie. That might be part of what makes you an exceptional officer of the law and what makes them monsters. It's the nature of the beast."

"So the barrier keeps all the bad creatures inside?" I said. "It doesn't work very well then, does it? We've got redcaps and vampires and all sorts of things running around New Fiddleham."

"The barrier is not perfect," Jackaby said. "It is to be expected that a handful of creatures slip through each year. Too many recently, it's true–but a fraction of those that lie beyond. It is the duty of the Seelie Court to seal the cracks as they occur. Think of that pond suspended above your bedroom on Augur Lane. Those creatures are like the tiniest drips beginning to form. They are nothing compared to the deluge that would await should the whole barrier ever collapse."

"That doesn't make me feel especially comfortable about our poking about here," I said. "Or about my sleeping arrangements, for that matter."

"I–I can feel it!" We all looked up. Finstern was nearly at the top of the mound when he flew back as though slapped by a giant invisible hand. He tumbled gracelessly, head over heels, until he landed, half-dazed, at the bottom of the hill.

"Mr. Finstern?" I rushed to his side.

"Observable phenomenon. Measurable reaction. Quantifiable." The inventor sat up, swaying slightly. He was smiling madly. "It's real."

My employer clambered up the mound. It was not overly large–ten, perhaps fifteen, feet from its base to its highest point. He stood where Finstern had been and felt the air all around him.

Nothing happened.

"I can't feel it. I still don't see anything." He looked down at the inventor with a critical eye. "Your father," he said. "What did your mother call him again?"

"Her magic man." Finstern sneered. "You can't feel it? It's in the air. I can feel it from here. It's humming like a generator."

Jackaby slid back down the mound. "No," he said. "I don't feel it. This mound is both a door and a lock, but neither one is meant for me. You, on the other hand . . . Whoever your father was, Mr. Finstern, I do believe the barrier exists to thwart his kith and kin."

Finstern pushed himself to his feet. "You're saying my father was part of your Unseelie Court?"

"I'm sorry," Jackaby said. "He may have been your mother's magic man after all; just not necessarily a good one."

"Good. Bad. Subjective," said Finstern coldly. "He made a bastard of me and left my mother ruined. You don't need to apologize to me for calling him a monster. How do we get inside?"

Jackaby nodded thoughtfully. "I wonder," he said. "Charlie, do you feel anything?"

Charlie stepped forward. "I don't know what I should be feeling, sir."

"Why don't you give it a try? Just there."

Charlie pulled himself up the grassy slope, reaching out in front of him as he climbed. Finstern's eyes narrowed as he watched. "I don't feel anything," Charlie said. "The Om Caini have always been neutral, sir. I'm sorry, but I don't think–" Charlie's outstretched hand suddenly vanished up to the elbow. He pulled it back abruptly. "Mr. Jackaby?"

We climbed up the mound behind him. Charlie reached forward again, and the air rippled like a mirage around his hand, swallowing it up to the wrist.

"There." Jackaby said. "Try to open it."

"Are we sure that's advisable?" asked Charlie.

"Nothing about my line of work is advisable," said Jackaby. "There are questions I need answered, and the people to answer them cannot be reached through standard channels."

"I don't know how," Charlie said. "I have no idea what I'm doing, sir."

"Please, Mr. Barker. Try."

Charlie took a deep breath and closed his eyes. For several seconds nothing happened, and then the hole in midair grew larger. It pulsed, stretching wider inch by inch. A wave of warm air washed over the mound, dancing through the tall grasses. It smelled sweet, like burnt sugar. Charlie's hand was suddenly lit from behind with sparkling sapphire and emerald light, and for a moment I feared we had opened a hole under some great magical lake, but then my eyes adjusted and I realized I was looking into a thick, vibrant wood.

"I really don't think I can–" Charlie opened his eyes and staggered back. Jackaby caught him before he tumbled down the hill. The portal was an archway now, rounded smoothly at the top and as tall as a church door. I stepped around it. From behind it was nothing at all. I saw only the dumbfounded faces of my companions gazing into thin air. I came back around to the front.

Finstern, in spite of the jolt it had given him earlier, was the first to step through the door. "Wait!" Jackaby called after him, but the inventor went on ahead, peering to the left and right.

"Charlie," Jackaby said, "I need you to stay here."

"Not a chance," Charlie replied. "You have no idea what you're walking into."

"What I know is that I'd like to walk out of it again. Do you know what heroes who enter the Annwyn are most known for?"

Charlie shook his head.

"Staying there," said Jackaby. "Whether they wanted to or not. Neither Miss Rook nor I can open this portal, Mr. Barker, and there's no telling if even you will be able to reopen it from the other side after it closes. I need you to maintain the doorway for all of us. You're the only one who can."

Charlie's eyes hunted for any alternative, but they found none. He turned to me, instead. "You know it isn't safe," he said. "You don't have to go."

I leaned forward on my toes and kissed his cheek. "We'll be back before you know it. I promise."

Jackaby stepped through the opening. "One more thing, Mr. Barker," he called back. "Try not to let anything out."

Chapter Twenty-Six

The Annwyn was vivid. I don't mean my experience of it–but the actual colors of the realm. The woods were strangely deep and intense, as though the whole forest had been painted by artists who refused to temper their vibrant hues. I spun around, taking it in. The leaves might as well have been cut from actual emeralds. Purple buds on the nearby bushes were so brilliant they almost seemed to glow, and even the sky above us was less of a robin's egg blue and closer to that of a ripe blueberry, although I could see only a few glimpses of it through the foliage.

The light filtering through the branches danced across my skin in patches of turquoise, flickering suddenly with the flap of wings high above us. All around, the chirps and squawks and constant rustle of wildlife layered into a steady, droning hum. If we had come looking for the land of the dead, it seemed as though we had taken a wrong turn. I had never been anywhere that felt so alive.

Finstern had already wound out of sight, and I hastened to keep up with Jackaby as we hurried after him. The forest was dense with ferns and ivy and all manner of brush, but there was a trail of sorts, where the plant life had been beaten back over time. I read a book once about an explorer in the islands who followed just such a path right into a den of angry wild boars. The only defense at my disposal was my employer's slim, ivory-handled silver knife, which was tucked in the pocket of my skirt, its sheath slapping lightly against my leg as I ran. The weight of it was a faint comfort, although it began to feel more and more like a letter opener and less and less like a real weapon the longer I thought about the sharp tusks and gnashing teeth that might lie ahead.

Here and there massive red stones littered the landscape. Some of them stood twenty feet tall, tilted upright like great crimson monoliths. As we passed by one of these, a glimmer of something white as snow just behind it drew my attention. I looked again, but there was nothing beyond the stone but the darkness of the forest. Another hint of white danced in my peripheral vision, but vanished the moment I turned my head. I shook my head. The forest was playing tricks on my eyes.

Gradually the trees thinned and the ground grew thick

with a tapestry of roots. Braids of living wood wove like heavy ropes in and out in inscrutable almost-patterns, overlapping and widening until each was so thick my fingertips could not have touched had I encircled one with both arms. At the center of it all was the largest living thing I have ever seen.

The roots spun around and around each other, coiling upwards until they melted into one trunk. It was a yew, though no ordinary tree had ever grown so massive. Its bark was a rich, raw umber, and the base of it was wider than a city block. Its branches stretched forever, until they seemed to fade away into the deep blue sky.

"They're like conduits," said Finstern from directly behind us, his Welsh accent colored with unmasked awe. "A battery of living cables. The earth as a single power cell. Genius, really. The principal is so simple. Can you not feel the energy field, Detective?"

Finstern climbed forward, stroking the bulging red-brown roots like a stable master might pet a prize stallion. Jackaby did not respond right away, but I had to admit there was an intangible energy about the place that sent prickling goose pimples up my arms like static electricity.

"There." Jackaby pointed toward the base of the impossible tree. A hundred meters off, nearly enveloped by the roots, two of the mighty red stones we had seen along the way stood like roman columns on either side of a deep knothole in the trunk. "That's where we're headed."

We clambered over the curling, weaving landscape. Jackaby was struggling over a root nearly as tall as he was when I caught sight of a patch of milk-white fur near the edge of the surrounding forest. It vanished again the instant I locked eyes on it, but I was certain I had seen it this time, a solitary shock of pure white in an oversaturated canvas of colors.

It occurred to me that spotting wildlife in a forest was not so peculiar. What was peculiar was not spotting any. The clamorous buzz of animal life had gradually died away as we neared the tree. Aside from that skittish beast, the fauna seemed to have given this tree a wide berth.

I was peering into the shadows in the underbrush and not watching my footing when my next step abruptly landed on nothing at all. I half dropped, half slid almost straight down, landing on my backside in a deep valley in the roots. The gap appeared to be natural, the coils of the yew simply having grown around the space, rather than showing any signs of having been cut or trampled. It formed a clear, straight path of dry earth, leading directly toward the crimson pillars.

Jackaby and Finstern joined me with slightly more finesse, and together we walked the last few yards toward the red pillars at the base of the tree. It was difficult to tell just how deep the knothole between them went. The wood formed a slit about three feet across at its widest and nearly as tall as myself. If it weren't for the red rocks on either side, my eyes might have dismissed the opening entirely as just another dark shadow in the unfathomable mess of intertwining roots.

"Watch your step," said a deep, dry voice.

I froze. Jackaby and Finstern drew up on either side of me. A little trickle of water snaked along the path, disappearing into the shadows at the base of the tree. I squinted.

There, amid the sprawling roots, sat a man. He wore ragged, red-brown robes and was leaning on his elbow; his back was hunched over the little flowing stream. We stepped forward cautiously, careful to skirt the trickle as we neared. The man was gaunt and almost as pale as Pavel. He held a bright green leaf in his slender fingers, lifting it over and across the water. His fingertips never quite reached past the edge of the shadow, but the sun shone bright on the very tip of the leaf. He touched it to the earth for a moment, and then brought it back, lowering it to the ground again on the shady side. He repeated the motion rhythmically.

As we closed the gap, I could finally make out a long line of ants leading up to the rivulet. With each pass, the thin man scooped up one or two ants and helped them over the trickle to the shaded side of the water, where an identical line was already marching steadily into the darkness of the tree.

"Why are you doing that?" Finstern asked.

"Because," said the man, his voice deep and rough, like

the grating of heavy stones, "it gives me purpose." He pushed himself up with great effort and stood. He was bone thin, with eyes shrouded in black shadows that only added to his skeletal countenance.

"Charon, I presume?" Jackaby stepped forward. "It's an honor to meet you."

"Not especially," replied the man. "Everyone does. Eventually."

"Yes, well," Jackaby said. "Expected or not, it's still a once-in-a-lifetime opportunity for most of us, isn't it?"

"The end of it," the man agreed.

"With just a few exceptions, of course. I imagine it's been a long time since anyone chartered a round trip, though. Who was the last mortal you met who hadn't shuffled off the old mortal coil? Herakles, Orpheus, Persephone?"

"Jack."

"Ah. Also good. I expect you've met a few of those, haven't you?"

"There are rules."

"Rules?"

"The four of you seek passage. There are rules."

"Three of us, Mr. Charon, sir," I said, instantly wishing I hadn't spoken. "Sorry–Charlie stayed behind."

"Four," repeated Charon. He looked at Jackaby meaningfully. "The bag."

"What?" Jackaby stumbled for a moment, but then caught on. "Oh!" He retrieved Jenny's brick. "Oh, this? I'm afraid we had a bit of a rough situation earlier. I don't think Miss Cavanaugh will be joining–"

"She is here."

As he said it, the roots around the gap seemed to quiver in the same way the pipes on Jackaby's boiler rumbled when it was bubbling to life on a cold morning. In a blink, Jenny was suddenly standing beside Jackaby. She gasped, looking as surprised as the rest of us.

"Jenny!" I said. "Are you all right?"

"Where on earth . . . ?"

"No," Charon answered her flatly. Finstern gaped and stared at the ghost, peering at her this way and that as a jeweler might a rare diamond. She was still translucent, the faintest outlines of the roots beyond her visible through her silvery features, but she looked more whole than I had ever seen her. Charon's haggard head cocked to one side. "What else is in the bag?"

Jackaby's eyes darted to Finstern and back to the robed figure. "Odds and ends," he hedged. "Some odder than others."

"It is a wrong thing."

"Which is why I'm keeping it out of the *wrong hands*."

Finstern, whose mouth had been open since Jenny's arrival, finally made use of it. "Wait. My machine? You have it?"

Jackaby frowned and sighed. "Yes. And my abode has suffered greatly for its safekeeping."

Finstern eyed the satchel suspiciously. "It can't be. Your bag is much too small."

"You said you studied Welsh folklore. Ever heard of Rhiannon? You see, she had a sack–"

"Gentlemen," I interrupted. "I believe we're getting a bit off topic, don't you? You have very nice toys, both of you, but we are at the gates to the great abyss right now." I turned toward Charon. "Or knobby wooden hole to the great abyss. You were saying something about rules?"

"No second chances," he said. "That is the first rule. You may ask for time, you may ask for favors, you may ask for mercy–but you are given what you are given. Make the most of it. It is all you will get."

"Understood," said Jackaby.

"Nobody enters the gate. This is the second rule."

"You might have opened with that one," Jackaby said. "Why have a gate at all, then?"

"Doesn't everybody enter?" I asked. "Like you said, eventually?"

"No. Every*one* enters. Every *soul*, but no *body*. If you enter, you must leave your flesh behind you."

"Well then," said Jenny. "For once I think I've got a leg up on the rest of you."

"You may enter if you wish, Jennifer Cavanaugh," Charon's voice rumbled. "But if you do, you may never re-turn to the land of the living. You belong below. You are a soul without a shell. Heed the first rule. This is your chance, your reprieve. You will not be given another."

"It's fine," said Jackaby. "You stay topside. I'll bring the answers back to you."

"Only mortals may pass. This is the third rule."

"Yes, that's all right. I am mortal," said Jackaby.

"You are, but a part of you isn't. Within you dwells a force unending. You may pass. You might return. Your gift will not. You cannot take it with you."

"I wouldn't be the Seer anymore," Jackaby said. "I would be technically dead. The sight would move on to its next host." It was hard to read my employer's expression, but some part of him seemed to be legitimately considering the notion. "I would be free."

Charon pointed a long finger at the inventor, who flinched. "For you it would be less pleasant. You too possess a spark of immortality, Owen Finstern, but it is woven through your core. The fair folk cannot enter. Should you attempt to cross over, your soul would be torn in two. I do not know if any shred of you would survive."

"I wasn't volunteering," Finstern replied.

"It's me, then," I said. My stomach fluttered. I had occasionally felt inadequate in the company of my extraordinary friends–like a rough stone among gems. I had always felt boring. Normal. Now it seemed my normalcy was what we needed. "I'll go."

"Abigail," Jenny said.

"No," said Jackaby. "It's too dangerous. I won't allow it."

"You don't have much choice, though, do you?" I said. "It's me or it's nothing. They've killed so many people already–more than we know, Pavel said–and a lot more might be coming. We need to know who's behind all of it. I can find out."

Jenny floated close to me. She reached her hand to my face, and I felt the faintest cool breeze on my cheek. "You've already done so much, Abigail. We can't ask you to do this, too."

"It's good that you don't have to, then. I've been digging my way into the ground my whole life, looking for that profound discovery that no one else has ever seen. Doesn't get much deeper than this. It's my choice. It's my adventure. I can find us the answers we need. I'm going."

"No," said Jackaby.

"No," said Charon.

I turned back to the ferryman. "Wait. No?" I said.

"You may not enter until you have severed your ties. This is the fourth rule. You may carry over no tethers connecting you to the world of the living, neither physical nor metaphysical."

"That's ludicrous," I said. "Of course I have ties to the world of the living. Everyone I know lives in the world of the living."

"You are permitted your emotions, Abigail Rook. You are not permitted a channel."

"A channel?"

"Your pocket."

I drew the silver dagger from my dress. "This isn't a channel. It's just a knife."

"Your other pocket."

"I haven't got anything in my other–" My fingers closed around a cool, round stone etched with simple, concentric circles. I drew it out. "Oh! How curious. I don't even remember bringing this."

Jackaby stepped toward me. "Where did you get that?" he asked.

"Pavel gave it to me when he gave me the sketch of Mr. Finstern. I must have already shown it to you–didn't I?"

"You most certainly did not." He produced a little red pouch out of the inner pocket of his coat and opened it. The lining on the inside glistened like silver, but it was empty. He held it toward me at arm's length. I plopped the stone inside, and he pulled the strings taut quickly, as though he were capturing a live squirrel and not a lifeless rock.

"Why? What is it?" I said.

Jackaby scowled hard.

"It has to have come from the council!" I said. "Charon says it's a channel. A channel to what, exactly? To whom?"

"I don't know," said Jackaby. "But I would very much like to."

I swallowed. "All the more reason to get those answers. Don't worry. I'll find Lawrence Hoole. He was at the heart of the council's project. He'll know more about those villains and what they're building than anyone."

Jackaby tucked the stone–the channel–away into his coat. "Wait."

"Sir, I appreciate your concern, but you can't fight every battle for me."

"No, I can't. But I can give you this." He took my hand and pressed into my palm a little leather purse. It was a dull gray-brown.

"What's this?"

"Four obols. They're ancient Greek currency. A number of cultures have traditions about paying the ferryman. Also, I packed the most appropriate relic I could find on short notice. You'll find a small length of petrified string inside. Sheep's gut, really. It has been passed down for a great many generations under the assumption that it was once a piece of the last lyre Orpheus ever played. I can't verify that, of course, but it does have an aura of divine contact, so it's entirely possible."

"Thank you, Mr. Jackaby."

"One more thing," he said. "The dead don't generally keep things in their pockets. It's traditional to . . ." He gestured to my face.

"To what?"

"You'll need to hold it in your mouth when you cross over."

"Lovely," I said, eyeing the faded leather.

"Do be safe," Jenny said.

"Don't worry. I'll be careful."

I tucked the pouch into my mouth as I stepped forward. It tasted like a salty strap of used boot leather. I tried very hard not to think too hard about the shriveled strip of gut inside it.

"Are you prepared?" Charon asked.

I nodded.

"Then come with me."

I stepped across the little trickle of water, moving out of the warm sunlight and into the cold shadows. Nothing happened for a moment, and then my legs buckled beneath me.

It was suddenly dark. I was falling.

And I was dead.

Chapter Twenty-Seven

I turned around. My body lay behind me in the dirt. It had not landed gracefully. My cheek was pressed against the cold stone floor, loose hair splaying across my eyes. One arm had folded behind me in an unnatural angle as I fell. I felt sick and numb.

"This way," said Charon.

I removed the leather pouch from my mouth as I followed the ferryman down the path, away from my lifeless corpse. My eyes were adjusting to the gloom, but there wasn't much except more gloom to see. The inside of a tree, it turns out, looks a lot like the outside of a tree, only darker. The cavern went much farther, deep into the earth. I could hear water flowing somewhere nearby as I followed Charon downward. The trickling little stream snaked into the cave, dribbling down a series of uneven tiers until it drained at last into a wide underground river. Mist swirled above the dark waters.

We descended the steps until we reached the river's edge, and Charon held out a bony hand. I retrieved two coins from the pouch, offering them up. Charon plucked them out of my hand, rubbing them together with a satisfied tinkling.

"Obols. It has been a long time since I was paid in obols." He sounded pleased, but his bony face showed no emotion. One of the coins glowed ruby red and then abruptly crumbled to ash between his fingers. He held the other up in the light from the opening above us, rubbing its weathered face with his thumb. "Eight chalkoi to the obol, six obols to the drachma, and one obol"–he handed the coin back to me–"to ride the ferry. I do not overcharge."

I took the coin and thanked him as I tucked it back into the leather purse.

He stepped out onto an ancient dock and picked up a long pole from where it rested against decrepit ropes. At the top of the pole hung three small rods from a short chain, like a sort of flail. Charon shook the stick as if he were trying to shoo away a fly. The rods vanished and for a fraction of a second it seemed as though a long, crescent scythe blade had taken their place, but then the pole was just a pole. It was a little wider toward the top, but otherwise just a straight staff hewn of ordinary wood.

He unwound a length of rope from the mooring and pulled firmly until an old wooden ship slowly cut through the veil of mist and came to bump against the dock. It was a long, shallow vessel, lined with weather-bleached cross-beams that stuck out like human ribs within a coal-black chest. It had a thin mast, but the sail, if ever it had flown one, had long since rotted away. The fore and aft of the ship curved upward, and the figurehead was a snarling dragon.

"That's your boat?" I said.

"Is there a problem?"

"No, of course not. It's just not exactly what I expected. In the paintings it's more of a simple gondola. Isn't that a bit large for one person to steer?"

"Vikings," he said. "They are stubborn, but they do make beautiful boats. This one is special. It handles rivers like a fish. You are correct, though. This is more than necessary. I had more souls to carry on my last trip. Please stand back."

He took hold of the ship with both pale hands and heaved upward. It tipped until it looked like it was about to capsize, and then folded impossibly into itself. Heavy timbers slid together like a collapsible jewelry box, each section slotting perfectly into place with a satisfying wooden clatter until it settled back into shape, bobbing gently on the water as a skiff half the size of the original. The boatman stood with his hands behind his back, rocking on his feet ever so slightly. "Yes," he said. "That is better."

"That's incredible!" I said. "How does it work?"

"Magic. Or science, or whatever they're calling it now. The smiths of Nidavellir constructed it. It was a gift from an old king. They used to call him the Father of the Slain. He was very popular. Do you still do Wednesdays up there?"

"Wednesdays?" I said. He had climbed into the fore of the boat, and I slid onto a wooden seat at the aft. The boat smelled of salt and firewood. "Erm. Yes, we still do Wednesdays."

Charon nodded. "That one's his. There is a channel in these roots that leads to his hall." Charon plunged his pole into the water and pushed off, punting the boat into the mist. "His men used to make a sport of skipping past me. There were days when this river was thick with their longships. They brought their own boats with them when they died."

"That all sounds like the Vikings," I said.

"That's right."

"I thought you were Greek."

"I don't bother much with politics. I am the ferryman."

"But you're real," I said. "And this place is real."

"Yes."

"So who had it right, then?"

"I do not understand the question."

"The afterlife. There are lots of different versions, and they can't all be true. Heaven, Hell, the Happy Hunting Ground–which is it? You're here, so does that mean there's a Hades with an Elysium and a Tartarus and everything?"

"Why would there not be?"

"Well, because a moment ago you were talking about Valhalla."

Charon pressed forward. The mist split around the masthead, curling into eddies that spun ghostly pirouettes over the surface of the river, the whole dance reflected below in the wine dark waters. "Do you know the fable of the blind men and the elephant?"

"I'm afraid I haven't heard that one," I said.

"A woman from the Hunan Province told it to me," said Charon. "Once upon a time a stranger came to a remote village with an elephant. Everyone got excited, including three blind men who didn't know what an elephant was. They decided to find out for themselves.

"The first man approached the elephant near its head. He reached his hand out and felt the leathery ear. The second man approached from behind and brushed the elephant's bristly tail. The third came at it from the side and stroked its wide midsection.

"'What a strange creature an elephant is,' the first man said. 'So flat and thin, like wash hung from the line.'

"'What are you talking about?' said the second man. 'That animal was hairy and coarse, like the bristles on a stiff broom.'

"'You are both wrong!' said the third. 'The beast was as broad and sturdy as a wall.' They three men argued and argued, but they never could come to an agreement."

Charon let the river drift past for another moment. "So," he said finally. "Who had it right?"

"They all did," I said. "Just not the whole of it."

"Good answer."

Charon guided the boat along, and I began to see things moving in the mist, shapes shifting along the shoreline, though I could not make out what I was seeing at first. We drew nearer, and I gasped. The silhouette of an enormous beast with a long snout lumbered along the bank across from us.

"Is that," I whispered, "a hellhound?"

"That is Ammit."

"Ammit?"

Charon gestured casually with his long pole, and the mist obligingly parted. The figure on the riverbank was not a dog at all—although it appeared to be trying to be every other animal all at once. It had the head of a crocodile, the mane and forefeet of a lion, and the heavy back legs of a hippopotamus. Its eyes shot up, red and piercing as we passed, but soon the mist closed back in and we moved beyond it.

I opened my mouth, but found no words with which to fill it.

"She is not what you were expecting?"

"She?" I said. "No, she's not what I was expecting. I guess I imagined little red imps or maybe choirs of moony angels with white robes and harps." I glanced back over my shoulder into the haze. "Ammit is a little different."

"They are here, also." Charon pressed onward at a slow crawl. Within the spinning mist I began to see all manner of shapes and faces, and it was difficult to determine if I was only imagining things in the billowing clouds or catching a real glimpse of what lay beyond them. "The imps are not my favorite, but we can take that route if you prefer."

"No, no. That's quite all right." I considered. "Is it hard to find your way?"

"I never lose my way."

"Do you think I'll be able to find mine?"

"I do not know."

"I'm looking for a man called Lawrence Hoole. Do you know how I might find him?"

"The river does not generally take you where you want to go," said Charon. "But it will always take you where you need to be."

"That's moderately reassuring," I said.

"There will be trials." Charon's tone betrayed neither sympathy nor malice. "There are always trials."

"I rather suspected." I took a deep breath. "What sort of trials?"

"I do not know what you will face. There are many. Ishtar once sacrificed articles of clothing at each gate until she stood naked before all the monsters of the underworld."

"That sounds like the sort of trial a naughty schoolboy would write."

Charon shrugged. "Ra had to slay a great serpent; Persephone had to abstain from eating. Some have crossed through fire, and others have simply found their names in a book. It is different for everyone. Death is a personal journey."

The boat suddenly rocked and lurched to a stop as if it had run aground. The mist roiled and condensed before us until it formed two pillars of solid ivory. Between them sprang coils of smoke that trickled upward toward the foggy darkness of the cavern ceiling. Somewhere in the distance a low note sounded, and the smoke trails snapped into tight, rigid bars. We bumped, bow to bars, against an ethereal gate.

"Ah," said Charon. "Here you are."

"What should I do?" I asked.

"–" said Charon.

"What?" I said, or tried to say. My lips formed the word, but no sound escaped.

The ferryman's mouth opened and closed, but I could hear nothing. Even the rush and drip of water all around me had stopped. I clutched at my ears frantically.

"Strain your ears to be sure I'm here," said a soft voice from beyond the gate. It was a woman's voice, low and quiet as a whisper, but still crystal clear in the absence of any other sound. "But say my name and I disappear."

I lowered my hands slowly. It was a riddle. I could do

riddles. If it were a choice between wordplay and swordplay in the depths of the underground, I would take words any day. "Strain your ears to be sure I'm here. Say my name and I disappear." I mouthed the clue as I thought. It sounded simple enough, although it was still unnerving to be enveloped by such absolute . . .

"Silence." I said the word out loud, and with it came rushing back all of the other sounds of the underground cave. The gate was mist again in an instant, and the boat shuddered forward.

Charon bowed his head in approval and returned to propelling the slender ship forward.

"Was that it?" I said. "Am I done?"

A voice came from my left. "I sure hope not, Abby darling."

I nearly fell out of the boat. Goose pimples rippled down my arms. Nellie Fuller stood beside us in the curling mist. She wore the same neatly tailored dress that had complemented her full figure when she was alive, her dark curls tucked up under a stylish black hat. She had been an ace reporter for the *New Fiddleham Chronicle*. She had been an indomitable force to be reckoned with. She had been my friend.

"It's real nice to see you, kid." She smiled. "But what's a hot-blooded girl like you doing down here?"

"Nellie!" I wanted to weep. "Oh my word! I'm so sorry!"

"Sorry?"

"For what happened–the valley–the dragon. It should never have been you."

She waved me away and rolled her eyes. "I don't need anybody apologizing for my choices. I'd been all around the world–it was time for a new adventure, anyway. There are some amazing souls down here. I met a woman named Anne Bonny on my first night. She was a real-life pirate, told me all about it! When they caught her, she snuck out of jail and went straight. Nobody ever found her again, but guess what? She died decades later, peacefully, lying in her bed, a mild-mannered great-grandmother! I met a boy named Elpenor, too. He survived the Trojan War–sailed with Odysseus himself! The actual Odysseus! I didn't even think any of that classic hero stuff really happened! Do you know how Elpenor died?"

"By the sword?" I guessed.

"He got drunk and fell off of a roof." She laughed. "I got to tell the both of them that *my* last dance was toe to toe with an honest-to-goodness dragon! We all have to go sometime, Abby. I'm happy I went out on a high note. I've got no regrets." She gave me a wink and I smiled. Death had not dulled her spirit in the least. "I didn't plan on having you follow me down so soon, though," she said. "What are you doing here?"

"I haven't died," I told her. "Dark forces are operating in New Fiddleham. People have been murdered, and Jackaby thinks that worse is on the way. I'm looking for answers."

"Oh, Abby!" Nellie held a hand to her chest. She looked like she was watching her child's first steps. "You followed a lead into the great beyond? God, you are like a young me. I'm so proud of you, sweetie. This place is great for answers. I tracked down the Borden parents right off. It turns out little Lizzie didn't do it, after all. They're a very nice couple, by the way. I hope their girl gets acquitted. She's been through quite enough. So, who are you looking for?"

"I need to find a professor, a man named Hoole. I don't suppose . . . ?"

"Sorry." She shook her head. "Never heard of him. There's a lot of underground to cover down here in the ever after. Good luck, though."

"Thank you, Nellie," I said. "We miss you, you know."

"Don't!" she chirped. "Just make it down here on your own terms eventually, and be sure you've built up a few amazing stories to tell me in the meantime."

The mist crept around her again, and Nellie began to slide slowly backward.

"Oh, one more word of advice." Her voice cut through the fog. "You want to catch the bastards? Use your peripheral vision. The real powers at play never take center stage. Don't follow the marionette, follow the strings."

"But I can't see who's pulling the strings! That's why I'm down here. Nellie? Nellie?" The mist folded behind us as the slim longship drifted onward.

Nellie Fuller was well behind us when the boat ground

to a halt again. This time it was not the white mist that coalesced into a barrier, but the dark shadows. As the gloom took solid shape, two obsidian pillars appeared to our left and right, followed by long strings of black, which dripped down from the roof of the cavern, stretching to the surface of the slow river like molasses from a spoon. The drips thickened, forming ink black bars. A deep chime sounded and the whole thing snapped into shape, just as the first gate had done.

"Here we go ag–" said Charon, and once more I was in a cushion of total silence.

The voice that issued from beyond the dark bars was small and meek, like a child's. "The more and more you have of me, you'll find the less that you can see."

I thought for a moment. "That's easy," I said. "It's darkness."

The gate lost solidity and the boat eased forward again as the sounds echoing through the caverns returned. The darkness of the gate did not dissipate entirely, but spread and hung in the air like a curtain. Charon's boat slipped through it like we were passing through a coal-black waterfall, and when we reached the far side the entire cave was as black as pitch.

I turned around, but the tunnel behind us was equally dark. "Charon?"

"I am here."

"I can't see a thing. Did I give the wrong answer?"

"I do not think so. You are doing very well."

Ahead of us a pinprick of warm light appeared. It grew by slow degrees as Charon pressed the vessel steadily forward. Soon I realized it was a lantern, and clutching it was the silhouette of a girl.

"Hello?" I called.

"Who are you?" she said, suspiciously. She had an American accent.

"It's all right. My name is Abigail," I said. "Abigail Rook. What's your name, young lady?" We drifted closer, and the girl's face came into view. She could not have been more than ten; she was blonde with a heart-shaped face and wide, wary eyes. The little spirit, I realized, looked like she had stepped straight out of the tintype in Jackaby's dossier. If I had had blood in my veins, it might have frozen. "Eleanor?"

"How do you know me?" she said. "Why are you here?"

The boat came to stop beside the girl, or else she was drifting along evenly with us now; I could see neither land nor water in the faint glow of the lantern. "We have a mutual friend," I said. "He speaks very fondly of you. And very sadly. You meant a lot to him."

Her brow crinkled. "I don't have a lot of friends."

"Neither does he, but he gets attached to the ones he has. Mr. Jackaby has the sight now. He's made a life of using it to help people, especially people who are different. People who are misunderstood."

Eleanor's expression faltered. A curious brightness flickered in her eyes, and then she giggled. "Mr. Jackaby? With a *mister* and everything?" Her smile was timid and earnest.

"That's right. He's grown into a very special man since you–since you knew him. He's a good man."

"Jackaby," said Eleanor. "He kept it."

"Kept it? You mean the sight?"

"I mean the nickname. He never let me call him Jackaby when the other boys were around. It was all right when we were alone in the library, but he was so embarrassed when we were out in public. My Jackaby."

"You mean Jackaby isn't even his real name?" I said. I had often wondered what the R. F. stood for, but I had assumed I knew at least his surname. "Oh, for heaven's sake, of course it isn't. Pavel was right. Mr. Jackaby does have a thing about names."

Eleanor laughed and caught her breath. The orange lamplight danced in her wide, wet eyes. "Names have power," she whispered, nodding. "And he kept the one I gave him. My dear, sweet Jackaby."

The lantern in her hands began to dim. Eleanor's head shot up, her expression suddenly intense. Her hand reached toward me, fingers shaking with urgency. "Oh no. If he has the sight, then they're coming for him, just like they came for me. They want it. They need it. Don't let them take it. It's important. You have to keep him safe!"

"Who's coming for him?" I said. The light was flickering

now, the cavern blinking into blackness and back with each sputter. Eleanor was beginning to drift away from the boat and back into the shadows.

"I never let them have it." Her voice was panicked. "I never let them. I couldn't. It's too important."

"Never let who have it? The council? Who is coming?"

"I could feel his eyes on me all the time, red as fire, waiting at the end."

"Where? The end of what?"

"At the end," she said, "of the long, dark hallway." And then the lantern died away and the cavern was pitch-black again. In the darkness I could hear the faintest echo of a whisper. "My poor, sweet Jackaby."

The sound of Charon's pole splashing softly in the water and the echoes of drips were all that punctuated the silence for several minutes. My chest felt tight.

"One more, I should think," Charon said at last.

"One more?"

"Yes," he said. "Three feels right. I've been doing this for some time. You begin to notice the patterns."

In another moment the boat shuddered beneath us. I still couldn't see anything, but I could tell that we had stopped. If there was a gate before us, I could not describe it. Everything was inky black.

"Here we are," Charon said.

A ringing note cut through the darkness, and then all

sound ceased. The voice that followed was a man's this time, clear and deep.

"My constant hunger must be fed, but if I drink, then I'll be dead."

Hunger and feeding and death—the notions felt uncomfortably close to home. A vampire? Vampires had to feed, but drinking wasn't what killed them. I tried to think, but my mind kept flashing back to little Eleanor and Nellie Fuller. What creature ate constantly, but could not drink?

"Fire!" I said at last. The word had barely left my lips when I was pressed back in the ship by a wave of hot air and a blinding light. Twin columns of flame bloomed to either side of us, and the surface of the river flickered with blue heat. We were coasting forward again down a channel of burning black waters, and this time we were approaching a dock.

"We have arrived." Charon nudged the ship forward until it bumped to a stop against the landing. The flames licked the sides of the old pier, but the ancient wood did not burn. "You did well, Abigail Rook."

Chapter Twenty-Eight

Charon stepped onto the dock and held out a hand. I accepted it and climbed after him. His fingers were calloused and rough, but his grasp was gentle and his arm steady. With one foot still in the boat and the other just stepping ashore, I felt a sudden chilling pressure wrap itself around my ankle. Without warning, the underworld spun and I began to slip backward.

Something from beneath the surface of the burning waters was pulling me down. My foot slid into a widening gap between the dock and the boat. Too startled even to cry out, I clutched desperately onto Charon's arm. To my unspeakable relief, his grip held fast. I hung in the air for a sickening moment, suspended between the ferryman above and the *something* below.

I craned my neck frantically to see shapes in the rippling blue flames beneath me. Tendrils of blue and black swam along the surface of the burning water, shadowy coils of smoke and flame, writhing and twisting and reaching out hungrily. They were eerily beautiful as they spun and beckoned. Their motion was hypnotic. The boat, the dock, the cavern walls around me all faded away as I stared, faded away until there was nothing but the tendrils and the infinite darkness beyond.

Charon pulled firmly, and I found myself suddenly lying facedown on the weathered old dock.

"I would advise against straying from your path," Charon said as calmly as if I had just stubbed my toe on the mooring. "There are things below that you might not care to encounter."

I pushed myself up and made for solid ground with alacrity. "What was that?" I asked breathlessly when the dock was behind me.

"I do not know."

"You don't–but you're the boatman!" I said. "You've been ferrying souls for hundreds of years."

"Thousands," said Charon.

"Then how do you not know?"

"In the same way, I suppose, that you can observe a rainbow without knowing its cause. Some things simply are."

"Refraction!" I said. "Rainbows are caused by light bending and splitting. It's called refraction–and we know because usually when people observe a curious phenomenon they want to learn more."

"Refraction." Charon tested the word out on his tongue. "Is that how it works?" he said. "I think perhaps someone should tell the Vikings."

"Thousands of years of traveling across a body of water that occasionally catches fire and tries to eat your passengers, and you never even learned what to call it?"

"You are in the underworld now," said Charon. "The natives here are as numberless as nightmares and equally unfathomable. To plumb the depths of such a place in an effort to understand it would be the paradigm of futility, Abigail Rook, and almost certainly the path to madness."

"You learned Ammit's name," I said.

"So I did," conceded Charon. "I will inquire about the fire at my earliest convenience. In the meantime, you should follow your path." He turned and walked back to the pier, leaving me to my quest. A stairway had been cut into the cave wall just ahead. It wound upward. Light poured down the steps from somewhere up above. I inched forward.

"Is that where I'll find Professor Hoole?" I called back to Charon.

He had already returned to the boat. He took up the long pole and pushed away from the pier. "That is where you are meant to be."

"Wait, you're going? How will I get back?"

"I will return when I am needed. Good-bye, Abigail Rook."

The ship drifted away down the river of living flames, wavering like a mirage until Charon had vanished into the distance. What had I gotten myself into? I had no idea what I was doing! I was completely alone, standing at the foot of a mysterious staircase in an underworld that had tried to kill me not five minutes earlier.

I took a deep breath. "Nowhere to go but up."

As I climbed the winding stone steps, I tried to imagine what I would say when I reached Lawrence Hoole. "Hello. We've never met, but some policemen I know fished your body out of a bunch of sewer muck and I'd very much like to know who put you there." Not exactly the sort of conversation they teach in finishing school.

Bleaker thoughts crept in and I began to worry that I might not find my way to the professor at all—or worse, that I might not find my way back again. The stairway seemed to tighten with each step as I ascended until I was sure it would seal me in before I ever reached the light. And what if it did? What if it locked me into place deep beneath the ground, my body above and my soul below? What would Jackaby and Jenny think if I never reemerged? What would Charlie? What would my parents? I closed my eyes. And what would become of them all if I failed? I took a deep breath and pressed onward.

The stairwell fell away behind me at last and I blinked into the light.

Had I breath in my body the sight before me would

have taken it. There was no ceiling at all in that space atop the stairs. The mantle of the sky bore not so much as a wispy cloud or field of blue, it simply went on forever into the cosmos. I could see whole worlds high above me, not mere pinpricks of light, but vast spinning globes in the heavens, some with pockmarked surfaces and others encircled by swirling gaseous clouds. There were shapes moving through the air all around me as well, intricately woven braids of matter and light coiling betwixt one another. They spun and pulsed, changing all the time. Where they touched, the threads twisted and rearranged themselves in an elegant dance.

What I took at first to be tremendous mountains in the distance whirred and clicked. They were not earthen mounds at all, but enormous brass cogs, spinning and glistening when they caught the light of the naked sun. The breathtaking view put every exhibit of science and industry I had ever seen to shame. The principles of chemistry, astronomy, and mechanics had been made manifest—magnified and heightened and woven together into the tapestry of an impossible living universe.

The ground was marked by long, sloping ridges that defined an enormous spiral, like the curves of a giant sidelong snail shell. The humps narrowed toward the center as they wrapped around and around one another in tighter and tighter curls. Movement caught my eye toward the center of the spiral and I stepped forward. My feet failed to meet the ground. I would have tripped and fallen had there been forces pulling me downward. Instead I found myself floating, weightless.

I blinked.

Back on earth, Jenny's feet never touched the ground either, I reminded myself. I had no body. I was technically dead now, and ghosts didn't need corporeal luxuries like gravity. I willed myself forward and found it fairly easy to direct my spirit into a smooth glide.

In the center of the spiral was a man. His back was turned to me as he hovered six feet in the air, fixated on his work. His shoulders heaved and his arms swung rhythmically, like a maestro conducting a symphony. In front of him, patterns emerged as three-dimensional waveforms, intertwining and overlapping–at once invisible and somehow brilliantly lustrous. It was like watching a billowing sheet of liquid diamond take shape. All the clever prototypes and models in the Hooles' house were to this place what Michelangelo's childhood scribblings were to the Sistine Chapel. The inventor's hands could finally keep up with his imagination, and the results were staggering.

"Professor?" I said, approaching. "You don't know me, but I–"

The soul turned. I froze.

He was not Lawrence Hoole.

Chapter Twenty-Nine

"You're . . . you're Howard Carson," I managed at last, when my words finally dislodged themselves from my throat.

"That's right," the spirit said. He wore a simple white shirt and gray trousers, his shirtsleeves rolled up. When I had seen him through Jenny's eyes I had felt drawn to him, Jenny's emotions flavoring my perception. Now that I saw him plainly I felt none of the same attraction.

"You don't know me," I started again. "My name is Abigail Rook. I'm from the world of the living."

"We're all expatriates here, aren't we, Miss Rook?" He smiled affably. It might have been a charming smile had I been in the mood to be charmed. Instead his demeanor only made me angry. I didn't want him to be pleasant and happy and playing with enormous magical science experiments in his own personal heaven. I wanted him to be devastated, racked with guilt at having conspired with villains and left Jenny for the slaughter.

"No," I said tersely. "I mean that I still belong there. I'll be going back. I'm only here to get some answers first."

His smile faltered. "You're serious?" He descended slowly toward the earth and looked me in the face. His feet touched down at the center point of the grand spiral. "You are serious. You've come a long way. What could you want to know that I might possibly be able to tell you?"

"I want to know who you were working for before you died, Mr. Carson. I want to know what you were building for them and how it worked. I want to know . . ." My throat tightened, but I gritted my teeth and took a deep breath, pushing through it. "I want to know who the woman was, and I want to know why you did it."

Howard Carson's expression darkened. "Who are *you* working for?" He stepped around me slowly. "You wouldn't have come this far just for a story. You couldn't have come this far alone." I could see the wheels turning behind his eyes. "They've rebuilt it, haven't they?"

I spun as he circled me. "Rebuilt what?" I demanded. "Tell me!"

The prismatic waves Carson had been creating still hung in the air, but now they began to spin more quickly, their smooth curves peaking in erratic spikes. "We were building the machine that would change the world, weren't we?" he said coldly. "I never met my employers, but you can tell them from me when you get back up there that I don't regret what I did one bit." My blood was pumping in my ears. I wanted to slap him. "And as for the woman–she was definitely worth it."

"Was she?" I said. "Was she worth dying for? Worth killing for?"

"Yes!" he said. "She was. Anyway, they got what they deserved." The stars above darkened, and the braids of crystalline light floating all around us began to crack and crumble as they collided, leaving sprays of sharp, brittle shards to glide weightlessly through the skies like flocks of wicked birds. "We all got what we deserved."

"Did Jenny?" My ire was nearly boiling.

The earth shook as the cogs in the distance suddenly ground to a halt. Carson breathed in and out slowly, his eyes downcast.

"What do you know about Jenny?"

"Jenny is a dear friend, Mr. Carson. So tell me, do you really think she got what she deserved?"

"Jenny." His head came up. His voice had lost its edge, and he looked as though he had been punched in the gut. "You'll have to tell me," he said. "Is she . . . is she happy?"

"Happy?" His concern seemed so earnest. I faltered. "You don't know what happened to her, do you?"

"How could I know?" he said. "I did what I could to

protect her, but in the end all I could do was hope the bastards would not come after my Jenny, too. I've taken comfort in the fact that she has not joined me yet, but there is not a day that passes that I don't worry that the mistakes of my past will be the ruin of her future."

I tried to make sense of what Carson was saying. "Then . . . there was no other woman?"

"What? Never."

"I'm sorry, Mr. Carson. I think you'll have to start from the beginning."

Carson nodded. The world around us melted away. The planets above faded to black. We hovered in empty space. "They are called the Dire Council," said Carson.

As he spoke, a familiar structure rose up around us. Tall walls stretched up on all sides, and soon we were inside the cavernous Buhmann building.

"How are you doing this?" I asked.

"Practice," said Carson dolefully. "I have relived each moment of it in my own mind often enough. It is no great undertaking to recreate the details for you now."

I gazed around me. This time the building was not empty but was filled with complex machinery and busy with workers moving to and fro. A familiar fat man with a curly mustache walked the floor like a foreman, his secretary scurrying after him with her clipboard. It felt like being inside Jenny's memories, but this time my head did not ache.

"The Dire Council," Carson repeated. "Mayor Poplin simply called them his benefactors, and for many months I knew them as nothing else, but I do pay attention. At first the work was glorious. I was encouraged to pursue the projects that inspired me. I was given raw materials and seemingly limitless funding. Gradually, though, directives came down with increasing specificity."

The Buhmann building fell beneath us, and we were suddenly floating over New Fiddleham. We coasted until we reached a stretch of paving stones I knew very well indeed–but 926 Augur Lane looked different. The garden was symmetrical and dotted with common rhododendrons instead of the more exotic fare I had become accustomed to. The structure of the building was simpler, as well. It was not the house of the mad detective I had come to know, riddled with irregularities and architectural augmentations–it was simply a house.

"Jenny's instincts were keener than mine," Carson said as we neared. "She wasn't comfortable with any of it. She wanted me to leave the project. I agreed with her, although later than I should have. We were going to be married in the spring, and I was fretting about saving enough money to support us. Jenny only fretted about saving me from myself. I went to Mayor Poplin and told him I was done. I thanked him for the opportunity and I left, just like that. But when I came to meet Jenny again the next day, she was acting strangely."

We drifted over New Fiddleham, and I spotted them in the street below. Jenny Cavanaugh was skipping down the cobbles ahead of Carson. He was stumbling to catch up, calling after her, imploring her to wait, but she kept constantly ahead of him so that as he turned each corner she was always just dashing around the next.

"It wasn't really her," I said.

"No. It wasn't," Carson confirmed. "I should have known. I did know. Something inside me was screaming, but it was Jenny's face–it was Jenny's voice."

Augur Lane whipped away, and we soared over the rooftops again until we came to a massive red brick building with a tall domed tower. It was incomplete, still encased in scaffolding, but once finished it would be easily one of the tallest buildings in the city. It sat on a hillside not far from Mayor Spade's neighborhood. Six or seven workers were struggling to move an elaborately constructed piece of machinery through a broad front doorway. I recognized the apparatus as one of the contraptions Carson and his associates had been assembling back in the Buhmann building in the Inkling District.

"I don't know that building," I said. "I've been all over New Fiddleham, and I've never seen it. Is it an observatory?"

"Mayor Poplin told us it was to be New Fiddleham's grand new Technology Center," Carson replied, "and I believed him. Maybe he believed it himself, I don't know. The Dire Council had other ideas."

We floated down until we were inside the building, where a colossal mechanical construct was taking shape. Owen Finstern's portable device was like a weed to an oak tree compared to that wonder of steel and copper and glass. Wheels spun and boilers hissed. Now and then a spray of sparks would burst from within the belly of the metal beast and workers would scramble to correct the problem.

"I followed her right into the heart of this place before she abandoned the ruse," said Carson.

Beneath us, the woman's hair rippled and lightened to a strawberry blonde. She spun around and Jenny's face was gone. I had never met the stranger, but something about her was eerily familiar. She had a hard chin and bright green eyes–the left ever so slightly higher than the right. The asymmetry struck a chord in my memory. She slipped out with a cruel laugh and slammed the door behind her.

"I tried to run, but it was too late," continued Carson. "The council's liaison was there, waiting. He was a despicable cretin, pale as death with a nasty temper."

"Pavel," I said as the pale man stepped out of the shadows.

"You've met?" said Carson.

"I may have planted a brick in his face earlier."

"I can see why Jenny likes you," Carson said. "Pavel told me that if I finished my task, no harm would come to Jenny."

"He was lying."

"Of course he was lying," said Carson. "And even greater

harm would come to a lot of people if I gave them what they wanted. I had never seen all the parts assembled–I hadn't dreamed that they were ever meant to be. I thought that all of us were working on separate projects. Andrews was developing a power generator with a capacity ten times the ones they were installing up in Crowley. Shea and Grawrock were turning the most far-fetched theories about energy field manipulation into realities, and Diaz had stumbled on a breakthrough in a wavelength transmission amplification that was going to make the most advanced studies in radio waves look like tin cans and bits of twine."

"And you?" I asked.

We floated down through the ceiling into a jumbled workroom. "The human mind," Carson's spirit answered. "Our full and limitless potential." The Carson from the past was beneath us, working frantically as the windows behind him bled from deep orange to a rich crimson in the light of the setting sun. He set down a file and blew metal shavings from a piece of meticulously machined steel, peering at it intently in the warm light.

"You didn't think it was perhaps a tad dangerous to go tinkering with the human mind using metal files and rolls of copper wire and all that?"

"I know it sounds mad. I guess it was–but it was meant to do great things. My final thesis at university had been designed to quell the surging fashion of mysticism and the occult, but I encountered the strangest results in my studies.

Even those purveyors who openly admitted to dealing in smoke and mirrors seemed to be doing more good than ill. Thaumaturgy and hokum saw recovery times plummet and chronic illnesses recede. Against all reason, I saw faith trump medical logic time and time again.

"That's where my real studies began. I pored over Haygarth's essays on the placebo effect and exchanged correspondences with Richard Caton in Liverpool about cerebral activity. It's all electricity, you see. The brain is essentially an electrical machine, regulating the rest of the body. Mind over matter. The human brain has the power to do amazing things–even surpass the furthest limits of the flesh–and it does so through electrical impulses. Given adequate stimulation, there are very few boundaries we can't push past. Empower the mind, empower the body."

"Please tell me you didn't electrocute people's brains to make them healthier."

"No, no, it was a field of influence, not a direct current. Electrical impulses can be amplified or dampened through the precise manipulation of concurrent energies. It was an exciting project. The early results were mixed, though. Some subjects responded astonishingly well to the treatment–increased strength, speed, stamina, even heightened motor skills and capacity for problem solving. A few showed adverse results, though–lethargy, and a sort of hypnotic state that left patients highly susceptible to suggestion."

"I can think of a few things a sinister organization could

do with a super-scientific machine that can brainwash targets with the push of a button," I said.

"Jenny had precisely the same concerns, but neither one of us had any sense of the scope. They were putting all of it together–all of our designs were culminating into one machine. They weren't housing an observatory; they were building a transmitter, one that overlooked a bustling metropolis. I began to understand it when I could finally see the thing up close. The power, the control, the range–it was a weapon unlike the world had ever seen. Or it was going to be."

"What did you do?"

"I did what they had brought me to do. I worked on my part of the machine. Pavel was my watchdog, but it was a wonder that simpleton could even work the buttons on his coat–he had no idea what I was creating. He watched me build it. He even helped. He had the chemicals I asked for delivered by the barrelful. By the time I had finished, it was too late to undo what I had done."

"The explosion! You're the one who sabotaged Poplin's project! That was you!"

We were hovering outside the building again now. The neighborhood was coated in velvet darkness until the bomb went off with the light of a miniature sun right in the heart of the city. Cogs and pipes and bricks rocketed past, and when the light died down enough to see anything, the building had been reduced to rubble and fused scraps of metal. A broad sheet of steel halfway down the hillside shifted, and out from underneath it crawled Howard Carson.

"You survived!" I said.

"Nearly–but we wouldn't be having this conversation if I had, now would we?" said Carson's ghost. Below us, a second figure whipped in front of Howard Carson with inhuman speed. Pavel's hair looked even thinner from above. He was short, and his clothes were old and frayed, but that made him no less intimidating as he rounded on the battered scientist.

Pavel was enraged. He gripped Carson's shirtfront and held the man's feet off the ground as he roared a stream of curses at him. Carson attempted to land a punch across the pale man's face, but Pavel batted his fist away like it was a pesky fly. Carson groaned. His hand hung at an unnatural angle from the wrist. Pavel snarled. Two sharp fangs glistened in the moonlight, and in another second they were buried in Carson's throat.

Beside me, Carson's ghost chuckled.

"You just *died*!" I said. "What about that is funny?"

"My last invention," the spirit replied. "It was crude, but effective." He nodded down at the scene and I saw Pavel reel backward. The vampire howled in pain and surprise, clutching at his mouth. When his hand dropped I saw that he was missing a tooth.

The Carson standing beneath us grinned at the small

victory. It was a tired, defiant smile, as though he knew it would be his last. Just beneath his collar glinted a glimmer of bronze. In another instant the pale man was upon him again. He ripped a concealed metal guard off of Carson's neck and hurled it down the hill with a clatter. His fingers buried themselves in the man's jugular and the scene went suddenly black.

Howard Carson's ghost hung in the empty void beside me. "And here we are," he said.

"That was very noble of you."

Carson shrugged. "I was a dead man anyway. I couldn't leave my Jenny with that awful machine hanging over her. The Dire Council had made me their puppet, but I would be damned if they were going to use my life's work to make puppets out of everyone I ever loved. It's best he finished me off, really. If I had managed to escape they would have come for me. They would have come through Jenny to get me. This is better. I hope she's living a happy life without me."

I cringed. "She hasn't been entirely unhappy," I hedged.

"What is it?"

"I'm so sorry, Mr. Carson," I said. "You did the right thing, but Jenny was already–" I swallowed. "They had already come for Jenny, long before you demolished the building."

Carson's expression hardened. "No. She isn't dead. I would have felt her cross over. I've searched!"

"She didn't cross over," I said. "She waited for you. She's up above. She's outside the gate right now."

Carson's eyed scrutinized my face as though searching for a lie.

"It's true," I said. "Come with me! Come and see for yourself. And I have more than enough obols left to pay the boatman to ferry us both."

"I couldn't."

"You could, Mr. Carson, and you should. You did the right thing all those years ago–but it isn't over yet. Help us stop the Dire Council from using your research. Help us lay your past mistakes to rest once and for all. Besides," I added, "you've left Jenny waiting long enough, don't you think?"

Hope crept into Howard Carson's eyes tentatively, feeling out the unfamiliar territory like a flame exploring the contours of a still-green branch. When it took hold at last it burned hot. "Take me with you."

Chapter Thirty

We descended the stairs toward the fiery azure light of the river. I felt gravity returning with each step until my feet once again found solid purchase on the rocky stairs. It was as though my soul knew that it belonged in those dark tunnels in a way that it had not belonged in Carson's private corner of the hereafter. As we approached the dock, I could see the ferryman's slender ship already approaching. I pulled out Jackaby's leather purse and passed it over to Carson.

"Here, take one of these," I said. "You'll need it for the trip." Carson peeked inside and pulled out the petrified string of sheepgut. "Why will I need this?"

I grabbed the strip and stuffed it in my pocket. "Not that–a coin. Take one of the coins to pay your passage."

Carson nodded and took out an obol. His eyes were on the water as he passed the pouch back to me.

Charon was pressing toward us with measured strokes. He was nearly at the platform before I realized the boatman was not alone. A tall figure stood in the boat behind him. The stranger wore a crimson shirt framed by a pristinely tailored suit in a shade of midnight black so pure that I could barely tell where his jacket ended and the darkness of the cavern began. Trying to make out any details made my eyes hurt.

I was so preoccupied watching their approach that at first I did not notice Howard Carson nearing the water's edge ahead of me. Tendrils of blue and black writhed within the flames at his feet, churning and swelling as he stepped up to the shoreline.

"Wait! Mr. Carson, don't–" I called out, but I was too late. He was leaning over, inspecting the ethereal flames, when an eager coil unfurled itself like a whip and snapped around his neck. Carson was hauled face-first into the Stygian waters.

I threw myself forward and seized his legs, pulling back with all my strength. The surface boiled spitefully in response to my efforts. Inches from my skin, the tendrils of liquid flame danced and taunted. I braced my feet against the dusty shore, but Carson only slid down farther. In the dark water below, the undulating forms took shape. Countless scores of marble gray hands–hands with too many fingers–all strained and grasped at him, clutching at his shirt and tugging him down by his hair. I pulled and kicked at the earth, but with all my strength I could not draw him back. I had taken Howard Carson from his eternal reward and delivered him to this.

And then things got worse.

As I struggled in vain, the leather purse shook and shifted in my grip. I was just adjusting my hands for another effort when the coins slipped out. My arms were full of Carson, and I could do nothing but watch dismally as the little obols spun end over end through the air to sink–plop, plop–into the dark water. At the same moment, Carson slid several inches farther down and a chilling cold clutched my wrist.

It had me. I realized with sickening clarity that the waters would claim us next. Plop, plop–just like the coins, we would fall into the darkness, never to be seen again.

Charon's boat clunked against the old boards a little ways away. Out of the corner of my eye I half registered that the dark stranger had stepped smoothly ashore. I heard footsteps tapping on wood, and then crunching across the dusty ground. The man's shoes reflected the roiling sapphire firelight in the shine of their polished leather as he drew up beside me.

"That's enough," he said calmly. His voice was fathoms deep and profoundly resonant. I felt it vibrating in my chest almost as much as I heard it. Instantly, the forces beneath the surface released their hold and I fell over backward.

Carson burst, gasping and sputtering, out of the water in front of me.

I looked up. The stranger was tall. Impossibly tall. I can recall in perfect detail the ruby-tipped tie pin affixed to his ebony necktie, can picture the sharp lines of his red lapel and his crisp starched collar–but as hard as I try to remember it, the man's face remains no more than a distant shadow in the mists of my memory.

"Hello, little mortal," he said. "You're early."

I swallowed and stood, looking up at where his face must have been–I'm almost certain he had one. "Just visiting," I said. "I'll be going back home straightaway."

"Of course," he said, graciously. His voice echoed disconcertingly through my skull. He swept a hand toward the ferry. "Charon will see you out."

I hesitated, glancing at Carson, who was pushing himself upright weakly.

"Ah. You wish to take this man's soul with you, is that it?" The stranger took two steps and was at Carson's side, looking him over.

"Yes," I said. "Please?"

The stranger circled silently for several steps. Carson stiffened like a schoolboy under the headmaster's gaze. "His place is here," said the man. "Here, he can have anything his heart desires, unlock mysteries of creation. Would he really want to leave that all behind? I understand the world above was less than kind to him before he left it. Why ever would he want to go back?"

Carson straightened. "For her."

"Hmm." The stranger turned back to me. "You must love him very much that you would come so far to retrieve him," he said.

"It's not like that," I replied. "But he's important."

"Every soul is important."

"Oh–I have this," I said, rummaging in my pocket.

"What's that?" the stranger said.

"A string from the lyre of Orpheus." I pulled out the petrified relic. Jackaby had made many claims about the origins of his eldritch artifacts, but I had never before hoped so hard that he was right.

The stranger did not reach for it. "And?" he asked. I could hear the grimace in his voice. "Are you looking for somewhere to dispose of it? Have you run out of refuse bins above?"

I blinked. "You–you don't want it?"

"What would I want with a crusty scrap of sheep intestines?"

"I don't know," I admitted. "As a memento, I suppose. A reminder of Orpheus and his lovely voice."

"Little mortal," the stranger said, "we don't need a string to remember Orpheus. We have the idiot's head. As it happens, I don't especially want your little friend, here, either, so I'll tell you what–I'll give you the standard bargain. Leave. Keep your eyes forward without wavering until you're both free from my domain, and he can follow you out. Don't peek. Don't doubt. Don't hesitate. Do we have an understanding?"

I swallowed and nodded. "Yes, sir," I said.

"As for you." The man turned to Carson. "You may follow in silence until you have crossed the final threshold, and then you will be free to leave–but know this. Should you hesitate, should you set even one foot back in the land of the dead, this realm will not relinquish you again."

Carson nodded.

"Very good. Now then, I believe you will be needing these." He gave a small gesture, and the blue-black tendrils surged out of the water and deposited my two lost obols into his hand. He delivered them to me.

"Thank you very much, sir."

"Good-bye, little mortals," the stranger said.

The fires dancing across the surface of the river suddenly flared white hot and leapt above our heads. Then, just as quickly, they were out and the tall dark man was gone. I resisted the immediate instinct to look back at Howard Carson. Keeping my eyes forward, I climbed back into the boat instead and handed Charon two obols.

"Thank you," said Charon. Both coins glowed a warm red this time and then crumbled to dust between his fingers. "So," he said. "Did you have a nice visit?"

The boat rocked as we cast off. Charon directed the dragon-shaped masthead into the swirling fog. I wanted to turn, to see Carson sitting behind me. It was maddening to imagine going through all of that only to lose him on the way out–but I stayed strong.

"I asked him," said Charon.

"You asked him?" I said. "Asked him what?"

"About the waters," said Charon. "I do not think that English has all the right words to explain it, but I will try, if you like. He calls it the Terminus. The End Soul."

"That thing is a soul?"

"Yes. All souls have power, you see. Every person has a unique soul–a spirit–and so too does every place. Human spirits and the spirits of the places they inhabit can become bonded, and their bond makes both souls stronger. Your friend, Jennifer Cavanaugh, has such a bond–and it is powerful enough to allow her to remain above. The underworld also has a soul. It has the End Soul."

"So," I said, "if we had fallen in, we would have become bonded to this Terminus thing the way Jenny is bonded to Augur Lane?"

"Not exactly. In a way, you already are. All souls are bonded to the End Soul. What they can become is *lost* in the End Soul. They can become a part of the single energy that powers all eternity, but at the cost of everything that makes them unique. For some, those who are ready, it is a great reward. For others–those who would prefer to remain distinct–it is less pleasant. Does that make sense to you?"

"I think it does," I said.

The dark waters lapped at the sides of the boat and shadowy shapes moved about in the mist all around us. We arrived more quickly than I expected back at the landing beneath the yew tree. The little trickle of water still snaked down from the entryway to drain into the river, and the glow of sunlight cut through the gloom from above.

"Charon?" I said.

"Yes, Abigail Rook?"

"Thank you for asking. You didn't have to do that for me. You're really very sweet."

"That is kind of you to say, Abigail Rook," said Charon. "I look forward to our next meeting." He slid the boat snugly up against the mooring. "But I hope that I do not have the pleasure for a very long time."

"Likewise," I said as I climbed out onto the dock. "Goodbye." I almost glanced behind me as I said it, but I caught myself and managed to keep my eyes fixed on the opening up above. If Howard Carson was behind me, he made not the faintest whisper of a sound. I ascended the stairs and stepped up to the bright threshold of the living world.

Chapter Thirty-One

Hell had been the lesser nightmare.

My body no longer lay face-down on the cold earth where I had left it. It had been dragged back into the sunlight and now sat propped up against the roots of the great tree. Owen Finstern was crouching over my corpse. My ivory-handled knife was in his hand and a zealous fury was in his eyes. "Carefully, now!" he demanded. "Secure the clamp plate over the collimating lens assembly."

Jackaby stood beside the inventor's machine. He had erected the device near the shadow's edge and he was making adjustments at Finstern's command.

"Do it right," Finstern barked. He pressed the silver blade against my lifeless neck. "Or the girl's soul won't have anything to come back to."

"You don't know what you're doing, Mr. Finstern," Jackaby said. "Please. Calm down."

"I know precisely what I'm doing. Turn it on."

"Don't you dare!" Jenny cried. She hovered between Finstern and Jackaby. "She helped save your life! Without our help those monsters would already have taken you captive. They're hunting you!"

"Let them!" Finstern roared. "I want them to come! I've been waiting for them to come since I was an infant! I said turn it on!"

Jackaby moved slowly around the machine. "To what end, Mr. Finstern? What do you hope to accomplish here?"

"My birthright." He pressed the blade against my lifeless neck. The skin bent under the edge. He was one flick of the wrist away from ending me for good. "Do it."

With a whir and a click, Jackaby turned on the machine. The mechanism hummed. "Power?" he said. "Is that all this is about?"

"It's all anything is about. It's the only reason you're alive, or haven't you figured that out yet?"

Jackaby scowled. "What are you talking about?"

"You haven't got a clue, have you? She told me all about what you can do." He tapped my body's lifeless cheek with the knife. From behind the threshold I cringed. I wanted to hit him, but now would be the worst time to burst back into my body, leaping under the knife. "She told me how it works, your sight," Finstern continued. "They're building something powerful, you said. You figured out that much. Well, I know what it's like, trying to work with powers you can't see or touch or measure. You're the missing element, detective. They need your eyes. The rest of us are working blind, but you can see it all as plain as day, can't you? Energy. Potential. Power. You can observe it and quantify it, can't you?"

Jackaby swallowed.

"You're no good to them dead. They would have to hunt down the next Seer if you died. I figure that's why they've kept tabs on you instead. That's the only reason you're alive. You're a worthless storage container for a priceless power." His eyes narrowed. "And I want it."

"You really don't," said Jackaby. "It is as much a burden as it is a gift. Trust me."

"Then let me lift your burden. It's what my machine does. Nobody has to die today, Detective. I'm not a monster, in spite of what you think of me. You cross over. I activate the machine. Your soul waits safely on the other side while I absorb the power of the sight instead of letting it flitter away to just anybody. With your eyes I can propel my work forward and take my place in the company of those who actually appreciate my efforts. Everybody wins."

Jackaby said nothing.

"There's another way, of course," Finstern added. "She dies. Then you die. Then I take it anyway. It's your choice."

Jackaby looked across the threshold and seemed to notice me, my spirit, for the first time. His gaze locked on mine, and he looked as helpless as I was. He was seriously considering going along with it; I could see it in his eyes. After several seconds, he turned soberly back toward Finstern and to my limp corpse.

My eyes blinked open.

They were my eyes, although not the ones I was using at the moment. I stared from behind the ethereal barrier as my corpse turned angrily to face the mad inventor. Jenny, I realized, was nowhere to be seen. Owen Finstern did not seem to have noticed.

"Go on, then," Finstern said. "Cross the line!" He gestured toward the gap in the yew tree where I stood, using the silver blade to point. He looked as though he were about to say something else when the corpse at his feet suddenly lurched to life.

Jenny was clumsy and stiff as she possessed my limbs, but the element of surprise appeared to be more than enough for the moment. She launched herself bodily at Finstern's legs, and he was thrown to the ground. The knife flew out of his hands as he slammed into the dirt.

"You shouldn't threaten my friends." They might have been my vocal chords, but it was Jenny's accent that issued from my lips. She lashed out, punching him hard in the neck and landing a knee in his ribs.

He coughed and deflected her next blow with a swat of his hand. He shoved her off of him, but Jenny clung to the inventor's shabby coat, and the two of them tumbled gracelessly together across the earth until they rolled to a stop with Finstern on top. He raised a hand to strike her, but Jenny raised the silver knife at the same moment, pointing it squarely at his heart.

Finstern dropped his hand and the two of them slowly stood. I felt a burst of pride at essentially watching myself win the fight. Jenny still looked a little unsteady in my skin, but she managed to keep the blade at his chest the whole time. "It's over," she said.

The words had scarcely left her lips when a tiny object flew over the towering roots beside us and coasted in a wide arc directly toward her. It looked like an acorn.

"Look out!" Jackaby yelled, but it was too late. The little nut missed Finstern's shoulder by an inch and landed on Jenny's chest—on my chest—with a flash of green light. She went instantly rigid.

Finstern stepped uncertainly aside. When the blade failed to follow him, he waved his hand in front of her face. Jenny managed to move my eyes a fraction to follow him, but otherwise she remained as still as a statue. Finstern turned to see where the acorn had come from. Twin mountains, one slate gray and the other dull brown, rose slowly above the mess of giant roots. The shapes unfolded and I realized I was looking at a pair of enormous men made of living stone.

"Elementals!" said Jackaby. "Oreborn. My word, look at the size of them! No quick movements." I'm not sure whom he was addressing. Jenny did not appear capable of making any movements at all, and Finstern hardly warranted the warning. The giants could have him as far as I was concerned.

The gray colossus reached down. His forearm was roughly the size and color of a fully grown rhinoceros. Around one massive wrist was strapped a huge steel cuff, and his fingers looked like articulated boulders. As he spread them out I realized there was a figure standing within. She stepped down from his palm as casually as a countess from a fancy carriage. Her elegant sleeveless dress was an iridescent blend of blues and greens that hugged her slim figure as though it were soaking wet. Around her neck hung a necklace with two thick beads, identical in color to the looming creatures, and around her waist was slung a navy blue belt. A knife was sheathed on one hip and an olive green pouch was strapped to the other.

She raised her chin and the sunlight played across her strawberry blonde locks. I recognized her. The hard jawline and the faint asymmetry to her emerald eyes—she was the woman who had mimicked Jenny all those years ago. As she stepped into the clearing I realized why she had looked so familiar in Carson's memory. It was the family resemblance.

"Hello, brother dear," she said to Owen Finstern. "It's been a long, long time."

Chapter Thirty-Two

Finstern's face twisted in a tortured mess of emotions. Confusion, anger, and something like hope rolled and crashed into one another as his twin sister walked toward him. His uneven eyes were wild and wary, while the woman's were bright and keen, but they were the same shape exactly, and the same vivid green. His unkempt hair was thin and ruddy orange while hers hung in graceful strawberry blonde waves, but otherwise the two were nearly identical. The curve of their noses, the cut of their jaws–there was no question that they were related.

"Morwen," he whispered.

"Not recently," she said. "Still, it's sweet that you remember. I've missed you." Her accent was American, without a trace of the Welsh tones that distinguished her brother's speech.

"How long have you been watching me?" Finstern demanded.

"Long enough to step in before you got yourself killed." She nodded toward Jenny—who was still locked in my frozen body. "It's a hex, by the way. It won't hold forever, but it will last long enough for our purposes. Our scouts in the Annwyn got word you had crossed over. You didn't use the Rend, either—you managed to open a veil-gate. Father will be very impressed. Where did you find it?"

"Don't tell her anything!" Jackaby yelled. "She's a nixie! They're tricksters, Finstern! Liars by nature!"

Morwen turned on her heel. "You're being very rude, Detective! Can't you see we're in the middle of a family reunion?" She put a hand to her chest and clasped the gray marble. "Alloch, would you please teach Mr. Jackaby not to interrupt me when I'm speaking?"

The ground shook as the slate gray giant closed the distance between itself and Jackaby in two wide steps. The hulking thing was twenty feet tall with hands that could palm a packhorse. Jackaby leapt aside, but the oreborn moved with remarkable speed for a landmass. It caught him in one huge granite fist and lifted him ten feet up in the air. Jackaby struggled, his feet kicking in vain.

"The stones!" he croaked as the oreborn's fingers pressed

into his chest. "The stones around her neck, Finstern–that's how she's controlling the elementals. They're bound by the bracers on their wrists. Break the–" Alloch tightened his hold.

"That's better," said Morwen. "Where were we?"

"You were about to explain why I should help you," said Finstern.

"We're kin, Owen." Morwen gave him a smile that seemed to be trying just a little too hard. "It's time you joined the family business."

"You left me to rot. You expect me to believe you suddenly want me back?"

"Who do you think sent you the invitation?" The smile was beatific, but it never quite melted the frost of her cold eyes. "It was my idea to bring you in. I want you to join us, Owen. Father wants you, too. He's been watching."

Owen's eye twitched. He swallowed and took a deep breath. "Father?"

"We want the same thing, brother. In fact, I'm looking forward to seeing you finish what you've started." She nodded toward Finstern's device. "It's about time you got a little magic of your own, isn't it? You've already proven yourself with science. Father was willing to bring you in on the merits of your work alone–now imagine what he would think of you with powers, as well. What a welcome you will receive as his rightful heir. Owen Finstern, the one true Seer and key to the coming kingdom."

"Rosemary's Green," said Finstern. "The gate we entered is on a mound in the northeast corner. One of their friends is keeping it open. I think he's some kind of half-breed. I heard the detective call him Seelie when he thought I wasn't listening."

An uneven smirk pulled Morwen's lips taut. She clasped the second stone on her necklace. "Autoch, dispose of the little nuisance at Rosemary's Green for us, please." The second hulking elemental stalked off into the forest, back the way we had come.

"No!" Jackaby managed to wheeze.

"What's that? You'd suddenly like to cooperate?" Morwen called up to him.

Alloch loosened his grasp ever so slightly and Jackaby gasped. "Leave Charlie out of this," he rasped. "He's done nothing to you."

"That's not how it works, Detective. You had your chance to play along. Now your friends are going to die. You can watch, if you like—before we kill you, too."

"I'll do it," Jackaby groaned. "I'll cross over willingly. It's the only way to do the thing cleanly. Just ask your brother. If he tries to force the sight out of me, he'll pull me out right along with it. He's seen what two souls can do to a body."

Finstern nodded, scowling. "It's true. It is unpleasant."

"I'll let him have the sight," said Jackaby. "Just call off your elementals and let Rook and Jenny go." The machine was still humming beneath him. "Please. They've been through enough."

Morwen scowled for a moment, and then a wicked grin spread across her face. "Rook *and* Jenny?"

"The girl," Finstern explained. "Her soul went underground, but they travel with a ghost. The dead woman has taken control of the girl's body."

"Jenny Cavanaugh?" The woman's skin glistened like rippling water, and she changed. Her blonde locks relaxed and darkened to a soft brunette, and her face transformed. She looked exactly as Jenny had in life. "Not sweet, innocent Jenny Cavanaugh?" she mocked, her voice becoming a perfect match for Jenny's.

She tapped my body's frozen forehead with a fingernail. "Are you really in there? This is rich. I heard rumors, but I had no idea . . . You can't get free of my little hex, can you? Oh, this is delicious. I've killed a lot of people in a lot of ways, but I've never had the pleasure of killing the same person twice. Did you get my little anniversary present? I carved it myself."

Jenny's eyes all but screamed from within my frozen sockets.

Morwen reached up to take my knife from my frozen hand, but the moment she touched the silver she cried out and pulled away. Her palm was blistered. It looked as if she had grabbed hold of a glowing coal.

Morwen swore under her breath. "Awfully ostentatious,

aren't we? Who carries around a silver knife? Fine. That's fine. If we're going to do this again, let's do it right, anyway."

With a ripple like a breeze over a still lake, her hair darkened further to a deep black and her dress became a crisp skirt and white blouse. A new face emerged, one I had seen before over the top of a clipboard. She was Mayor Poplin's secretary. She had been there ten years ago, hiding in plain sight. She reached to her belt and drew the long dagger from its sheath. The metal was as black as midnight and curved slightly, like an Arabian scimitar. She was hardly one to complain about ostentatious weapons.

"There we go. Remember this one? Just like old times, isn't it?" she taunted. "Better, even. Last time I killed you I was in such a rush. I'll be sure to savor it this time."

She drew the black blade down Jenny's cheek–down my cheek. Her brother's threats had only been for effect, but Morwen did not hold back. The edge pierced my skin and cut a line of deep crimson from the corner of my eye down toward my jaw. Jenny's eyes screamed from within my frozen sockets. My head swam. I couldn't watch. I felt sick and trapped and helpless.

Abruptly, the ebony blade shot backward. It landed in the dirt behind Morwen, glowing red hot at the tip as though just plucked from a forge fire. She clutched her already injured hand and snarled with indignant rage. "What?"

I didn't understand it myself. Blood ran down my body's

unmoving face, but what force had stopped her blade was beyond me.

On the other side of the clearing, Jackaby grunted. He wrenched an arm free and, with a flick of his wrist, flung a little red stone—the last of the Cherufe's tears—toward his captor's rocky arm. It hit the inside of Alloch's elbow, and at once the giant's granite flesh boiled. Alloch bellowed. The stony arm glowed red from the curve of his shoulder to the steel brace around his wrist. Great gobs of charred molten rock were sloughing off and dropping to the earth.

"Do it now!" Morwen commanded her brother. "Turn it on!" Her secretary façade slipped away, and she was herself once more, strawberry blonde with furious panic playing across her eyes. She retrieved the black blade with her uninjured hand.

Finstern had scrambled to the machine. "I can't!" he said. "His soul needs to leave his body first!"

"Alloch!" Morwen clasped the gray bead on her necklace with her free hand. "Throw him over the line! Now! Ouch!" The little stone bead was glowing like a hot coal.

The enormous elemental moaned—a sound like the echoing rumble of a rock slide—but he obliged, his arm swinging toward the gate. At the same moment, Finstern activated the machine.

I felt a pressure at my back, and then I was suddenly across the threshold.

Time held still.

An unseen force pulled me toward my body. I drifted past Jackaby, who was still pinned in the monster's grip, unable to stop himself from plunging toward the threshold as I left it. I drifted past Finstern, lit by the unearthly glow emanating from his device, and past Morwen, her expression furious and frantic.

I spun as I drifted into my own sorely abused body, a new perspective snapping abruptly into place before me. The world burst back to life in the same instant. The bead in Morwen's hand exploded, fracturing in a burst of gray shards right in front of me. She cried out in alarm and nearly dropped her wicked black blade. At the same moment, Alloch's forearm broke free from the rest of his body, carrying Jackaby with it to land with an earthshaking thud just shy of the shadow's edge. Finstern's machine pulsed with a blinding white-blue beam of light for several seconds, and then it sparked and went dark again. Finstern doubled over on the ground. I was looking through my own eyes again, watching the madness around me, but I could not move.

I felt a flood of fear and fury bubbling out of control inside my skull. I could barely hear myself think. I focused. "Jenny," I thought. "I'm here. You're not alone."

The storm of emotions softened. "I'm afraid," she thought. "I'm so sorry. I tried. I can't move."

"Let's try again," I thought. "Together."

Alloch clutched the stump of his arm, which stuck out at a gruesome angle from his broad torso, charred and broken.

He shook his head and roared, loud and deep. The sound echoed through the forest, and then the colossus stalked away, shaking the ground with each step.

Owen Finstern staggered and fell sideways as he attempted to pick himself up off the ground.

"Brother?" asked Morwen, sheathing the blade at her hip. "Did it work?"

Owen stood. "Yes." he said. "No!" He twitched and clutched at his temples. The inventor's legs betrayed him and he toppled to the ground again.

"The sight, brother–do you have the sight?" Morwen demanded.

"No! No–he's in my head! It hurts! Help me!" Forces within Finstern were working at cross purposes. With each frantic step he seemed to be pulling himself against his own will closer and closer to the underworld.

With tremendous effort I felt my fingers flex. My hand clenched into a fist. I could sense the magic of the hex beginning to splinter.

"Keep pushing." The thought echoed in my head, though I don't know if it was mine or Jenny's. "Keep pushing." I poured every ounce of will I had into the effort, and from somewhere inside me I felt Jenny's energy building, resonating like an orchestral crescendo. And then we were suddenly pushing against nothing.

The hex broke. We were free. I felt Jenny's presence leave

me and I fell to my knees, once more alone in my own head. The world spun and I fought against the dizziness. My eyes tried to focus on a glittering shape that lay on the ground before me. When it had slowed to a gradual spin, I reached out and picked up the silver knife.

"Impossible!" Morwen wrapped the fingers of her good hand around the remaining bead on her necklace. "Autoch. Get back here. Now!" From within her grasp, the second bead cracked audibly.

I have had to piece together the events that had been taking place beyond my sight on the edge of Rosemary's Green that day. What follows is my best interpretation of Charlie's account of his experience, with his modesty and brevity removed.

Charlie had maintained his position as promised, safeguarding our veil-gate atop the grassy mound. The first creature to approach him was a jackrabbit with a little pair of antlers affixed atop its head. Charlie shooed the timid creature back into the forest with little difficulty, but there were more to come. A silvery owl as tall as a man coasted down out of the leaves to investigate the portal with suspicious eyes before flapping away. Three stocky fairies with wings like moths chose that moment to make a break for it, but Charlie batted them away. Next came a sort of scaly chicken, which startled easily and hurried off, and then a tawny stag with antlers of polished gold. Charlie had stomped, snarled, and swatted back a dozen strange species by the time the forest shook and a flurry of leaves spun to the ground.

The oreborn, Autoch, was twenty feet tall if he was an inch, his skin made of living, dusty brown rock. The boulders that made up his knee joints ground together with a rough, grating scrape as he stalked toward Charlie.

Charlie took a deep breath. "We don't have to do this," he said evenly.

"GRRAAAAAUGH!" countered Autoch with all the eloquence of an avalanche.

"Or perhaps we do." Charlie slipped his suspenders down from his shoulders and kicked off his shoes as the oreborn pounded closer. The window into the Annwyn filled with megalithic muscles and the forest shuddered with each heavy footfall, but by the time the behemoth was upon him, Charlie had changed. He met the rock monster in his canine form, muscles rippling beneath a coat of chocolate brown and black.

A heavy fist slammed down where Charlie had been standing, flattening nothing but empty clothes as the hound whipped aside. Charlie's instincts, although always keen, were sharpest when he was on all fours. He wasted no time vaulting atop the craggy arm, his eyes hunting for a weakness of any kind. He bounded to Autoch's shoulder in one leap and went straight for the brute's eyes, which glistened like jet marbles in the shadow of his heavy brow.

Autoch did not even flinch as Charlie's claws glanced off of the polished obsidian orbs. The attack left not so much as a scratch on the great elemental.

Charlie hit the ground again and bounded back to place in the portal. Whatever came, he could not allow that gap to close. The veil-gate only extended as high as Autoch's broad slab of a chest, and the giant had to stoop down to see Charlie. It made a sudden grab for him with fingers as thick as a grown man's waist. Charlie dodged again, and the creature gave him a meaningful nod, those glistening eyes sparkling like gems.

Charlie wasn't sure if he had seen it correctly, but Autoch repeated the motion. It was as if the creature were trying to communicate. The hound followed the elemental's gaze to a sturdy steel cuff affixed to Autoch's wrist. The band was fastened by a single seam along the inside of his wrist, a long hinge with a fine silver pin holding the two sides together.

"Now why would anyone with skin like yours need to wear something like that?" Charlie wondered. The stony creature swung again, and Charlie barely managed to duck under the quick strike. Autoch's expression was annoyed, although his anger seemed to be directed not at Charlie but at his own hands–almost as though they were acting against the elemental's will. "I really hope I'm right about this," Charlie thought to himself. The hound fixed his eyes on the silver pin and pounced just as Autoch reached for him.

Autoch moved faster. He caught Charlie in one rocky fist and pulled him off of the mound and into the Annwyn, dangling him upside down. The elemental squeezed and the air rushed out of Charlie's lungs in a wheeze. He felt his ribs screaming in protest. As Autoch lifted him high into the air, Charlie caught a glimpse of the portal behind them. Either his vision was going dark or the window into the human world was closing. With the last of his breath leaving his body, Charlie changed.

His muscles shuddered and his bones rearranged themselves. For a moment he wore neither one form nor the other. In that fleeting instant he slid through the creature's stony fingers and onto its wrist. His human lungs expanded. The moment his fingers had fully formed, they began to pull at the pin, working it loose from the fixture.

Autoch shook his heavy arm widely, and Charlie sailed through the air to land on his back in the dirt and leaves. The hulking figure plodded forward to loom over him.

As the figure stalked up, filling Charlie's field of vision, Charlie held up his hand. Clutched in his trembling fist was a long, thin silver rod. Autoch stopped. He held up his own hand and regarded his wrist. The bracer clinked open, loosely. The giant reached up with his other hand and ripped the metal off of his arm. He flexed his fingers experimentally and tossed the cuff away into the forest.

Charlie stood, nervously. "Feel better?" he asked.

Autoch turned his obsidian gaze toward the policeman for a few seconds, and then lunged forward without warning. Charlie fell backward, but the giant's hand sailed high above his head. When Charlie looked up, it took him a few seconds to understand what he was seeing. Autoch's outstretched arm hung perfectly still, and one stony finger seemed to end abruptly at the knuckle. A halo of light shone around the stump.

The portal! During the scuffle Charlie had been thrown away from his post, and the veil-gate had all but sealed behind him. Autoch's finger was all that held it open now. With his other hand, Autoch gestured Charlie forward.

Charlie stepped cautiously up to the oreborn's hand, which less than a minute earlier had been doing its best to crush the life out of him. Autoch removed his huge finger gently and Charlie took his place, using both hands to hold open the impossible hole in midair. The window into Rosemary's Green was barely larger than Charlie's head.

He looked back over his shoulder. "Thank you," he said to the elemental giant.

Autoch pounded a fist against his chest with a sharp clack, and, without further explanation, plodded off into the blue-green forest.

Concentrating hard, Charlie managed to coax the entrance to grow larger and larger until it was once more wide enough for a body to pass through. Shaken though he was, he slipped back into his clothes and resumed his place as a sentry. His heart thudded in his chest as he caught his breath.

He was not alone. A snow-white hunting hound with ears of bright crimson stood watching him silently from the underbrush. How long it had been there by the time Charlie noticed it, he did not know. It was lean and angular like a greyhound, far smaller than his own canine stature–but something about the beast made Charlie feel as though he ought to kneel or bow or roll over and show his underbelly. He straightened up instead.

"Hello, friend," Charlie said.

The dog stared deep into Charlie's eyes, and then in a flash of milky white fur it was gone, and Charlie was alone again.

Back beneath the towering yew tree, Morwen gasped. The little brown stone on her necklace splintered and fell apart, nothing but tan pebbles and rock dust trickling through her fingers and down the shimmering blue-green dress. "No!" she shrieked. Her hex broken and her minions free, the nixie panicked. She fumbled with the pouch at her side, pulling out a handful of acorns.

The whole world was still spinning around me, but up close I could see that scraps of folded paper had been stuffed inside each of them. More hexes. She loosed one at me and I managed to duck away from it without falling over. Morwen snarled and let fly the whole handful. There was no chance that I could dodge them all.

A sudden gust of wind whipped up before the projectiles could reach me, sending them tumbling harmlessly into the roots. "LEAVE MY FRIENDS ALONE." Jenny was nowhere to be seen, but her voice was everywhere and hard as steel. Dust began to form little eddies as the air spun all around us.

Morwen cursed and ran for the machine, slapping the brass fixtures into their traveling straps clumsily and folding the legs shut. Across the clearing I could see Jackaby's body still trapped in the grip of the giant's unyielding fingers, and Finstern still fighting his own limbs.

"Sister!" Finstern cried. "Help me!"

"We needed a demonstration," she called across the windy clearing. "And you have provided that. Father will be very pleased with your efforts on our behalf, dear brother. I'll take your little toy, but your presence"–she secured the last strap and hefted the device over her shoulder–"is not required."

Finstern cried out desperately, but Morwen turned her back on him and ran for the forest. I willed the world to hold still and flung the silver knife at her as hard as I could. The blade whipped through the air. It caught her leg a glancing blow, slicing a hole in her shimmering skirts and bouncing off into the roots. She glared back at me icily for just a moment, but the attack did not even slow her down. In another moment she had vanished into the woods.

Jenny Cavanaugh materialized in the center of the clearing. Freezing wind whipped around her.

"Jenny!" called out a familiar voice through Finstern's mouth.

The inventor's foot stumbled across the threshold just as Jenny turned. She eyed Finstern angrily. "Jackaby?" she said. "Are you in there?"

Finstern shook his head violently. "Argh! Get out! Get him out of my head!" he hollered furiously in his own Welsh accent. Then, in an American voice much softer and kinder than that of the insufferable cretin we had come to know, the man spoke again. "No. Not Jackaby. It's me, Jennybean."

The wind stopped.

I realized what had pushed me across the threshold, what was fighting Finstern in his own skin. Howard Carson. He had followed me after all, only to rush into the path of the machine and channel his own soul into the mad inventor's body.

Jenny's eyes were wide. She hung motionless in the air. For several seconds the only sounds were the creaks of molten rock gradually solidifying in ashy lumps beside us. Swirling tendrils of blue-black mist were beginning to creep up out of the cave in the tree. One of the wisps of the Terminus, the End Soul, clung to Finstern's foot and climbed his leg, winding upward like a smoky snake.

"Howard?" whispered Jenny.

"Keep back," he said. "I can't stay. It's already pulling me down. I can feel it. "

"Howard? Howard–I looked for you. I waited for so long." Jenny's voice shook.

"Don't wait any longer," he said. "You've lost enough time waiting, and it's all my fault. I should have listened to you from the start. I would give your whole life back to you if I could, and mine right along with it." The mist grew thicker, moving, swirling, undulating all the time as it coiled around the inventor's waist. "I can't. What I can give you is a little more time. Usc it well. Every second. Find Poplin. Mayor Poplin was the only one of us to meet the council face-to-face. Find Poplin and you'll find your answers."

"I don't want you to go," Jenny breathed. "I'm not strong enough to lose you again."

"You're stronger than you think. You always have been. Listen to me now–losing Finstern will only slow them down. It won't stop them." The shadowy tendrils had coiled around his chest. "Stop waiting," he said. "You've always been strong for me. It's time for you to be strong for you."

"Howard–"

"Good-bye, Jennybean. Be amazing."

And then Owen Finstern fell backward across the threshold.

His arms flailed once, as though he were waking from a nightmare, and his startled scream was cut short mid-breath as his body collapsed to the ground, just as mine had done when I crossed over. Above the man's still corpse not one but two spectral figures appeared. The spirit of Howard Carson drifted serenely backward into the darkness of the yew tree. He reached into his pocket and flicked a single coin in the air and caught it. The obol I had given him. He had managed to keep it after all. He stared lovingly at Jenny until the mist had claimed him.

The departure of Owen Finstern's soul was not so peaceful. His mouth broke open in an anguished snarl, and it was clear he was fighting forces against which he could not win. Behind him, in the shadows of the great tree, a figure appeared, dressed in an impeccable black suit. The stranger watched as Finstern's soul spasmed, watched as his head shot back. It was as though invisible chains were dragging the inventor's ghost forward and backward at the same time. He twitched and bucked, then shuddered wretchedly, coming apart at the seams. By the time his broken soul finally tumbled backward into the hole, it did not look much like a man anymore. Something else–no more than a sliver of darkness–skittered away into the roots in the opposite direction like an angry black insect.

Charon had warned us. The part of Finstern that was inhuman could not enter, and the part of him that was human could not escape. The crossing had completely torn Finstern apart.

"What will become of them?" I called to the dark stranger

in the shadows. "Will Mr. Carson get to go back to his afterlife?" The stranger did not answer right away. "Is Owen Finstern just gone, now? Does whatever is left of his humanity get its own special place in the underworld? Does he join the End Soul?"

"Ask me those questions," said the echoing voice, "when next we meet again, little mortal." And then the shadows were empty. The stranger was gone.

With a clatter of crumbling stones, Jackaby finally kicked his way free of the Alloch's ruined hand. He brushed off his coat and crossed the clearing to stand beside Jenny Cavanaugh.

"Jenny?" he said.

"I told you there was no other woman," she said, her eyes still fixed on the tree.

"You were right," Jackaby conceded. "It looks like the only thing that could tempt that man away from you was you. She's a nixie. Nixies are shape-shifting water spirits."

"He was a good man," said Jenny. "You would have liked him."

"I think you're right," said Jackaby. "He gave himself up to keep you safe."

"Twice," said Jenny.

I stepped forward hesitantly. "Are you all right?" I said.

She took a deep breath. "No," she said. "But I will be. It's good to know the truth. I saw what Howard told you in the underworld," she said. "I saw everything the moment you got back. I saw it in your head. I can't thank you enough for what you've done for me." She smiled at me and then cringed. "Oh, Abigail, your face!"

I reached a hand up and felt the cut. It was long and tender, but it wasn't deep. Morwen had struck a line straight across the middle of my existing scar. Each investigation I pursued with Jackaby seemed to leave me with larger and more visible injuries. At this rate, I would be escalating to decapitation by our sixth or seventh case if I wasn't careful. "I'll live," I said. "I'm sure it looks worse than it is. Really."

"You can't fool me. I was in there when you got it," said Jenny. "I'm so sorry."

"That scar is nothing to apologize for," said Jackaby. "It may very well be the only reason Miss Rook is still alive. Look. Just like the devil going after old Will o' the Wisps, Morwen managed to inscribe the mark of a cross without meaning to. Unseelie Fae don't handle religious iconography well. It's in their nature to reject contradicting powers. Come on. We'll get you patched up back at the house."

"No," I said. "Carson was right about that, too–we can't wait. Finstern's machine in those monsters' hands is bad enough, but the Dire Council is already constructing something else–something capable of enslaving entire cities at a time."

"Did you say the Dire Council?" Jackaby asked. His tone told me he had heard the name before, and his eyes told me he had hoped he wouldn't hear it again.

"Yes. The Dire Council. That's what Mr. Carson called them. As the Seer, you're the best chance we have of hunting down the council before it's too late–and their favorite slippery assassin just stole the only machine in the world capable of taking you out of commission. We need to act fast. We can't let her get back to her father."

"I'm all for putting a stop to that nefarious nixie," said Jackaby, "but she's long gone by now. It would be easier to pick up a trail back in our world, but the Annwyn is saturated with Unseelie energies. Tracking her in here would be like finding a drop of water in an ocean."

"Then we don't track her at all," I said.

"You have something in mind?"

"Yes," I said. "We need to stop watching the marionette and start following the strings."

Chapter Thirty-Three

The sky was already beginning to darken by the time we reached the veil-gate. Charlie stood like a palace guard as we stepped through, but his face betrayed the relief he felt at our return. His expression faltered as he caught sight of the line of red running down my face.

"It's fine, really." I gave him a kiss on the cheek and he smiled, a confused medley of contentment and concern, as he followed me across the threshold. He paused, taking notice of Jenny, and then glanced back through the portal.

"Hello, Miss Cavanaugh. What about Mr. Finstern?"

"He isn't coming," answered Jackaby. "He made choices."

"I'll explain everything along the way," I said.

The portal closed silently as soon as Charlie climbed down from the mound. We put Rosemary's Green behind us and wound our way back into the city proper. Along the way I told Charlie about the tree, about the underworld, and about what I had learned from Howard Carson. "Mr. Carson called them the Dire Council," I said. "Jackaby, you know something about a Dire Council, don't you?"

Jackaby scowled darkly. "Yes," he said. "I do. I know that there are monsters grown men only dare whisper about, and those monsters only dare whisper about the Dire Fae. They are chaos incarnate. The Dire Council is worse–they are insidiously clever chaos. Organized chaos. Redcaps and dragons and vampires are nothing compared to what will come if the Dire Council achieves their goal."

"What goal?"

"According to tradition, Dire Fae have a passion for havoc. The Dire Council gives that passion scope. They have sought in the past to tear down the barriers between realms. To bring the Anwynn crashing into the earth. The Seelie Fae served nobly the last time–and suffered terrible losses to ensure the Dire Fae did not succeed. Think of your own Guy Fawkes, only instead of blowing up some stuffy parliament building, the council set their sights on the human race. Not even the Old Testament boasts any plague to compare with the onslaught of every species in the Unseelie Court unleashed on the world all at once."

"It's the fate of all mankind, then, sir?" I said. "Grand. That's grand. Let's make sure that doesn't happen, shall we?"

"I still don't understand," said Charlie. "Where are we going?"

"We're visiting an old friend," said Jackaby.

"An old enemy," added Jenny. She had vanished from sight as we wound our way through the streets, but her voice remained clear and close at hand.

The sun was easing toward the horizon and the sky was warming to a rich burgundy as we made our way into the heart of the city. While we walked I finished the story, telling Charlie about what had happened after I emerged from the underworld, about Finstern and his treacherous sister, Morwen, and about her underhanded escape.

"It's Morwen we're after now," Jenny added darkly. "We will finish this tonight."

"Don't leave off the clever bit," Jackaby piped in. "Miss Rook put all the pieces together. I'll have to give you a raise if you've got it right."

"You always just tell me to pay myself whatever sounds reasonable from the accounts," I said.

"Well, I will instruct you to pay yourself slightly more."

"I didn't do anything all that impressive, anyway," I said. "I simply took what we already know about Morwen and connected a few strings. We know that she was raised by her father—a secretive, manipulative *magic man.* It's a fair wager he's our puppet master, or one of them, at least. We also know that she was already here in New Fiddleham over a decade ago, doing his dirty work. In those days

Morwen worked for Mayor Poplin in the guise of his secretary. Poplin had a history of corruption, and my guess is he was an easy mark for their plans. His Technology Center was nothing but a cover story for their sinister science project."

"Which is why Mr. Carson destroyed it," said Charlie.

"Right, but that wasn't the end of it. Poplin had bled the city dry to fund the project, so when it went up in flames he went up in smoke. He lost favor fast and an idealistic candidate named Philip Spade was elected in a landslide to take his place."

"You think Mayor Spade is connected to all of this?" Charlie asked.

"I think the clandestine Dire Council had lost more than a building and a half-finished machine," I said. "They had lost their political hold on New Fiddleham. They had to regroup. They needed a firmer grip on the city, and I don't believe for an instant that they just cut their losses and moved on."

We had arrived at the mayor's estate. Jackaby took the lead as we marched past the immaculately trimmed gardens and up the walk until we came to a white door framed by broad marble pilasters. "The thing about idealists," he said, knocking on the door, "is that they have a habit of being hopeless romantics, as well."

"Which is why we believe that the nixie, an experienced temptress and a shapeshifter, was ideally suited to infiltrate

Mayor Spade's personal life and become the real power behind the throne."

"Wait–Mary?" Charlie said. "Mary Spade?"

"Two simple words, yet as much a command from her superiors as a new identity," said Jackaby. "Mary Spade."

Spade's butler opened the door and sighed audibly.

"Bertram, my good man," said Jackaby, "Do show us in."

"No," Bertram said. "Mr. Spade is not seeing guests at this hour, Mr. Jackaby, and certainly not you. If you wish to conduct business, you will need to make an appointment with the mayor's office in the morning, not harass him in his personal residence."

"Ah, but you see, we're not here for the mayor this time. We're here for his wife–only I imagine we've just missed her, haven't we?"

Bertram raised an eyebrow. "Mrs. Spade is not available."

"Getting awfully late in the evening for the lady to be out, isn't it? I imagine she has a perfectly reasonable explanation for–"

"Mrs. Spade is indisposed, Mr. Jackaby," Bertram interrupted. "That does not mean she is not on the premises. Oh, good heavens. What has happened to your face, young lady?"

"It's fine," I said.

"Indisposed?" said Jackaby. "She's called for a bath, hasn't she?"

"Not that it is any of your business what my lady is–"

"No! She can't!" Jackaby shoved through the door. "Quick, we need to stop her before she gets into the water!"

"How dare you!" Bertram exploded. "Stop right there!"

"What's the meaning of this?" Philip Spade stood at the top of the broad, curving staircase, his bald head and bushy beard jutting over the banister as he adjusted his glasses. He had already changed into a pair of navy blue pajamas for the evening.

"Hello, mayor!" Jackaby leapt up the stairs three at a time. "Delightful to see you again."

"Why on earth are you here?"

"You've been a great ally in the past and helped me out of more than a few tight spots. Now we're here to help you out of one of your own. You can thank us after."

"What are you talking about? Hold still, would you!"

Jackaby had ascended to the landing and was already sweeping past Spade and down the high-ceilinged hallway. "You gave me my current home and place of business when I was still operating out of a shabby two-room apartment. Tell me–why did you offer me that splendid building on Augur Lane?"

"I don't know. It seemed like a good fit," said Spade. "It was going to waste due to its rather sordid history, but you didn't seem the sort to be scared off by ghost stories."

"No, indeed. It was your idea then?"

"Well, no," he admitted. "Mary suggested it, now that you mention it. Why?"

"Awfully benevolent of the lady to suggest you just give away a valuable piece of real estate to little old me, especially given how upset she was about those rosebushes. I imagine she was probably more upset about my torching the nest of brownies residing within them, actually. They're practically cousins, after all. Still, it did provide her with a handy excuse to dislike me and a convenient reason to avoid meeting face-to-face."

"What? That's ludicrous. You've met Mary. Haven't you?"

"Strangely, no–I haven't. I've never thought much of it–but she has always been conspicuously absent when I came calling. She's always been taken ill or been visiting an aunt or, most often and most telling of all"–Jackaby threw open the door at the end of the hall with a flourish–"taking a bath!"

We peered inside. "Sir," I said, "I think this is a sitting room." From within the room, a startled maid had ceased dusting the coffee table and straightened up.

"Whoops!" Jackaby spun, counting doors on his fingers.

"What is he raving about?" Spade said. "Why would it be suspect that Mary offer you the house?" Spade spun around as Jackaby whipped off between Charlie and me, stalking back up the hallway.

"The sordid history of that place," I informed the mayor, "isn't just history. The people who killed Jenny Cavanaugh are still here in New Fiddleham. They had been through her house already, so they knew the ins-and-outs of the property. Their wickedness didn't end with the murder on Augur Lane ten years ago–it had barely begun. When Jackaby showed up in New Fiddleham, he posed an immediate threat to their operation, but they couldn't simply kill him. They needed him alive, so they did the most logical thing. They kept tabs on him and kept him busy."

"That's right," Jackaby agreed. "Meanwhile they were biding their time and rebuilding, waiting until the whole mess seemed to have washed away. But–as those Mudlark boys could tell you–everything that washes away has to wash up somewhere. And speaking of washing . . . here we are!" He wrenched open another door triumphantly. A simple white bathtub with brass feet stood empty before us. "She's not here!"

"Of course not," said Bertram. "Mrs. Spade never takes her bath in the east wing."

"Mr. Spade," said Jackaby, "you have an impractically large abode."

"Will you just tell me what on earth is going on!" Mayor Spade was turning red around the collar.

"Certainly," said Jackaby. "Last year you appointed Mr. Swift, a bloodthirsty monster, as the commissioner of the entire New Fiddleham Police Department. Remember that? Yes, of course you do. The question is: why? Why Swift? I doubt the job was his idea. Redcaps are notoriously solitary creatures. So whose idea was it?"

"What? Swift had papers. We contacted references. He came highly recommended," Spade hedged. "He deceived us all. You can't blame me for–"

"I agree entirely," Jackaby said. "So, whose idea was it?"

Spade swallowed. "Well, Mary did introduce us. She said he had served in the war with her father. At least, the real Mr. Swift had served in the war with her father. But it's not–"

"Not a total lie," said Jackaby. "He was serving in a war they're trying to start."

"No!" Spade shook his head.

Jackaby started off down the stairs again, making rapidly for the west end of the mansion.

"No, Mary wouldn't do that. Not on purpose. She was duped as much as any of us. She's nothing but sweet and friendly."

"I'm sure she is," I said, hurrying to keep up with Spade and my employer. "In fact, I imagine your wife is often social on your behalf, yes? Throwing parties and having tea with important families?"

"Yes! Yes, that is much more her sort of thing. She makes friends so easily."

"She has been establishing a network of social and political contacts," Jackaby said. "A spider weaving her web."

"I beg your pardon–that's my wife!" Spade said.

"I understand the late Mrs. Beaumont was one of the most influential socialites in the city," I said. "Mary didn't, by any chance, meet with the late Mrs. Beaumont before the poor woman's death, did she?"

"How can you even suggest such a thing! Mary was with me that whole evening! She was devastated when she heard the news. She and Mrs. Beaumont had been so close! Mary even bought the woman a cute little kitty to keep her company after Mr. Beaumont passed away."

Jackaby and I exchanged glances. "Mrs. Wiggles," I told him, "is the reason Mrs. Beaumont was killed. She wasn't really a cat, mayor. She was a dangerous supernatural creature in disguise. One of her brood became the fifty-foot dragon that nearly wiped Gadston off the map. Mrs. Beaumont was silenced before we could trace the thing back to its source."

Spade huffed in frustration and disbelief. A maid slipped out of a door at the far end of the hall, closing it gently behind her. She was carrying a large empty pitcher. Steam issued out of the ceramic mouth as if it had been only recently emptied.

"She's in there!" I pointed. Jackaby was a dozen paces ahead of us already.

"Absolutely not!" yelled Spade. "You will not barge in on my wife while she is—"

And then Jackaby threw open the door.

Mary Spade had wrapped a towel around herself and was just testing the steamy water with one hand as her husband, the butler, a completely baffled maid, a wanted fugitive, a mad detective, and I all came to a stop and peered in at her. Mary was a beautiful woman with gentle brown curls framing a face that belonged on the cover of a saccharine dime novel.

"Philip dear?" she said, taking our entrance remarkably well. "What's going on?"

"It's over, Morwen," said Jackaby firmly. "He knows."

"He damn well does not know!" Spade spluttered. "This is madness! Shut that door!"

"No," said Jackaby. "That woman is not your wife, Mr. Spade. She's not really a woman at all, and she's not called Mary. She's a creature called a nixie, and she's been pulling your strings from the moment the two of you met."

"That's impossible."

"It's really not. She showed us her true face less than an hour ago, and even if you can't see her as I see her, there can be no question as to her species. Miss Rook had the foresight to equip herself with a silver knife for our outing. Silver is notoriously effective against fairies of the Unseelie Court. The slightest touch burned her hand badly. We saw it happen."

"Burned?" Mary lifted both hands and turned them around so that everyone could see. Her skin was flawless. "How perfectly ridiculous. My hands are just fine. Now if you don't mind–"

"Of course they're fine; you've had them in the water. Like mermaids and selkies and water spirits of all sorts, nixies need only return to their element to become rejuvenated. Miss Rook also caught you a cut on your leg with the silver blade before you fled, though. It's just a nick, but I see you have not had time to attend to that. Had we gotten here two minutes later, you would've had time to soak the injury away."

"This is absurd," said Spade. "You're talking nonsense! Now stop looking at my wife's legs this . . ." he faltered, ". . . this instant." Mary could not lower the towel to cover any more of her legs without sacrificing modesty, and an angry red cut was just visible beneath the edge of the cloth.

"I have no idea what that man is talking about," said Mary. She sounded so earnest and innocent–something deep inside of me almost wanted to believe her, but I had landed that cut myself. "Oh, Philip, what's going on?"

"How did you hurt your leg, Mary?"

"It's nothing, darling. I had an accident with the washbasin earlier. It just slipped and cracked while I was–and you were . . ." She trailed off.

"Oh, to hell with it." Mary Spade stood up straight and let go of the towel. It rippled, and before it could fall to the floor it became the same sleeveless blue-green dress the nixie had worn in the Annwyn, right down to the black blade hanging from her belt. Her eyes lost their perfect symmetry, her brown curls softened to a shimmering strawberry blonde, and her face became Morwen's again. "Let's just get this over with already."

Chapter Thirty-Four

The maid dropped the pitcher. It shattered on the floorboards behind us and Mayor Spade staggered back a step. "What have you done with my Mary?" he managed.

"You ignorant little gnat." Morwen rolled her eyes. "At least Poplin was sharp enough to just demand a bribe. There is no Mary. There's only ever been me."

She lifted her knee and plunged her injured leg into the steamy bath. The water climbed her dress, holding itself together like beads of dew on a leaf, collecting and rising upward until it swirled in a coil around her waist. It was mesmerizing, like watching a liquid boa constrictor.

She pulled the leg out again and spun gracefully. Before I knew what was happening, a tunnel of steaming water whipped through the air and slapped into my chest with all the force of a beam of lumber. My feet slid out from under me and I flew back. My head cracked against the hallway wall so hard it made my eyes hurt.

I blinked my vision back in place in time to see Charlie lunge toward the door. Morwen spun in another elegant twirl and the snake of water hammered into him. He was pelted sideways into Bertram, and the two of them toppled to the floor. Jackaby reached for something in his coat, but Morwen did not give him the chance. He was lifted completely off his feet by another blast of living water, tumbling sidelong down the hallway in the opposite direction.

The maid had long since fled, and the rest of us were still picking ourselves up off the ground—all but Spade, who straightened and held his chin up. The mayor looked alone, his eyes full of hurt and pain. "I trusted you," he said quietly. "I loved you."

"That was the idea," said Morwen flatly. "Don't give me that insufferable look. We've just reached the 'death do us part' moment in our relationship, honey pie."

The temperature dropped abruptly. The steaming water that had soaked my shirtwaist suddenly felt like ice. Morwen spun again, channeling the water back up her body, and whipped her arm out toward Spade. He flinched, bracing himself for the blow, but it never came.

"What . . . ?" Morwen's voice shot up an octave and she shuddered. The water, which was coiled around her from shin to shoulder, had frozen solid.

"Neat trick, I'll give you that," she said. "Is that you, Jenny?" Morwen flexed and shook until the ice cracked and broke apart, tumbling around her in heavy chunks. She slid one hand to her hip and pulled the long black blade from her belt as she scanned the room from side to side. "That's adorable. I took your meaningless life and now you're going to pay me back with what? The chills?"

The air shimmered on the other side of the bathtub and Jenny appeared. "I couldn't see it before," Jenny said. "But I see it now. You're afraid."

"Afraid of you?" Morwen laughed. "You were pathetic when you were an idiot girl. Now you're just the shadow of an idiot girl. You're nothing. I can see why your boyfriend was so eager to give you the slip. You really think he didn't know it was me? He knew."

"Don't listen to her," Jackaby grunted, and pushed himself to his feet.

"It's all right, Jackaby," Jenny said evenly. "I can handle her."

"You think so?" Morwen scoffed. "Because I think you're a damn ghost. You think I'm afraid of being haunted? Haunt me. I'm going to gut every last one of your friends in front of you while you haunt me. I'm going to start with the girl." She jabbed her black blade at me to punctuate the threat. "And then I'm going to work my way up to lover boy over there, and you're going to haunt me through the whole bloody slaughter, because that's all you can do."

"Leave her alone!" Jackaby pulled a slender chain from his coat. It was a dull iron-gray and no thicker than the chain for a pocket watch. He wound it around his hand several times until it formed a band of links across his knuckles when he clenched his fist.

"No," said Jenny. "It's my turn." She did not flicker. She did not slip into an echo. Her voice was steady and calm.

Morwen laughed. "That's hilarious. What're you going to do to me? Make the curtains wiggle?"

"I can manage a little more than that."

The whole house shuddered.

Morwen sneered. "If you think a little tremor is going to scare me, then you haven't met my fa–"

Morwen's sentence was cut short as the bathtub flipped suddenly upward and launched itself with a deafening crash through the bathroom wall and into the adjacent room, taking the unready nixie along with it.

I stared at Jenny. She drifted through the wreckage as calm as anything, not a hair out of place. "My brick. My house. My whole wide world." She slid through the demolished wall. "My turn."

We hastened to follow, clambering over broken plaster and cracked beams. The bathtub had carved its path into Mayor Spade's study. It now lay with its brass feet pointed at the ceiling, splintered enamel shards littering the deep red carpet. Morwen's groans echoed from within.

"I've always been strongest when I was being strong for other people," Jenny said casually. "And that's not a bad thing. I would have made a marvelous wife." She gave the slightest wave of her hand. It was no more effort than she had devoted to swatting at a handkerchief when we had first begun practicing together, but now the bathtub flew off of Morwen like a piece of dollhouse furniture, smashing into Spade's desk with a clamorous clatter of enamel pieces and splintered wood. "But somebody reminded me today that it's okay to be strong for myself."

From the mantel above the desk, the portrait of Mrs. Spade smiled placidly down upon the chaos. The perfect, elegant face behind the frame could not have looked more unlike the manic, furious madwoman lying crumpled in the middle of the carpet. Her uneven eyes glared up at Jenny, her hair was splayed out like Medusa's vipers, and her lips curled in a spiteful snarl.

Morwen pushed herself to her knees, swayed, and nearly toppled back down again. She held fast to her wicked weapon with one hand and pushed a mess of red-blonde hair out of her face with the other.

Jenny drifted slowly toward her.

"I remember every detail of it, you insignificant cow," Morwen panted, affecting a crooked grin that failed to convey the same confidence it had before. "You screamed. You cried and blubbered like a baby before you died."

"It won't work," said Jenny. "You can't rile me anymore."

"No? You should have seen your handsome Howard Carson after our vamp got through with him," Morwen went on. For all her venom, she looked as though she might pass out at any moment. The trip through the wall had left several gashes along her arms, and her eyes appeared to be having difficulty focusing. "You could barely recognize his butchered corpse in the end," she hissed. "We pitched what was left into the fire like greasy table scraps."

Jenny did not rise to the bait. She only drifted slowly to a stop, looming over Morwen. Morwen gripped her dark dagger so tightly her knuckles whitened. She lashed out wildly at the specter, but the blade met nothing more substantial than moonlight. The effort cost the nixie her balance, and she collapsed again onto the carpet.

"It's frustrating, isn't it?" said Jenny calmly. "Not being able to make contact." She reached down and easily plucked the blade out of Morwen's grasp. She shifted the weapon from one hand to the other, regarding the dark metal curiously. The solidity of the thing sat at odds with her translucent fingers.

Morwen pushed herself up with great difficulty, swaying to an unsteady slouch on one knee. The fight had left the nixie, but not her fury. Her dress was torn and she had plaster ground into her hair. Her voice was hollow. "Just get it over with."

"It is over," said Jenny. She dropped the blade onto the carpet behind her with a soft thump.

Morwen narrowed her eyes. "Don't waste your pity on me, ghost," she spat.

"I won't," said Jenny. "Nor any fear nor fury. I'm done with you, Morwen. My friends, however . . . are not. Mr. Jackaby?"

Jackaby stepped forward. He unwound the chain from his hand as he moved around toward Morwen.

"Done with me?" Morwen spat. "You only exist because of me, ghost! You're nothing but a ripple in my wake, you worthless trash. I made you!"

"You didn't make me," Jenny said gently. "I made myself, and I will continue to make myself forever after. What you did to me? That made you. It made you a murderer and it made you a monster. They buried the girl you killed, Morwen. I'm the spirit you couldn't kill. You have no power over me."

Jackaby was approaching with the chain held taut. Morwen snarled and tried to swipe it out of his grasp. Jackaby managed to keep hold of one end as the other spun and coiled around Morwen's wrist. "This binding is made of Tibetan sky-iron," he said as she tried to pull away. "Very pure. Very sacred. This may sting a little."

"What?" Morwen cried. "It burns! Get it off!"

The more she struggled and fought, the tighter the chain wound. The links slipped together with a series of quiet clicks, forming a seamless band.

Morwen gritted her teeth and snarled. Her gaze drilled into my employer, and her fingers were tensed like talons. She was shaking with anger. "Why won't my hands work?" she demanded.

"Because of the work you would put them to," Jackaby replied. "You're bound by my will until I give you leave to go."

He inspected the pouch at her side and found a single remaining hex-acorn within it. She growled as he relieved her of the trinket, but she could do nothing to stop him as he tucked it away into one of the myriad pockets of his coat. Behind him a piece of plaster the size of a dinner plate slipped from the demolished wall and landed atop the debris with a crash.

Mayor Spade stood watching from the ruined bathroom, looking rather like the bathtub had flattened him instead of his wife. He opened his mouth and closed it. He stared at Morwen. The damage done to his home was slight compared to the ruins that had just been made of the poor man's life.

"Mr. Spade," I said. "I'm so sorry you had to find out this way."

The mayor only hung his head. "I have been a terrible fool."

"Yes," Jackaby said gently. "Yes, you have. Well then, I think we're finished here. Sorry about the mess, Mayor. Let me know if you need a good contractor for that wall, I'm happy to call in a favor or two. Don't trouble yourself, Bertram. We'll see ourselves out."

Chapter Thirty-Five

The mayor's estate was not the only property to have suffered that day; Jackaby's house at 926 Augur Lane looked as though it had barely survived a war. The damage around us felt raw and personal as we stepped back inside. I tried not to think about the fact that the worst of it was still nothing compared to the carnage that would ensue if the earth and Annwyn became one.

Toby skittered into the foyer and wound several circles around Charlie's legs. Even Douglas flapped up onto the bookshelf and bobbed happily from one foot to the other. We had a lot of work ahead of us, but ransacked or not, it was a relief to be home.

"What are you going to do with her?" I asked. Jackaby

still had Morwen bound with his chain of sky-iron. She had said nothing since we had left the mayor's estate.

"We're going to ask her a few questions," said Jackaby. "We'll start with finding out where she stowed her brother's machine and then move on to the rest of her family. It may take time. This chain prevents her from actively fighting against me, but it can't compel her to cooperate any more than that. For now, we will simply keep her out of trouble." Morwen narrowed her eyes but said nothing. "The cellar is still the most secure chamber on the property. It was originally meant to keep undesirables out, of course, but it should serve just as well to keep this one in until we're ready to deal with her."

"It was *originally* meant to store jam," said Jenny, "but in light of our current state of affairs, I suppose it's a good thing you renovated."

"Mr. Barker, would you be so kind as to see our guest secured soundly in the cellar?" Jackaby commended his prisoner into Charlie's care, and Charlie led her off through the house and toward the back of the building. Before they turned the corner, Morwen shot one last acid glare at Jenny. Jenny did not return the woman's venom, but simply watched them with a blank expression until they had stepped out of sight.

"How do you feel?" Jackaby said.

"Good." Jenny considered the question earnestly. "I feel

good. I thought I would hate her. I thought I would want to hurt her, but I don't. Not really. It feels strangely liberating."

"Excellent," Jackaby said. "That's excellent."

"And then there's Howard," she continued. "After all these years of wondering–it's strange to just know. I hadn't realized how much I needed to, and now I know. Howard is dead."

"He died a hero."

"Of course he did." Jenny smiled. "I only wish you could have known him. The two of you are more than a little alike."

"You're handling all of this well." Jackaby said. "I must admit I wasn't certain you would be here to have this conversation. I was afraid . . ."

"Afraid?"

"Of losing . . . Afraid that you . . ." He took a deep breath and tried again. "There were some very big questions keeping you tethered to the land of the living, Miss Cavanaugh. I was afraid that finding answers–finding closure–might cut your ties to this world."

"I should have moved on to the other side by now." Jenny nodded. "I wasn't certain about that, either. I might have crossed over straightaway if I had found those answers years ago. I guess I wasn't satisfied with just being that girl who died. She's a part of me, but I do believe I'm more than an echo now. Maybe I'm not supposed to be more, but I am. I have new thoughts and feelings." She bit her lip and looked away from Jackaby. "They're maddening sometimes–but they're mine, and not hers. They're emotions the woman I used to be never knew, and that means I must be somebody right now. Whatever else I am, I'm my own somebody–and I'm not done figuring out who that is just yet."

I have seen Jackaby look through people and over people. I have seen him regard people like science experiments and like puzzle pieces. While Jenny spoke, he looked into her eyes like I have never seen him look at anyone before. It was unexpectedly tender.

"Perhaps I should excuse myself," I said.

"No, Miss Rook." Jackaby turned away, pulling the little red pouch out of his coat and setting it on the desk. Inside was the strange stone that Pavel had given me. "We need to talk."

"I'm afraid that may have to wait," said Charlie from the doorway. We turned.

"Was there a problem?" Jackaby stiffened. "Morwen?"

"Is secured in your cellar. She was very compliant. We could use chains like that one on the police department. The thing is, the cellar was already occupied. Do you know this woman?"

He stepped aside, and the widow Cordelia Hoole came forward. In her arms was a little girl in a yellow dress. "Mrs. Hoole," I managed. "We weren't expecting–Is that Mrs. Wick's child?"

"No," said Jackaby. He stepped up and tickled the chubby little toddler on her chin. "She's not."

"You're right," Mrs. Hoole confirmed. "I know that you don't like secrets, Mr. Jackaby. Forgive me. This is Hope. She is my secret."

"Why ever should a child be secret?" asked Jackaby. "Children make terrible secrets. They are much too conspicuous. Loud, stinking, prone to fits."

"Sir," I said. "Mrs. Hoole and the professor were only wed for a year."

"Yes? So?" said Jackaby.

"That girl is at least two years old. She isn't Professor Hoole's daughter, is she?" I asked. "That was your big secret."

Mrs. Hoole shook her head. "I wasn't born into Lawrence's world," she said. "I've lived through things–things I never want my child to see." She took a deep breath. "It was for the best she never knew her real father. I wanted a better life for her than the one I had known. I looked to marry someone with money, someone on the way up. After Hope was born I began hanging about the college, looking to court a naive, wealthy student. Someone with prospects.

"A bit by mistake, I caught the eye of a kind but rather lonely professor instead. I kept my old life hidden from Lawrence, kept Hope hidden. Mrs. Wick looked after her while we courted. After he proposed–I'm so embarrassed–I was just in too deep. I was never disloyal. The fact is, I had accidentally fallen in love right back. I loved Lawrence, but I loved Hope too much to risk his leaving me should I ever tell him the truth. As soon as we were married, I begged Lawrence to hire a live-in housemaid. I told him I knew a woman who had been good to my family, and that she had a little girl to look after. Mrs. Wick came to live with us, and with her came my little Hope.

"That's why I didn't bring her with me when I came to meet you. I didn't know if I could trust you. But then you stopped that terrible man from killing me and you gave me shelter from the creatures. I heard them up above me after you had gone. It was a terrible noise. They came to the cellar door, crashing and thudding–but they couldn't get in. Your protection may be the only reason I'm alive, Detective. I left to bring Hope back, to keep her under that same protection, if you'll permit it."

Jackaby looked dour. "I cannot."

"Please, Detective. My little Hope didn't choose to be who she was. She didn't choose to have a woman like me for a mother. She didn't ask for any of it. I'm not perfect, Mr. Jackaby, but I would give everything for my daughter."

Jackaby nodded. "Thank you for your honesty, Mrs. Hoole," he said. "I like honest. Alas, I'm afraid I cannot keep my promise to you or to your daughter. The situation had changed. We have made targets of ourselves and by extension this house. Your own assassin has taken your place in the cellar. My home is no longer safe."

Mrs. Hoole sank. "Where will I go?"

Jackaby pursed his lips and closed his tired eyes. After several long seconds he opened them again. "I want you to memorize an address. Memorize it–never write it down–and reveal your destination to no one." He leaned in and whispered in her ear. "Got it? There are good people who live there. They will help you."

"Sh-Should I tell them Mr. Jackaby sent me?" Mrs. Hoole asked.

"No. Tell them–" Jackaby took a deep breath. "Tell them their son sent you. Tell them that he misses them." A tingle rippled up my spine as I realized what he was saying. "Most of all, tell them to get ready. I left a box with them a very long time ago. A cigar box tied with twine. Tell them to use it. All of it. They will need everything they can muster."

My employer–a man who never spoke of his past, who hung no portraits over his mantel, who did not even share his name–had parents. He had a mother and a father who were real people and lived in a real house somewhere in the real world. I found the notion almost mystifying. What could they possibly be like?

Jackaby attended to Mrs. Hoole, outfitting her with a satchel full of charms and wards, a roll of spending money, and some fresh fruit and a few slightly stale biscuits. He offered to fetch some pickles and jam from the cellar, but the widow declined politely. She thanked the detective profusely before departing with little Hope on her hip.

"Wouldn't it be safer to travel with them?" I asked when the door closed. "Just to be sure they reach their destination?"

"They would be no safer in our company," said Jackaby. "They are better off alone."

"That isn't really why you didn't offer, though, is it?" Jenny's voice preceded her appearance. She came into view beside Jackaby. "When was the last time you saw them?"

Jackaby stared out the broken front window, watching the widow walk away. "I have not seen my family in roughly two decades, Miss Cavanaugh. We do not correspond. The sight does not discriminate when it takes a host, and it does not make accommodations for family. I found my own way after it took me."

"But you were so young then," I said.

"I was ten years old."

"They didn't believe you, did they?" Jenny said. "You were just a boy who had lost his friend. You were confused and afraid, and your parents didn't believe you. So you ran away?"

Tears welled in Jackaby's gray eyes. "No, Miss Cavanaugh," he said. "They did believe me. They believed every word. They never doubted me for a moment, my parents, even when I was sure I was mad myself. My parents are not perfect, but they were prepared to give up everything for me. And they would have had to, if I had stayed. So I left."

He watched Mrs. Hoole turn the corner with her daughter and vanish into the lamp-lit streets of New Fiddleham.

"I don't like secrets, but I understand why she kept hers," he said. "My parents are my secret. I didn't hide my name for my own protection–I hid it for theirs. They are about to need more protection than my absence has afforded them. Some locks cannot be unbroken, and what we've unleashed is going to be big."

"Where do we start?" I asked.

"Poplin," said Jenny. "Howard told me to look for Mayor Poplin."

"That's a good lead, but Poplin has been ten years on the run. I'm interested in something a bit closer to home before we go chasing the past again." He pulled the little red pouch from his coat pocket. Within it rested the stone Pavel had slipped me. "The Dire Council is planning something massive, something melding magic and machinery, and they are employing the sharpest scientific minds they can lay their hands on, and for all we know they could be ready to unleash it tomorrow. We need more than ever to know who's behind it."

"And you think that stone is the key?"

"I think it's a channel," he said. "I think it's the reason for your blackouts, your unexplained behavior, even your attack on Pavel . . ."

"You said all that was the aftereffect of a possession," I said. "That I was feeling Jenny's emotions and acting on them."

"I said that before I saw Jenny and you together. Layering

one's consciousness is like layering colors, but instead of blending blue and yellow to make green, you blend two auras to create a third. With Miss Cavanaugh in your mind, you were brighter. The two of you melded easily, and I could see both of your energies, distinct yet intertwined. You make a lovely and indomitable pair. What I saw the day you knocked Pavel out the window was something else entirely. You were overshadowed and something else entirely was there. I have never seen a possession firsthand. I didn't realize what I was seeing then. Now that we know all the details, the truth seems painfully obvious. The Dire Council has been in your head, Miss Rook."

I didn't want to believe it. I felt sick and angry. More than angry, I was furious. Coming into our home had been violation enough, but the thought that some evil wretch had been creeping around inside my head was too much. It made my skin crawl.

"They were the ones who opened my safe, I'd wager," Jackaby continued. "Mortal locks are paltry things to a mage of even middling caliber, and they were the ones who attacked Pavel, not you. He must have said too much, or else his benefactors were afraid he might. It explains why Finstern's device overloaded, as well. His machine wasn't pulling energy out of you, it was pulling it through you. Without even knowing it, Finstern stuck his tap clean through the barrel and started emptying the reservoir on the other side of it. Whoever's on the other side is powerful, too. Beyond powerful." He gritted his teeth. "We need to know who's over there."

"How?"

"The stone appears to function in the same way possession does. It opens a window. When Miss Cavanaugh possessed you, you said you saw her memories. What did you see when you were under the Dire Council's control?"

"I–I don't . . . nothing. I just felt woozy and everything went dark."

"There has to be something! You can look both ways through a window. Think, Miss Rook!"

"Let her be," Jenny said, floating down beside me. "It's a lot to take in."

Jackaby shook his head. "The council has been ahead of us every step of the way. This may be our only chance to close the gap." He loosened the cords on the little purse. "I'm going to look through myself. You two watch me closely. If I so much as lift a finger, you knock the stone out of my hands."

"What? No! Are you mad?" Jenny said.

"Time is running out."

"No. Not you," I said. Jackaby and Jenny both looked at me. "It can't be you. You're the one they're after. They need your eyes, and if you're right, you'd be giving them exactly what they want. No, it has to be me."

"Abigail . . ." said Jenny.

"Besides," I said. "I can't see if anything comes through

from the other side, but Jackaby can. He can watch for the aura and remove the stone the second anyone tries to take over."

"Abigail, no . . ." Jenny pleaded.

"I can't ask this of you," said Jackaby.

"You don't have to. They used me. I want to return the favor."

I sat down at the ransacked desk and Jackaby picked up the pouch. I held out my hand. Very carefully, he dropped the stone into my outstretched palm. I could see Jenny drifting back and forth behind him, worrying the translucent lace on her dress. At first nothing happened. I stared at the carved circles and imagined opening a window. I pushed with all my mental muscles against the stone. Still nothing for several seconds.

The sensation came abruptly. The scar on my temple felt hot, but I ignored the pain and focused on the little stone, concentrating hard. The room spun and the edges of my vision dimmed. A tunnel of darkness closed in until all that remained were the stone's rough circles. The lines were suddenly more than carvings. They curved high above me and described the outline of a long tunnel through the darkness. The walls to either side were made of shadows and gloom. I moved through the passage–falling or flying, I could not say–drifting through a series of uneven rings. Something shimmered ahead of me, a single star in the sea of black. I drew closer.

Pure white light punctured the darkness, and in the center of it stood a man. The figure was almost lost in the blinding brightness. His features were inscrutable–a charcoal silhouette against the halo of light. I suddenly wanted to be anywhere else, but I willed myself to inch closer, trying to discern any details.

THE AGE OF MEN HAS ENDED. The thought had no voice, no accent. The words simply sprang from inside my head, echoing like cannon fire. I AM THE KING OF THE EARTH AND THE ANNWYN. I AM DONE WITH YOUR KIND AND I AM DONE WITH YOUR WALLS AND I AM DONE WITH WAITING. The figure lunged forward and I saw his eyes in the darkness, blood red and full of malice.

The stone clacked against the desk. The dark tunnel fell away and I was back in the house on Augur Lane. I blinked. My cheek was on fire. Jackaby slipped the channel back into the red pouch and pulled the cords tight.

"Well?" he said. "What did you see?"

I held on to the desk with both hands to keep from spinning off the chair. "He's there. He called himself a king. It was like he was waiting for me at the end of a long–" I caught my breath. "Red eyes and the end of a long, dark hallway. That's what Eleanor was seeing all those years ago! The hallway wasn't a place at all. It was a channel, straight to him."

"He was in her head?" said Jackaby. "For months, he

was in Eleanor's head." His hands balled into fists. "But she resisted. She died resisting. They needed her. The Dire Council needed her sight and she died rather than let them take it."

"And now they need you," said Jenny, quietly.

"He spoke to me," I said. "The *king of the earth and the Annwyn.* He said he was done with walls and he was done waiting."

"Good," said Jackaby.

"Good?" said Jenny.

"Good. All this time we've been chasing shadows while he was building war machines and murdering innocent bystanders. Not anymore. We took his teeth when we bested Pavel and we bound his hands when we bested Morwen. If this king wants my eyes he'll need to come out of the shadows to get them himself. We're finally forcing *his* hand instead of the other way around. He's tired of waiting? Good. So am I."

"Sir," I said. "You know we're with you, but we're not ready to fight a war. They want to tear down a wall we can't even see and unleash an army we can't begin to imagine. We're not ready for any of this."

"They killed Eleanor because she stood against them. They killed Howard Carson. Lawrence Hoole. Nellie Fuller." He looked up at Jenny. "Jenny Cavanaugh. How many countless others? Good people have lost their lives every time they've risen up against the Dire Council's villainy. I will not let those losses be in vain, nor will I stand idly by while countless others meet the same fate. We don't know how long our window will last, and we cannot give him time to rally. He could be at our doorstep before we know it."

"Well then," I said, summoning the strength to stand up without wobbling. "Let's go save the world."

Supplemental Material

It was well after midnight when Jackaby passed by my room. He paused in the hallway before doubling back to poke his head through my open door.

"You haven't slept," he said.

"No, sir. Not yet." I sat up, hugging the blankets around myself. My stomach was a tightening knot. "I–I'm–" I sighed.

"You're what?" Jackaby stepped inside.

"I'm–" I took a deep breath. I didn't want to say it out loud. Saying it out loud somehow made it true. I dropped my head, letting the words fall in sheepish whispers on the blanket. "I'm afraid."

"Of course you are," said Jackaby flatly. "You're intelligent and you're aware. Why shouldn't you be afraid?"

"That's very reassuring, sir. Thank you," I said. "Are you afraid?"

"Constantly," he said. "It's the reason I'm still alive. Fear keeps us sharp. Listen to your fear."

"And what if my fear tells me—what if it tells me I should run away?" I asked.

Jackaby leaned against the battered old dresser and regarded me with a bemused smile. "Then you should probably run away. I told you as much when I hired you. This line of work comes with heavy risks."

"Why haven't you run?" I asked.

His smile faltered and he swallowed. "I ran once," he said. "In a way, I haven't stopped." He crossed the room in silence before dropping into a threadbare armchair in the corner.

"What did you run from?" I asked.

He raised an eyebrow at me but did not reply.

"It's hard to imagine," I said. "What could scare a man who fights monsters?"

His expression hardened. "Being a man who doesn't." He closed his eyes and leaned his head against the chair-back. "Being a man who lets the monsters win. I've been running from that for a very long time."

I nodded, not knowing what else to say. The clock in the hallway ticked out a stoic rhythm that echoed through the house for several beats. Jackaby broke the silence at last.

"Have I told you the story of the two pennies?" he asked.

I shook my head. "Another folktale?"

"A memory," he said. "I met a man that day."

"Which day?" I asked.

"The day I ran. The sight was still so new to me then, and I had so much to learn. I was a rudderless boy with the weight of the world on my unready shoulders. I didn't know where I was going, just that I needed to be gone.

"I walked for hours before reaching the nearest town, which is where I met the man. He wore stained overalls and a faded cap. His hair was gray, and his moustache bushy. He had a muddy cart at his side and a long-handled brush in his hands—he was a simple workman, cleaning a fountain in the town square. I don't know why, but I stopped to watch him. There was something calming about the way he worked.

"The workman was just packing up when a married couple passed by with a little girl in tow. The old workman set his brush aside and greeted them with a kindly smile. He showed the child a penny he had fished out of the fountain. He told her an impromptu story about wishing wells and lucky coins. I listened from my bench. The girl's parents seemed to find the man charming. The girl was riveted. The story was a lot of nonsense.

"When he was done, he handed the coin to the girl. She closed her eyes solemnly and tossed it into the water. The old man tipped his cap, and the family went happily on their way.

"I watched them as they walked off down the lane. I had seen the coin. It was a penny. Unexceptional. No aura, no halo, no magic. And yet–

"Impossibly, the girl was changed by the experience. There was a new glow around her. I could see it as plainly as you can see the glow of a candle. It was a blue aura, but a warm blue. It was as though she had been charmed, and I suppose she had been. I would wager anything that little girl got her wish after all.

"The workman was looking right at me when I turned back. He gestured for me to come forward, so I climbed down from my bench and approached him nervously. He hung his rag on the cart and merrily pressed a second salvaged coin into my palm.

"It was a penny, just like the first. Just like countless others. A scuffed Indian Head. Brown. Small. It might have been the least special penny ever minted. The man told me to make a wish. I smiled warily and tossed the thing into the fountain."

"What did you wish for?" I asked.

"Nothing," Jackaby said, rubbing his neck. "My life as I knew it was over. I was alone. I was afraid. I wanted nothing that a wet penny could give me. The nice man patted my arm and pushed his cart away down the cobblestones.

I watched my penny sink to the bottom of the fountain. That's when I saw it."

"Saw what?"

"The first penny, the little girl's. It was glowing blue, but a warm blue, just like the girl's aura–a hopeful blue. My own coin came to rest beside it, brown and lusterless. Her coin had been as dull as mine, but the wish had changed it. It was now shining with a raw and radiant optimism–a lucky penny, indeed."

"Missed opportunity, then," I said. "The man's story was real, after all. You should have made a wish."

Jackaby opened his eyes, and a smile gently returned to his cheeks. "I did not need the wish so much as I needed the lesson," he said. "I learned what I needed to learn. I learned that we make our own luck, Miss Rook. It wasn't the coin. It was finding something to believe in. There is real power in that."

"I like that," I said. "So, what have you found to believe in, sir?"

Jackaby looked at me for a long time. His storm gray eyes bore into mine, but his expression was curiously gentle. At length he rose to his feet. "Good night, Miss Rook," he said. "Until tomorrow comes."

In another moment Jackaby would be out the door. Soon I would hear his feet pad down the carpet, hear his door click shut at the end of the hall. For that instant, though,

I felt a curious sensation ripple over me. I felt the knot of fear inside me loosen. I felt as though if I looked down I might see myself aglow–blue, perhaps, but a warm blue, a hopeful blue.

"Good night, Mr. Jackaby," I said. "Until tomorrow comes."

Acknowledgments

I must thank Elise Howard, Eileen Lawrence, Brunson Hoole, and all of the amazing minds at Algonquin Young Readers, without whom the Jackaby series would not be the Jackaby series; my brilliant wife, Katrina, who continues to be my first and most trusted reader; and my agent, Lucy Carson, who remains Jackaby's stalwart ally. I would also like to acknowledge all of the brilliant students who grace my classroom with their presence and who provide me with tremendous hope for the future. Keep reading, love odd, and celebrate strange!

Read on for a sneak peek at the final novel in William Ritter's Jackaby series, *The Dire King*

"The devil's come for me," the old man wheezed. "He's come for me at last!"

Jackaby knelt beside him, offering him a steady hand. "There are no devils here," he said. "Catch your breath a moment. That's it." His eyes narrowed. "Hold on, now–you're familiar."

"We have met, Detective," the man croaked. "The church–" But he collapsed into a fit of dry coughs.

Recognition dawned and Jackaby cocked his head, startled. "My word! It's Gustaf, isn't it? No, Grossman? Grafton!" The old man nodded weakly. "Father Grafton. Yes. Good God, you've grown old!"

"Sir," I chided.

"Miss Rook, allow me to introduce Father Grafton. We last met–what was it–three years ago? When Douglas and I were investigating a rather grisly series of killings on the outskirts of town."

"Not my doing," Grafton managed. "The killings."

"No," confirmed Jackaby. "The pastor was doing everything in his power to prevent any further harm from befalling his parishioners. Made a good show of it, too. Of course, he was at least thirty years younger then." He whipped back to the old man. "Three decades in just three years? Have you been meddling with the occult? You know firsthand how dangerous that is! I'll have you know Douglas hasn't been the same since he left that church of yours!"

"Put the fear in him, did it?"

"A bit. Mostly it turned him into an aquatic bird."

"*D-dim Hud*." The man's eyes seemed to be having trouble focusing. He shook his head, blinking. "No magic. Not anymore." A patch of wispy white hair fell from his head and drifted to the floorboards.

Jackaby peered intensely at Father Grafton. "You're getting older by the second!"

Grafton nodded weakly.

"I don't understand." Jackaby peered into Grafton's ear and then took a sniff of his wispy hair. "I don't see any sign of a curse, no traces of paranormal poisons, no visible enchantments. Who did this to you?"

"Time," Grafton rasped. "Not much time." Wrinkles cut across the man's face like scars and milky white cataracts formed in his eyes. His shoulders shook. "*Harfau o Hafgan*," he breathed.

"*Harfau o Hafgan*? What does that mean? Is that Welsh?"

"*Mae'r coron, waywffon, a darian,*" Grafton mumbled, his head drooping with each word–and then he lurched up so suddenly it made me jump. He clutched Jackaby's arm.

"The crown, the spear, the shield. You cannot let him collect them. He has already taken the crown. The spear . . . it was destroyed, but I fear it has been remade. The shield . . . the shield . . ." He was gasping with each breath, his whole body shuddering. His eyes were wide and wild. "He trusted me. Now I have to trust you. The shield is in the Bible. The Bible of the zealot."

"The shield is in a Bible?" said Jackaby. "What Bible? Whose? Are you the zealot?"

"Not much time. The shield. In the Bible. You must stop–stop–*stopiwch y brenin.*" Father Grafton crumpled to the floor, and with one last rattling breath, he was still.

Jackaby delicately turned him over. Grafton's skin had gone as dry as parchment. The old man's body looked as though he had been mummified. I put a hand over my mouth.

"Is he–" I whispered.

"Quite," said Jackaby.